Chronicle

of

Dagothar

Histories of the Characters, Clans, Kingdoms and Races of the Inhabitants of Dagothar

Chronology covers 679 events within 420 dated entries in the 22,032 years leading up to The Oraclon Chronicles

A PreHistory Timeline in Appendix

Jason M. Breshears

The Oraclon Chronicle

2018

Preface

The following letter was addressed to Cephan, found tucked between the pages of this most extraordinary book.

Dear Cephan,

I leave with you my greatest possession, my gift to posterity. In this, my *Annals,* I was but an heir to far more reputable archivists and chronographers. My friend, herein are the answers you seek. Within these pages are hidden the secrets of the gods. In discovering the past, dear Cephan, the future can be known. The following is a list of books and sources of high antiquity, many no longer extant.

Tread carefully in the dark.

Imaricus Arcanacraft of House D'Vordred

Sources

Broken Moon Apocryphon: When the Sun Darkens

Haddar Epos: Red Anvil Chronology of Groblis Giltbeard

Wickerug Tapestry: of Vulena the Thorn Maiden

Book of Bark and Battles: Caedorian author unknown

Testimony of Laer'garoth the Old: Dragon Chronicler of Caedoria

Mythlore and Legends Past: Annals Historium, Castle Demarsculd

The Lost Scriptures of Achuzan: Writings taken from Mount Talisman

Barristan Records: Early History of Western Poltyria: Redshield Book Depository

The Book of Giants: Nikkolo Ord Magi Library

Annals of Dalen the Seer: Before the Barad-ai Wars

Records of Hinterport: Haberdag Quillminster

Ashadulan Tablets of Xakkiun Temple: scried by mage-archivists of the Deep Men

The Late Caedorian Empire: Yald'bold Whitlock, scribe

Odagathus yith Omalacrul: Forbidden Book of Mind and Magelore

Broken Moon Annals: Chanoch the Chronicler od Daethalon

Inscriptions of Macewise: Runic Histories of the Haddarim Dwarves

Dathari Antiquities: Chanoch the Chronicler of Daethalon

Plea to the Brard: Erythiul the Prophet of Daethalon

Observations of the Broken Moon Disasters: Praetus the Archivist of Daethalon

Annals of Uthril: excavated from Barrowen [Boldur Hill]

Codex Caerea: relic texts preserved from the *Book of the Ancient Lost*. Holy Scriptures of Dagothar

Omens and Prophecies of Caedoria: Yald'bold Whitlock, scribe

Forgotten Histories of Borderealm: Evander, Archivist of Everleaf

Poltus Antiquities: Royal Annals of Appletrot Conservatory

Oral Traditions of the Dwarves: Matthias, loremaster and Borderealm Ranger

Knightshade Antiquities: Annals Historium: Castle Demarsculd

Oracular Inscriptions of the Shadowitch: Imaricus Arcanacraft's notes from visiting her throne room

Saga of the Sundered Ones: Emim Histories: Tholgamog Hammerworn

Chronicles of Enchandrus: Nabor the Anchorite, halfling sage

The Early Years: Silthani Records of Sigils Arch from library of Lady Ardruna of Shannidar

Chronicle of Dagothar

*Over twenty-two thousand years before The Oraclon Chronicles
story unfolds, the realm of Dagothar was already very old. The
Death of the First World had been so long ago there were but
scant memories of that time. A world-destroying burning
mountain crashed into A'DIN and in the wake of the planetary
ruin an ocean drained leaving behind the Great Desert of
Eternal Sands and the lands of Dagothar were cut off from Aroth
Beyond. This vast destruction was long before a second
catastrophe known to historians as The Cataclysm.*

14,688 Before Cataclysm: Before humans existed on A'DIN the
continents of Dagothar and Aroth Beyond were populated with
scattered descendants of creatures and beasts from the Old
World, with animals that flourished, the seas teeming with life.
In this year at the height of night a great black darkness blotted
out a third of the stars in the sky. A massive shadow in the
heavens that made the ground tremble. This event interrupted a
conflict between demonic overlords called Throne-Banes and an
ancient race of powerful beings living in Dagothar descended
from those who had thrived in The World Before. Both factions,
the Dark Reliquars and the Minions paused while animals fled to
their hiding haunts as *millions* of figures of all shapes and sizes
fell from the sky to impact the ground.

The night skies were filled with singing as the elemental races
arrived upon A'DIN as rains of thick loam and soil fell with them
to blanket whole regions of Dagothar. As the gigantic shadow in
the heavens moved away the stars began reappearing and for

many hours it did rain seeds, pods, bulbs, cocoons, larvae and dirt upon an already ancient world.

A dense concentration of layered patches of earth fell upon a certain area where appeared a Golden Pillar with the hint of a face. Air, water, cloud, earth, stone, mineral, fire, crystal and metallic elementals converged around the Pillar of A'DIN singing as they set to their tasks of building a fantastic sanctuary around their god.

The reign of the Elementals over the wilds of Dagothar endured in this way for 2448 years, when something unusual took place.

12,240 Before Cataclysm: During the past two millennia the Golden Pillar had very slowly taken on a new form, the pillar changing to that of a massive tree trunk that had sprouted large limbs. In this year a branch grew heavy with a pine cone that turned into a cocoon that dropped to the ground. The elementals were astonished to see a slender, beautiful female unfold from the wrappings. They watched as she stood and looked up at their golden god and spoke, calling him *Elderboughs*...this god whom they knew of as Gomirr'un.

The elementals befriended Sharassa, first of the Branchborn, she being Keeper of the Soul of Elderboughs but the elementals did not understand. Sharassa would one day be widely feared as the Mycomaiden. Three months and eighteen days later a small cocoon dropped and Sharassa excitedly watched a bright-eyed green turtle pop out. She named him Mabbu.

In the year of Sharassa's birth did Elderboughs send the elementals away with instructions. They traveled to a large granite mountain and carved it into a four-sided prism, etching the symbols upon its surface told to them by Gomirr'un. Inside and below it they carved out great galleries of rock and covered the walls with the knowledges of the past and future. In this way was Mount Talisman made. For 264 years did Sharassa and the elementals continue with Elderboughs.

11,976 Before Cataclysm: The Great Cedar of A'DIN now a magnificent golden-hued pine tree, in this year his branches grew heavy with myriads of pine cone cocoons that the elementals tended until the husks were removed to reveal a new race upon Dagothar- the Ha'akathrals, or Athaki. The First People. Tall, strong, nature-wise with the essence of the elementals running through their veins who took a strong liking to them instantly. Under the guidance of the elementals, the Athaki were trained to deal with the many Old World dangers that still lurked about. The First People were regarded by the elementals as their own children and for this reason they were called the *earthborn* race.

The Ha'akathrals were not human, nor was Sharassa whom they regarded with awe and reverence. In these days humans, elves, dwarves and faeries did not yet exist.

9216 Before Cataclysm: For two thousand seven hundred and sixty years did the Athaki wander far and wide across Dagothar following the herds. Though dragons had grieved them for a spell a hero among the First People emerged who slew the Addanc and ended the oppression of the wyrms. In this way was begun the reign of TAL'NIK of the Two Horns.

With the threat of the dragons ended, Elderboughs in this year sprouted fifty and then two cocoons from which produced his faery daughters. Ashrey was firstborn of the fifty Shars but Dhishra was firstborn of the two High Shars, her and her sister who would later become the Queen of Everleaf before she changed into the Shadowitch of Splinterdark.

The fifty-three females, Elderboughs, the Athaki and elementals lived in peace for seven hundred and twenty years before something astonishing occurred.

8496 Before Cataclysm: At the beginning of the year ten thousand eight hundred cocoons sprouted and quickly fell upon the ground in the garden of Elderboughs. The First Birthing of the Bough-wrought were dryads, nymphs, nixies and sylphs, females all. In the summer these throngs of female faeries and the shars worked day and night as Elderboughs grew pine cone cocoons that produced the hundreds of thousands of faeries, male and female. This was the Second Birthing of the Bough-Wrought. Among the many thousands of pine cones were dropped four that were of unusual size and great of weight, each shining with its own golden illumination. They were set before the face of Elderboughs and when they emerged from their cocoons the Great Cedar of A'DIN told the shars that these four were the Pillars of Everleaf. All males, Manax the warsloth was first among them. Over seventeen centuries would pass as the fey lived and explored the world with the elementals and animals, though little dealings did the faeries have with the Athaki.

6792 Before Cataclysm: The entire faery world is summoned to Elderboughs and they are commanded to make pilgrimage to Mount Talisman, to behold its four sky-facing effigies, to wander its galleries of stone and learn the mysteries contained inside written upon all the gallery walls. Many go immediately, though the Great Tree gave them a thirty year period to carry out this sacred obligation.

5415 Before Cataclysm: In this year the world grew cold, flowers did not blossom. A few unicorns and pegasi vanished and many faeries saw beasts unknown to them wandering in the hills at night. Snows began that did not stop. Thus began the *Age of Shadowed Ice* and many among the fey were shamed, thinking this cold was brought upon the world because they had not made pilgrimage to Mount Talisman with the others. During this period many faeries, elementals and creatures on the surface world found refuge in the warmer caves and caverns of the underworld, where they found it already teeming with animals and plant life. Some referred to this period as the Dark Time. Many elementals were frozen solid on the surface only to die or become mindless or insane when they thawed out centuries later.

During the *Shadowed Ice* a thick vapor canopy enshrouded all of A'DIN in a dim light that caused the cold. The sun was not seen in centuries. The Dark Reliquars saw the scattered clans of the Ha'akathrals as a problem interfering with their own work across Dagothar so they slew all they could find. Many of the First People were killed, survivors reduced to hiding from the hordes of the Kal'ud Bor in service to the Dark Reliquars.

4896 Before Cataclysm: Sharassa, firstborn of Elderboughs, by this time had journeyed into the underworld three times despite the warnings of the other faeries. In this year she made her descent a third time into the Deep since the onset of the Shadowed Ice, accompanied by two other very powerful faeries named Webol and a nymph who would later be called Necralissa. These were joined by several others and none returned to Everleaf.

4632 Before Cataclysm: In the 783rd year of the Shadowed Ice the Athaki under leadership of TAL-NIK of the Beasthorn built the last of the sky-pillars in Dagothar. Many pillars had already been destroyed by the Kal'ud Bor, their enemies. The elementals, friends of the Ha'akathrals, brooded patiently in anger, wanting to make war against the Kal'ud Bor but

Elderboughs told them that the wickedness of the Kal was not yet full. These hordes would later be known as the Cloudborn, named after the vapor canopy that hid the sun.

4497 Before Cataclysm: The Age of Shadowed Ice ends as does the Age of the Ha'akathrals, who are so decimated in numbers by their conflicts with the Kal'ud Bor they are now but one large group led by TAL'NIK. As the world thaws and plants reappear the fey who remained above ground and in the sanctuary of Elderboughs are astonished to discover a *new* race living in Dagothar...humans. No one, not elemental, Athaki or fey knew when and where the first men appeared but they were found living in villages clustered close together under the mighty snow-covered trees of Dimwood. They wore animal skins for clothes, with furs, used spears and flint knives, had their own peculiar language and regarded the faeries suspiciously. Already they numbered in the thousands.

3888 Before Cataclysm: The Minions from The World Before that was destroyed long prior to the birth of the faeries, secretly enter Mount Talisman's massive galleries to search the prophetic knowledge carved onto the walls as they sought to understand the identity and purpose of this new race called humans. While in the subterranean corridors they happened upon several faeries who had arrived to fulfill their oaths to Elderboughs, albeit late. Those faeries were taken by the Minions and never seen again.

3456 Before Cataclysm: Humans discover a vast, perfectly level plateau of basement rock, basalt, perfect for the laying out of an expansive city. In this year Men began building Talan Dathar. Men are unaware that directly below this basalt plateau was located the perfectly preserved (in stasis) Navigator platform containing the first Oraclon and the first Planescape Portal, all architecture from The World Before.

2664 Before Cataclysm: In the seven hundred and ninety-second year from the founding of Talan Dathar, the first city of Men, an expedition of humans returned from Mount Talisman with a train of tablets covered in the prophetic inscriptions from under the mountain. Upon their return Men laid the foundation stones and flooring to the Temple of Eternal Lore which housed the tablets which came to be called the Codex.

2592 Before Cataclysm: Temple of Eternal Lore completed in Talan Dathar.

2544 Before Cataclysm: In this year one of the Minions, the only female, from The World Before, led an invasion of underworlders against the gates of Talan Dathar. They were allied to the frostlings that came down from the mountains and too sieged Men in their city. Hordes of animals, monsters, creatures descended from the lost faeries and elementals that had descended into the Deep during the Shadowed Ice period broke themselves on the shield walls of humans. The underworld invaders had not seen the surface world in 28 centuries and were unprepared for the valor of Men. For five days raged the *War of the Black Tides* until the Men of Talan Dathar slaughtered the hosts of the she-Abominid before she fled to the mountains.

2481 Before Cataclysm: In the *War of Mygok the Titan* we have the first historical account of both dwarves and titans in Dagothar. In a series of battles the Nimbolc dwarves of Darkfrost Peaks expelled the Titans from their region. In humiliation and rage the host of Titans fell violently upon Talan

Dathar in Dimwood and ruined much of the city of Men. The Titans continued in haste eastward and humans rebuilt their city upon the ruins of the old.

2448 Before Cataclysm: Elderboughs the Goldenlimb pronounced judgment against Mygok the Titan for the sack of Talan Dathar and the elementals, faeries and Ha'Akathrals prepare to execute this punishment on the field of battle but in penance Mygok and his Titans build an incredible stronghold next to Mount Talisman and dedicate it to Elderboughs. In this way was war averted and Ricanor Keep built.

1859 Before Cataclysm: The monstrously large pet of the Abominids in the underworld escapes the Abysshicar Sea in the Deep, swimming up through the salt rivers from the surface world into the Spawnsea. In this year did Imigorn the Triton-whale appear in the seas of Dagothar.

1512 Before Cataclysm: In the 19th year of the reign of Dagith Malacrul, the Mage-King of Talan Dathar, the Nimbolc dwarves came down from Mount Thokax and attacked the city, for Men had for some time been mining minerals and metals out of the lower peaks. The dwarves were repelled before the mighty walls of the city and soon after several outposts and villages of humans in Dimwood were attacked by the Silthani elves. In this year Men made first contact with both dwarves and elves as defenders of their own territories. The wood elves retreated when large hosts of human soldiers were sent to garrison the posts and townships.

1307 Before Cataclysm: The buildings of Talan Dathar suddenly trembled as the ground rumbled for a short moment.

Within days the Men of the city found themselves defending the walls against another horde of underworld creatures, again led by a hideous Minion female. The army of the Deep was driven off and scattered throughout Dimwood and rangers reported that a new lake had appeared in the forest and all the settlements in the area had been wiped out by the invaders before they reached the city. This was the beginning of Lake Mir Dol'hinnon and Blackmar Deeps.

1152 Before Cataclysm: TAL-NIK leads his people to an isolated hill not far from Elderboughs' sanctuary. The Athaki dig deep under and through the hill and then erect walls and structures on its surface, including massive stone doors in the hillside. Far below the hill in the tunnels is found a cave system that leads down into the Deep. In this way was Doorwood Hill of old built by the Ha'akathrals in the center of Borderealm.

1104 Before Cataclysm: In the 427th year of the Malacrul Dynasty of Talan Dathar, the Minions of the Deep attacked again in two separate forces. Underworld armies were led by an Abominid from Hollowrealm far below Dagothar but a second host was allied together by the machinations of the female Minion who had organized the two prior sieges of the city. She had raised the firbolgs of Darkfrost, the three-eyed gnomes of northern Devilspire called the Draer and the forces of Shintosh the draconarch of Winterfang, the lost city of dragons against Men at Talan Dathar.

The Magelords of House Malacrul led the city's defense and quickly captured the Draconarch himself to the astonishment of the other dragons who kept back when Men threatened to open their ruler's throat. But the battle that raged along the walls was lost, several breaches opened as underworlders spilled into the city. The indecisive dragons now emboldened to renew their assault on the interior were suddenly halted by the peal of a powerful horn and shook the air with power. The forest quietened and the breaches emptied of enemies leaving Men bewildered. A terrible onslought was fought in the trees and the underworlders fled toward the mountains with the firbolgs as the Draer fled eastward.

Witnesses saw a gigantic earth elemental holding up a tall bearded figure who blew a strange double-horn. The enemies were cut down and chased off by the Athaki and their elemental allies as TAL'NIK observed their retreat. Hissing at the power and noise of the Addanc horn whom TAL'NIK slew in the past, the wyrms took flight and left their master Draconarch a prisoner of Men. None among dragonkind would oppose the Slayer.

The Magelords received several dragon eggs as security for the release of the Draconarch and in this way did Talan Dathar begin its own line of wyrms. TAL'NIK and the elementals gave chase to the she-Minion and Men erected statues of him throughout their city that would later become objects of worship.

1008 Before Cataclysm: A group of fey traveled together and departed the world of their kin to live isolated from the other faeries. The majority of these were they who had either neglected to make their pilgrimages to Mount Talisman or those who did so but not in the time allotted by Elderboughs. The controversy was initiated by Da'nelia, one of the High Shars, sister of Dhishra, who accused them of being bad faeries. While few other among the fey agreed with this pronouncement, as many more faeries entered the discussions over a period of days, these fey grouped together and departed their kin. They would eventually spread throughout the Deep and the haunts of Dagothar as the dreaded *shadowfae*.

930 Before Cataclysm: Overpopulation in the metropolis of Talan Dathar and the surrounding towns in Dimwood prompted an exodus of 20,000 people who departed in a days-long train of loaded wagons. Passing out of Dimwood they were never heard from again. In Caedorian records is found a single reference claiming that the Men of the Scorched Earth in northern Borderealm and the cave folk of Deep Ore Peaks are the descendants of those people who had wandered into Splinterdark and were scattered by numerous orc attacks.

893 Before Cataclysm: Out of the caves and caverns of Darkfrost Peaks emerged armored dark-skinned dwarves called the Hul' Ekkan. They flooded into Dimwood razing several human settlements and towns before attacking Talan Dathar. They used magical explosives and blew apart sections of the walls to begin fighting street-to-street. When more than half of their forces were inside the city the Magelords magically summoned ice walls to trap them inside the gates as a hidden human army inside the Temple of Eternal Lore precinct rushed out to engage the dwarves. On the walls the humans doubled their forces who were hid inside nearby buildings thus keeping out those dwarves that tried to rescue their doomed kin within the trap. Hearing those slaughtered inside, the Hul' Ekkan retreated through the woods harried by human archers and rangers all the way to the foothills of Darkfrost.

828 Before Cataclysm: Ish'layyar, one of the four heroic Pillars of Everleaf forest, fought and slew the dragon Orthilok the Ironscaled when the wyrm thought to take by force the Solace Sanctuary in northern Everleaf from the faeries.

792 Before Cataclysm: First regnal year of Manusa Goldenheart, human regent of Talan Dathar, widely heralded as the Friend of Elderboughs and first human king to send a delegation with gifts to the Court of Elderboughs in far away

Everleaf. This marked the beginning of the time called the Peace of Manusa, a seven hundred year period of growth and expansion of human settlements with no invasions. During this time the Minions and their hosts were silent. It was during Manusa's life on the throne that the other races began calling Men the Dat'hari, later rendered Dathari, meaning *from Talan Dathar.* In those days, far from the population centers of Men, humans and faeries did engage in friendships and communion.

656 Before Cataclysm: The fortress-city of Sigils Arch in Shannidar is finished, built before the Citadels spread throughout the region of the Silthani elves who departed Dimwood. At that time Shannidar was a thick forested land.

641 Before Cataclysm: An unknown civilization of Men according to the faeries began constructing a gigantic pyramid in the forest far to the south of Shannidar. The megalithic blocks were hewn to perfection and the purpose of the monument was a mystery. The Silthani spies claimed that it took almost the entire civilization of humans in the southern forest to a century to finish the pyramid.

552 Before Cataclysm: While camped at Cindereach as the athaki men were out on a hunt the females of the Ha'akathrals camped there were attacked and butchered by a horde of ogres though they took great losses. Among the lost was the mate of TAL-NIK of the Beasthorn.

551 Before Cataclysm: One year after laying the final blocks into position on the pyramid, the southern Men sealed the entrance and laid the gigantic prism-shaped topstone using two domesticated dragons to hoist the stone.

515 Before Cataclysm: For thirty-six years the southern Men of the Pyramid maintained communication with the government of Talan Dathar using emissaries on courier drakes. But in this year communications did not come, expected as they were three times a year. The Men of Talan Dathar sent rangers on dragon steeds to the pyramid city far in the south but they found a waste of putrifying bodies littering the streets and buildings shut up with the dead. Strewn about the city were the carcasses of snakelike figures, a serpent people originally from the underworld. The Silthani elves recorded this to be the first appearance of the Silapenti race.

438 Before Cataclysm: Garotha Shadowskin hatched from the brood of the white wyrms of Talan Dathar in service to Men, sired by a black dragon of the wilds. Garotha would become famous and his name would change to *Dracomancer* for his ability to cast spells taught to him by the Dathari Magelords of House Malacrul. He is father to the equally famous dragon, Laer'garoth the Old, and Garotha was grandsire to Navaniz the Bold,a wyrm of Caedoria.

81 Before Cataclysm: From tunnels and caveways around the world spilled forth starving and haggard survivors from a series of wars raging in Hollowrealm far below Dagothar. In the Deep battles were fought and entire races in the underworld were enslaved while others having no utility were eaten. Others were forced to integrate and hybrid races were created by the Minions. Overpopulation in the underworld led to wholesale slaughter and the Mrul, overlord of the Minions, imposed his rule over all of the Deep.

7 Before Cataclysm: Eight Abominids, one a female, emerged from the underworld leading eight armies of beasts, creatures and soldiers from the Deep. They surrounded the walls of Talan Dathar by night, none knowing how so many could approach the city so quickly and undetected. Whole camps turned into trenchworks and burrows and beasts dug under the walls but were stopped mostly by older stone ruins below the city. The Men of Talan Dathar led by the Magelords and aided by the dragons defended Talan Dathar but could not drive off the invaders from Dimwood.

For seven years the Minions and their armies killed off all humans in the expansive woods separated from the city and seiged Talan Dathar, renewing their efforts to enter the city week after week but repelled. The heroic Dathari fought back with intensity unexpected but for seven years no other races came to the aid of Men in the *Siege of the Minions.*

The Cataclysm That Broke the World

The Cataclysm: In the 7th year of the Siege of Talan Dathar a great host of elementals fell upon the camp-cities of the underworlders in Dimwood that surrounded the city as all eight Minions pushed their armies in a wave of armored bodies over the walls of Talan Dathar. The battle raged in the streets and the dragon Garotha Dracomancer lost an eye to a Minion as he defended the gates to the Temple of Eternal Lore. Since that time he was known as Garotha One-Eye. From the south the Titans entered the battle against Men not knowing that the elementals were even then decimating the hordes of the Deep outside the walls. As the Titans approached the overrun walls seven races of Ayr shapechangers fell upon them with violence led by the mighty Eganosh Faerymane. The ariel faery led the charge of ten thousands of apanthoi and bruun. At the turning of the battle, when the hordes from the Deep realized their peril, suddenly all eight Abominids vanished leaving them behind.

A moment later the whole world shook. Buildings rocked and fell, some collapsing. An earthquake rocked the whole of Dagothar from the mountains of Darkfrost to the Uraku Peaks in the east, from Mount Ogrori in the Eternal Sands of the north to the islands in the far south of the Spawnsea. The quaking tore apart the foundations of Talan Dathar, splitting in sections even the two earlier foundations of the city which was already 3456 years old. This was the 2592nd year since the laying of the foundation for the Temple of Eternal Lore. This last siege of the Minions lasted seven years and was the seventh time Talan Dathar in its long history had been invaded.

The Cataclysm is agreed by all ancient chronographers to have been a great divide in the history of Dagothar that began another Age. Since this seven year occupation of the armies of Hollowrealm, Dimwood has been home to foul and fell creatures, monsters and aberrations. A dark pall has since hung over Dimwood and the greatest concentration of strange plants and beasts is in the region of Blackmar Deeps.

Age of Forgotten Years

also known as

The Scattering Years

It has often been said that the Age of Forgotten Years was so named because no histories were written but this is untrue. Many records survived to later be incorporated into the annals of descended peoples and kingdoms. What was lost were the dates these events occurred. The Cataclysm broke the world, ended order as chaos ensued and brought many changes.

Cities of different races, settlements, cave systems and underground dwellings collapsed. The following events are known to have happened during The Scattering Years but the dates they transpired are unknown. A few events are indeed dated during this period and they are listed when in the series of other events they are believed to fit.

> The Men of Talan Dathar began separating themselves into twelve families, or tribes. It is unknown how many of these tribes departed the city during these years. Ancient ruins of human settlements and civilizations are spread throughout vast Dimwood, Splinterdark, Treehelm, along the edges of the Great Desert of Eternal Sands, the jungles of the Silapenti to the south and the coasts of Hinterealm to the plains of the Scorched Earth.

> a tribe of Men settled in the Eternal Sands around a great oasis. They were later bewitched by an ancient evil and became the wicked Sand Kings in The Burning Years.

> a tribe of Men called the Sildari who had many dealings with the elves found a permanent home in the far southeast of Borderealm, beyond Harrowood and the Dathom Peaks. These are the red men called Sylnadorians.

> three tribes of Men migrated together. The people of Kaidor, Brard and Pol'tr. They settled in Splinterdark and built a great kingdom with colonial outposts in Treehelm and Arborealm. These were the ancestors of the Caedorians, the Barad-ai (Deep Men) and the Poltyrians.

> More than two tribes remained at Talan Dathar and rebuilt another level of the city on the ruins of former occupations. A small army of elementals remained with the humans and aided them in the rebuilding, the Men of Talan Dathar not aware that this was ordered by Elderboughs. The Great Tree sent them with precise instructions and the rock, crystal, metal and fire elementals erected an odd seven-sided temple structure in the center of the city, its inner walls covered in strange symbols. The Dathari has no understanding about this Navigator temple but they vowed to protect it.

> 217th Year After Cataclysm: In the Court of Elderboughs the petition of an injured wickerworl was interrupted by the sudden appearance of a tall figure wrapped in shadows so dark not even the golden light of the Ancient Tree dispelled it. the High Shar Dhishra and shars Sionya and Yanla tried to advance against it but were unable to move. The intruder of darkness spoke-

"It is spoken that you are the Pilot..."

"I AM." At Elderboughs' admission the shadow nodded as the alarmed faeries gathered around listened.

"Below Talan Dathar is silence."

"THIS IS GOOD."

"Below Hollowrealm is noise." Hearing this the Great Cedar's eyes widened and this was noticed by the fey. The shadow continued-

"Below the chasm...Goriok Maw. An enemy thrives." The figure vanished and as it did so the shadows tightened and the warsloth Gano'tax noticed a dark metal scepter strapped across its back. The god of the faeries provided them no explanation for the visitor's presence.

> an old story is told of this time claiming that a single Minion came with an army to end Talan Dathar, a hideous female Abominid. A great battle was fought in the forest and as in the

past the she-Minion was driven off again by the valor of the Dathari and their wizards. It is said that she did not return to the underworld but remained on the surface, taking her residence in Blackmar Deeps. She would later be known as the Witch of Dimwood.

> the Dathari of Dimwood buried the original Temple of Eternal Lore and laid a new foundation over it, adding supports and new buildings above it to conceal its place. A second Temple of Eternal Lore was constructed, less magnificent, but placed above ground but at a different location.

> during this Dark Age, or Scattering, came the first reports of goblins, orcs, trolls and ogres

> as with Men, so with dwarves. The Nimbolc dwarves of Mount Thokax in Darkfrost Peaks had a vast underground network of undervein highways connecting Upper Nimbolc to its two major stronghold colonies far to the east in Devilspire Mountains- Dijin Castle and Ebrog Keep. Nimbolc was abandoned because in the quaking a chasm opened in Lower Thokax and a cave in lead straight into a nest of deadly underworld monsters. The nest caves themselves went down further into the domain of the Minions so the Six Clans of the Nimbolc resettled in The Scattering abandoning their metropolis in Upper Thokax.

> the dwarven clan of the EM'M occupy Dijin Castle and northern Devilspire Mountains, ancestors of the dwarves of Emim'gard.

> dwarven clans of GAL'DR and the HAD.DR remain together during The Scattering and occupy Ebrog Pass's two fortresses at the southern terminus of Bholbash Valley in the Devilspire range. These were the dwarf ancestors of the Galdirim dwarves of Deep Ore Peaks and the Haddarim, or dwarves of Red Anvil.

> dwarven clan of VAL'DR settled the caverns and valley of Bholbash between the Dijin and Ebrog strongholds. The ancestors of the Silverbeard and Silveraxe clans.

> only the GA'RM clan of Nimbolc in Darkfrost remained in the western mountains. At some point they came in contact with the she-Minion in Dimwood at Blackmar Deeps. They were not seen on the surface again. These were the ancestors of the dreaded Grimh, the red race of gigantc dwarves of the Deep.

> It was during these Dark Times that the elementals at instruction of Elderboughs sealed shut the galleries of knowledge hidden below Mount Talisman. Men has already gained access and produced the Codex from these inscriptions of the past and future. TAL-NIK is said to have been in attendance when the Great Tree commanded this of the elementals. Scholars studying the Codex many years later would discover an obscure reference to a secret door cleverly designed by these elementals leading into the forbidden galleries below Mount Talisman.

> During this period occurred the first Bone Kingdom War, the dwarven description for those restless hordes of orcs, goblins, trolls, ogres and cave giants united by their chieftains in Devilspire to rid the mountains of the dwarves. The masses of Bone Kingdom armies attacked the EM'M at Dijin Castle, the VAL'DR of the valley and the GAL'DR and HAD'DR of Ebrog Keep. The unified dwarven clans descended from Nimbolc defeated the Bone Kingdoms.

> Many years later the Second Bone Kingdom War was a series of assaults on Ebrog Pass, tribes of minataurs now allied to the Bone Kingdoms. Though repelled it was known that another vast hordes was amassing. The dwarves were constantly harried by giants of the Bone Kingdoms and finally the GAL'DR with the HAD'DR migrate out of the mountain range, both clans departing with a burning hatred for giants. The GAL'DR traveled to Deep Ore Peaks, the HAD'DR to Ettertooth mountains to later be known as the dwarves of Red Anvil.

> In the Third Bone Kingdom War the VAL'DR were overrun in the valley of Bholbash and lost their caverns to the orcs. In flight they were further decimated but groups of survivors made it to Deep Ore Peaks to join the GAL'DR in their cavernholds.

> In the Fourth Bone Kingdom War the EM'M dwarves defended Dijin Castle and slaughtered the orcs, minataurs, ogres and cave giants in two decisive battles.

> During the Forgotten Years it was said that a man of Kaidor hunted down an Azura Wyrm named Svaldurhulk Sky-Lord that had eaten two of his horses. It is said that this unnamed human was the first among Men to become a dragonslayer and that this dual was the origin of the Heroic Code.

> Four hundred and fourteen years after TAL-NIK stood with many elementals in the Court of Elderboughs on the issue of the sealing of Mount Talisman, the leader of the Ha'akathrals returned to the ruins of Cindereach and arranged the death of the lubarts for the Silthani trade guilds hurt by the highway robbery along the road to Dimwood.

> The final Fall of Talan Dathar transpired during the Forgotten Years. The aged dragon Garotha Dracomancer, Guardian of the City, arrived in the east among the people of Kaidor and Brard with the sorrowful news of the final overthrown and ruination of the First City of Men, which by the dragon's reckoning happened in the 1509th year since his hatching. Chronographers estimate this Fall of Talan Dathar was about a thousand years After Cataclysm, when the Minions ultimately succeeded in ending the City of Men. In Garotha's possession, harnessed in heavy netting to his underbelly, were the treasured archives and holy books of the last Dathari. Garotha remained his days with the Kaidorians.

> 1009th Year After Cataclysm. The faeries of Everleaf stilled as a rain storm came out of a cloudless sky. A darkness fell over the woods and faeries pressed in to the Court of Elderboughs as a visitor armored in swirling shadows appeared before Archaic Tree. For a long time the Ancient Cedar and the dark intruder

stood quietly and all realized they were communicating mentally. The stranger disappeared and the weather returned to day light. Elderboughs said nothing to the fey about this exchange.

> *The Plague of the Minions* occurred toward the end of the Forgotten Years. A terrible epidemic killed off humans all over the west spread out in colonies and settlements of Dathari in Dimwood far from the ruins of Talan Dathar. The dark forest was left with not one human inhabitant. The elementals, fey, elves and dwarves were perplexed, for disease and epidemic at this time was as yet unknown to them and they were unaffected. The Plague afflicted the populations of other human civilizations but the infection seemed to lose its potency the further from Dimwood these victims were found.

> At the edge of Dimwood a vile and powerful witch appears, taking up her residence in an abandoned fortress tower once occupied by humans before the Plague. In orcan the site was called Yalda'bok. She drew to her domain many wicked and dangerous creatures.

> *The Titan-Wyrm War* was a mysterious conflict that began with a single small fight between a green dragon and an armored Titan, names unknown. But the dragon in mid-battle was maimed horribly by a second Titan and word spread of the murder throughout Devilspire, Dimwood, Splinterdark, Deep Ore and Darkfrost Peaks. In the weeks that followed more and more Titans and dragons entered the conflict and suddenly full battle erupted in Bholbash Valley. The struggle became epic as over a thousand Titans found themselves at war with three thousand dragons of all kinds and sizes. The greatest part of the conflict occurred inside the huge, hollow mountain later to be known widely as Kag'Ar Grul of Devilspire, which in Old Gyant simply means *Where Titans Flee*. The Titans, losing half of their numbers, these magnificent figures who stood over fifty feet in height and thousands of years old, fled as more and more dragons arrived from lands unknown. This war was about 1500

After Cataclysm and is the final event according to the ancient chronographers to transpire during The Scattering Years.

End of the Age of Forgotten Years

Chronological Record Continues

1519 After Cataclysm: This year noted for two events connected together, and for this being the renewal of the historical record after The Scattering. In the Siege of Dijin Castle, also known as the The Fall of Mygok the Titan, the Titans sieged the EM'M dwarves of northern Devilspire, aided by local cave giants and cyclopean barbarians. The EM'M dwarves had prepared by making special slings when the Titans had become a threat. These slings catapulted specially trained and armored dwarves protected by spells. Whole companies of these dwarves were launched at the surprised Titans like flying ants with hooks and blades that were grooved to hold the potent venom extracted from the manticores of the EM'M. Mygok the Titan was felled in this way and chopped apart to the horror and astonishment of the other Titans. At his fall the Bone Kingdom allies dispersed and the dwarves took as their trophy the mighty hammer of Mygok.

1530 After Cataclysm: The EM'M dwarves of Dijin Castle melt down the hammer of Mygok the Titan and forge the spell-crafted war hammer called *Quakemaker*.

1554 After Cataclysm: Elaborately feathered and robed figures, humans from the Great Desert of Eternal Sands, traveled across the face of Dagothar in large entourages visiting the courts, holds, caverns, camps and kingdoms of all races. These strangers appeared in Darkfrost, Dimwood, Wandering Elms, Shannidar, Devilspire, Dijin Castle, Ettertooth Mountains, in Splinterdark, Titan Oaks, Deep Ore Peaks, Treehelm, Arborealm, Feyknot-on-the-Water, the Scorched Earth, Burning Flats, the Isin Plain, Enchandrus and even in Everleaf Pines to the Court of Elderboughs. The Men of the Eternal Sands arrived astride sleek coppery dragons as envoys of one who was called Zrakiul Plagueborn, King of the Eternal Sands. All other kings and rulers were to vow their allegiance, pay homage to his emissaries and send tribute to him at his desert palace amidst the magnificent city of Gotsduin. When the envoys appeared before the Barkwalk demanding entrance into the Court of the Great Tree, Lycrops and Ish'layyar, two of the Pillars of Everleaf, gave them battle and slew them for their insolence.

1556 After Cataclysm: The HAD'DR dwarves occupying a series of caverns in western Ettertooth range far from the domain of their enemies, the stone giants of Il-Makkabor, suddenly found themselves sieged by a massive army of strange humans, many riding copper dragons and mounted astride great lizard beasts. Almost overrun and unprepared to fight a host so immense, the HAD'DR engineers collapsed their cavern entrances after retreating in to the network of tunnels and caves deep underneath Ettertooth mountains. The dwarves escaped to hidden haunts and began a major exploration of the cave systems below Ettertooth.

1558 After Cataclysm: The EM'M dwarves of Dijin Castle found themselves surrounded by a major host of the Men of the Eternal Sands at the same time that a second huge army invaded Splinterdark making war against the faeries and humans of Kaidor, Brard and Pol'tr. This began *The Burning Years,* so named by the ancients for two reasons. First, it was the policy of these desert marauders to burn with fire the homes of those who resisted, even entire colonies and townships. Second, their war against all others in Dagothar coincided with a drought when the sun burned hotter. Many feared that it was the Sand Emporer who held power over the rain. Emporer Zrakiul of Gotsduin could not penetrate Dijin Castle's defenses but he vowed to end the dwarves of Devilspire mountains when he returned.

1559 After Cataclysm: Two Sand Kings under Emporer Zrakiul of the Eternal Sands lead their armies again the Men of the Scorched Earth. In this devastating conflict the Scorched Earth clans were only able to repel the invaders when the mighty faeries of Everleaf joined them. In this war the heroic King-Slayer named Fenrix the Mighty, a warsloth general, was torn apart by copper dragons.

Also in this year the HAD'DR dwarves of Ettertooth engaged the stone giants of Il-Makkabor in the Battle of Three Cliffs. The dwarves were defeated and had to retreat back into the caves below the mountains. Though the HAD'DR were the aggressors, now the stone giants made sport of hunting them.

1560 After Cataclysm: In the Battle of Illyriac Plains the Men of Kaidor, Brard and Polt'tr amassed a great army and met the hosts of the Sand Kings in the region that would later be called the Gnolldom Plains. During the battle another host emerged onto the field from Ettertooth, a horde of Etterorcs allied to Emporer Zrakiul of the Eternal Sands. The humans of Splinterdark and the men of the desert engaged in mutual slaughter as the Kaidor-led army retreated back into the woods. The Etterorcs would not venture far from their caves so returned to the mountains and the Sand Kings departed the field back to their desert.

1563 After Cataclysm: In the Battle of Midnight Pass the HAD'DR dwarves engage the stone giants with a ferocity that alarmed their much larger adversaries. Unable to effect a greater victory because the narrowness of the pass the HAD'DR break their assault with a new knowledge about the giants. The dwarves learned that the stone giants never adopt new strategies nor alter their barbarian tactics, but newer weapons designed for larger opponents and new attack methods aided them in felling more giants than usual. The HAD'DR begin extensive weapons manufacturing and training.

1565 After Cataclysm: Four separate Sand King armies invade the faery-occupied and sacred forest of Enchandrus Domain in what is now called the Moonfurrow War. Many faeries were killed but the Moonfurrow Gardens were protected until the host of Manax the warsloth, a Pillar of Everleaf, arrived and drove the Men of the Eternal Sands out of the woods. The enemy gathered again outside Enchandrus and Manax with his raging faeries broke their order and sent them retreating across the Illyriac Plain. Copper dragons dropping reinforcements from the skies had the Sand Kings again regrouping at the edge of Ettertooth and Manax, joined now by the Men of the Scorched Earth, broke their lines, slaughtered them without ceasing day and night and pursued the survivors all the way to the Eternal Sands where Manax's army fell upon the host of Gotsduin at the city gates in the desert. The faeries and Scorched Earth humans cut through this army completing a road hundreds of miles long littered with the bodies of the dead from Enchandrus across Dagothar to the gates of Gotsduin. The slaughter outside the city walls was at the turning of the year.

1566 After Cataclysm: As the Men of the Scorched Earth clans and faeries with Manax made war against the people of Gotsduin, the warsloth general Manax and his sloths located, beat down and rounded up the five Sand Kings with their Emporer whom the wily Mithix the warsloth captured. The powerful Sand Kings and Zrakiul were discovered to be Minion-touched. As the entire civilization of Gotsduin was put to the sword, spear, talon and teeth, Manax and the more powerful faeries led by Violia opened the old tombs and cast each Sand King into a vault and sealed them inside, trapped and sealed with faerylock enchantments. In this war Manax rose to prominence as the chief of the Pillars of Everleaf and was henceforth titled The Mighty. He is said to have ended The Burning Years. Since those days the ruins of Gotsduin have been called the Crypts of the Olden Sand Kings. This ended the last human kingdom called by the name Dathari, or *from Talan Dathar*. This war caused faeries to distrust Men.

1569 After Cataclysm: Preparing a major offensive against the stone giants of Il-Makkabor, the HAD'DR found themselves unexpectedly under attack by a large horde of Etterorcs now free from the bewitchery of the Sand Kings. This is known as the First Etterorc War, the orcs driven off after they overran a few cavernholds of the dwarves. This unforeseen campaign set the HAD'DR back in their designs against the giants.

1571 After Cataclysm: After twenty-seven years of making the mountain habitable and fortifying the caves and accesses underneath, the GAL'DR dwarves in Deep Ore Peaks move their population into their new home, the mountain city of Grol-galdir. Engineers begin work of Daggerhold fortress and the immense Chainway Bridge defense system. The VAL'DR, from which came the famous Silverbeard and Silveraxe clans, are given Mount Forknost and the dungeon mines as their new home. Already the dungeon mines were full of captives- orcs, goblins and cave ogres.

1574 After Cataclysm: The Second Etterorc War against the HAD'DR. The Etterorcs this time brought with them a tribe of violent cave trolls but the orcs were not ready for the battle discipline of the trained dwarven soldiers and the hacking to pieces of every single large trolls put the orcs to flight. A grand victory for their were very few dwarven casualties.

1575 After Cataclysm: The Year of Two Winters. As the year warmed into spring, a second winter occurred and lasted till late in the year merging with the winter following. Men were affected the most, hunger and even starvation in some regions, for the crops did not grow.

1578 After Cataclysm: The Siege of Grol-galdir, also remembered as the War of Webol the Evil, who had lived in Deep Ore Peaks long before the arrival of the dwarves. Webol's hordelings and snakelike warriors were unable to drive out the Galdirim.

1581 After Cataclysm: The HAD'DR accidentally happen upon a group of stone giants that had ranged far from Il-Makkabor. Using new military techniques the dwarven patrol defeated the giants, even killing one. News of the victory emboldened the HAD'DR resulting with more and more dwarven patrols being sent further out.

1584 After Cataclysm: The Fall of Il-Makkabor. The HAD'DR dwarves formerly challenged the stone giants to battle, a contest for the possession of the great cavern of springs called Il-Makkabor. The giants laughed and met them in open battle but were quickly overwhelmed by the advancing dwarves protected in thick metal armor and using long weapons. Many giants fell as others fled and the dwarves occupied the cavern and escorted the giantesses and their young ones out of the mountain. Honoring their gigantic adversaries the HAD'DR kept the name Il-Makkabor and the dwarves were ever after known as the Haddarim.

1609 After Cataclysm: Following the emergence of a strange cult of goddess worshippers in the southern mountains of Devilspire, a major resurgence of the Bone Kingdoms occurred. The orcs, goblins, trolls, ogres, minataurs and cave giants were now led by seemingly undefeatable axe-wielding chieftains. They occupied the dwarven-abandoned citadels at Ebrog Pass and Bholbash Valley and for the first time the orcs explored and occupied the vastness of Kag'Ar Grul where the Titans and dragons had made war.

In this year the Bone Kingdoms attacked Dijin Castle. In the battle the axes of the orc chieftains cut down many of the great ones among the EM'M dwarves, more than a few mighty dwarves wielding the magically-forged war hammer *Quakemaker* to little effect. A young son of the patriarch of the Hammerworn clan named Theol saw Quakemaker lying on the ground amidst the chaos of battle. Picking it up he swung the mighty metal hammer of Mygok the Titan and completely knocked an axe chieftain out of his armor as a potent energy crackled and pulsed from the impact. The EM'M dwarves rallied behind Theol Hammerworn and the Bone Kingdom invaders were driven off.

1611 After Cataclysm: The Hammerworn clan at ascendancy in EM'M dwarven society it held a special council where it was decided that it was time for them to join their brethren in finding a new home in the east. News of the taking of Il-Makkabor by the HAD'DR and the building of Grol-galdir by the GAL'DR prompted the EM'M leaders to agree that Dijin Castle was not fit to settle, for the Bone Kingdoms would never rest until they were driven out or destroyed. In this year the EM'M vacated Dijin Castle and passed out of Devilspire Mountains toward Deep Ore Peaks.

1612 After Cataclysm: The migrating trains and army of the EM'M dwarves passed through the dried floodplain of Feymark'ul and found their passage opposed by the Titans of the forest, Titan Oaks, where they had retreated after their decimation by the dragons. As the EM'M led by Theol Hammerworn prepared to defend against the Titans, a serpentine, black and white tiger-striped faery dragon bearing a single rider descended from the sky. Dhishra, High Shar daughter of Elderboughs, addressed the Titans, ordering them to allow the dwarves to pass into the mountains, for "...such is the will of Elderboughs." The Titans returned to their wood and the dwarves perplexed that a god of the woodland beings would intercede on their behalf. Long are the memories of the dwarves and the name of Dhishra was entered into their lore.

1613 After Cataclysm: Webol the Evil and his hordelings attacked the Galdirim dwarves in the Battle of Deep Ore Mines as the Druil'kin trolls of the Fingers of Deep Ore Peaks sieged Mount Forknost of the VAL'DR dwarves. While these battles were fought the orcs of Deep Ore amassed at Daggerhold above the mines at entrance to Grol-galdir and attacked. The assault was long planned by Webol the Ancient but unknown to him, his loyal dark faeries, the trolls and orcs, not far away was the mighty host of the EM'M dwarves located in a series of caverns northwest of Grol-galdir , given to them by the Galdirim for a temporary home in their migration. As the Galdirim drove off Webol's hordelings of serpent folk, the EM'M dwarves fell upon the trolls around Mount Forknost and the orcs who were unable to enter Daggerhold. By the end of the year the EM'M were settled in the caverns they took from the Druil'kin trolls.

1621 After Cataclysm: The Third Etterorc War began with the rise to power of a half-ogre orc chieftain who unified all the Etterorcs together, with local trolls, cobble goblins and even some cave giants. But no stone giants joined their cause against the Haddarim dwarves. The half-ogre orc leader was smarter than most orcs and challenged the Haddarim to open battle on the opposite end of the valley at the foot of Il-Makkabor mountain, where a second and much larger host of Bone Kingdom orcs and goblins awaited to trap the dwarves. The battled raged a whole day resulting in the death of the half-ogre but the Haddarim had to retreat into Il-Makkabor due to the sheer numbers of Bone Kingdom adversaries still alive after ten thousand were felled. Third Etterorc War would last three years.

1624 After Cataclysm: Dwarves of Il-Makkabor defeat the Etterorcs and capture thousands of them in a series of raids into Etterorc territory. An enormous anvil is made with a huge, ceremonial maul which are then used to crush the skulls of the orcs and their allies. In this year the Haddarim became the Dwarves of Red Anvil.

1692 After Cataclysm: after discovering the vast halls and undercaverns of Ricanor Castle empty, the EM'M dwarves finding the ancient structures intact, megalithic blocks Titan-laid that marveled the dwarves, the Hammerworn Dynasty under King Theol relocates their people to Ricanor just outside the legendary Mount Talisman. Here the EM'M dwarves would make their home for centuries under the Hammerworn kings.

1700 After Cataclysm: The Fall of Garotha Dracomancer, the ancient wyrm of Talan Dathar, formerly called Shadowskin and The One-Eyed. This protector of Kaidor fell in defense of Haddons Gate in Arborealm when the Horned Wyrms of Southwood attacked. Southwood no longer exists, buried under the waters of the Spawnsea.

At this time the Kaidor Protectorate were black dragons of draconarch blood from Dimwood antiquity. Those wyrms in service to the Brard were green dragons and the wyrms of the Pol'tr were snow white. With the death of Garotha the dragons of all three groups convened in council among themselves, forbidding Men to choose for them their own draconic ruler. A wyrm of the blood of Garotha was chosen, named Laer'garoth. The Men of the Three Tribes assembled for war against the dragons of Southwoods but were forbidden this by their own wyrms...the dragons explaining that Men need not meddle in affairs not their own.

1701 After Cataclysm: led by their new leader of the combined Protectorate, Laer'garoth the Black, the wyrms of Kaidor, Brard and Pol'tr took to the sky and attacked the haunts of the Horned Wyrms of Southwoods in retaliation for their trespass on Haddons Gate. Over fifty enemy dragons were killed or severely maimed and twenty female younglings were brought back and divided among the three groups of dragons in service to Men. This year saw Laer'garotha given the title of Hornbreaker.

1719 After Cataclysm: The shocking news spreads far and wide that a human named Greric du'Brard slew one of the dreaded axemasters of Devilspire in single combat before his patrol then slaughtered an entire orc company. From Sigils Arch to Deep Ore all along the trade routes the name of Greric became known. The Galdirim traveled to the spot where the axemaster fell and erected a stone monument and statue of Greric, the inscription reading, "...in this the 175th year from the founding of Grol-galdir."

1724 After Cataclysm: Webol the Evil again attacks with his serpent-like hordelings, sieging Mount Forknost of the VAL'DR dwarves in Deep Ore Peaks. The dwarven defenses were breached and had not the Galdirim soldiers arrived in time to chase off the surprised invaders the VAL'DR would have fallen, their survivors ending up in the dungeon mines of Webol. The VAL'DR were escorted to Grol-galdir where they live until this day, known as the Silverbeards and Silveraxe clans.

1725 After Cataclysm: In this year the Witch of Yald'bok on the edge of Dimwood was killed by a Silthani Moonshadow assassin by a stratagem of the famous human hero Greric du'Brard. The dwarves of Grol-galdir, hearing of the death of Commander Greric sculpted a statue in his honor still seen at Daggerhold this day.

1728 After Cataclysm: the Aelvanar elves of Splinterdark had by this date become too populous for their communities. The Aelvani family of elves migrate to Everleaf and take up residence among the faeries around the Barkwalk and Court of Elderboughs. This arrival was initially opposed by the fey but the Great Tree approved and the matter was settled. This is the origin of Ti'el City.

1744 After Cataclysm: Men experienced a population explosion, already filling Arborealm, Treehelm and the coasts of the Spawnsea with villages and settlements. The city of Haddons Gate was a vast wooden metropolis surrounding a central stonework district with a huge fortress. Long weary of the political and military dominance of the Kaidor, the Pol'tr people break out in a civil war and a major battle is fought at Haddons Gate in which the Brard did not participate. The Pol'ty were subdued and instigators were publicly executed. This year marked the Ascendancy of Caedoria.

1792 After Cataclysm: Early in the year an army of scorpinids lead by their Mound Barons from the jungles of the Silapenti attacked the south citadel of Shannidar, overrunning it. The Silthani elves, knowing that these invaders were heading toward Sigils Arch, moved an army through the underground corridor system connecting all the citadels to the Arch, emerging behind the scorpinids. At Sigils Arch the other Silthani warriors were prepared and pressed between the two Silthani elven armies the scorpinids were slaughtered. At this time the Silthani had no knowledge of the teeming colonies of scorpinids in the southern jungles.

1797 After Cataclysm: Silthani elven scouts along the jungle frontier learn of a great war fought deep in the jungle interior between the scorpinid Mound Barons and a race of serpent people, the Silapenti. The victor in this war is unknown, but later in the year the Silthani received reports of a large host of scorpinids approaching Sigils Arch by keeping far away from the southern citadel. Prepared, the elves fended off the attack and the Mound Barons returned to the jungle.

1801 After Cataclysm: The faeries in the Court of Elderboughs instantly grow quiet at the intrusion of a foul-smelling humped-back devil, obviously petrified with fear at seeing Elderboughs' gigantic face. The devil whimpers.

"Masssta! Pleesss! Cast me not backward! Not back to Abysss...messsage I have!" It's knobby nose peeked out from its wing-enwrapped body. Several warsloths closed in, weapons ready but the unbearable stench of the devil was like armor keeping them away.

"WHAT HAVE YOU, IDRU?" Hearing this the devil winced and moaned.

"My masshta be watched! He canna come! No...too many eyesss, he sayeth." Hearing these words spoken in high sylvan by a devil the warsloth Gano'tax remembered the shadow with the scepter that visited long ago. The devil continued.

"Th' Banes! He sayeth...in twenty and three yearsss. Yesss. A plan of returnsss. They shalt come...The Great Goddesss, sshe callsss them."

"WHO IS THIS GODDESS?"

"Sshe is Ashadula! Masshta sayeth th' Pilot will know..."

The faeries listened in alarm, none having heard the name Ashadula before and many wondering who this master of the devil was. The fetid devil vanished, none knowing that Elderboughs sent him to banishment in the Abyssal Planes.

1824 After Cataclysm: This was the *Year of the Second Sun,* according to human records, also known as the Broken Moon. But the faeries remembered this year as the *War of the Star People.* The historic accounts gathered from the memories of the fey, traditions of elves, runic pillars of dwarves and records of Men as well as the ancient book of the dragon, Laer'garoth the

Old, the Dragon-Chronicler, are so fantastic they are often relegated to the status of myth and superstition. Much has been forgotten.

It is said that in this year a second sun appeared in the heavens, shining even at night, and that gods in the thousands appeared like burning stars and fought among themselves with spears of light that destroyed this new sun...turning it into the Broken Moon that soon disappeared out of sight. As gods among the starry canopy battled, the sons of gods descended in fiery chariots and fought among themselves in a great battle above and in the ruins of Talan Dathar...the First City of Men.

During this sky war a burning mountain fell upon Dagothar in the far east. Later it was said that this piece of a god crashed into what is now called Lake Fellstar amidst Sunkenwood.

The incident was over as quickly as it had begun, forgotten by most almost as soon as it occurred, the inhabitants of Dagothar having no reason to remember it. A small group of men in Caedoria recorded the events and after a while they died leaving their writings to be discovered centuries later.

[See Appendix: Year of the Second Sun for additional details about this event that were unknown to Imaricus]

1832 After Cataclysm: Shannidar of the Silthani elves is again invaded by the Mound Barons of the scorpinid armies who brought with them from the jungle swamps the dreaded Kraxa'kin trolls, the formions who were another branch of the insect people, and enormous cyprian bog giants. In the Battle of Shannidar South the elves lost and retreated to reinforcements at the walls of Sigils Arch where they lost again and had to hide inside the city. The Mound Barons sieged the Arch and this prolonged affair reached the ears of others in the jungle who came to aid the Barons, smaller forces that together greatly added to the scorpinid host. In Dimwood the centaurs told King

Thalleus the Yak-Centaur faery ruler of the Silthani plight and Thalleus thundered across Shannidar to their aid; centaur spearmen and archers, raging elm treants, groups of faeries and a countless mass of hopping toggl'ids. The Mound Barons broke under the assault and fled back to the Jungles of the Silapenti.

1843 After Cataclysm: Druldosh the Draconarch of Darkfrost declared himself king of Dimwood forest, setting his seat of power in the ruins of Talan Dathar nine and ten years after the War of the Star People who fought among those ancient buildings. Druldosh was a polar wyrm and had as his subjects many other dragons, the frost giants of Darkfrost Peaks, the Hama'kin trolls, the Bone Kingdoms of those same mountains. The upper ruins of Talan Dathar became the capitol of Druldosh's domain.

1846 After Cataclysm: After repeated requests to yield to his authority were unmet, Druldosh sent a large army of Hama'kin trolls and cave ogres against King Thalleus of the faeries. Not one troll returned to Talan Dathar and rumors persisted that the forest had come alive and swallowed his army as the yak-centaur roared with laughter. Over half of the entire race of Hama'kin trolls were lost to the treants of Dimwood, this battle earning them the title, Elmlord Guardians.

1857 After Cataclysm: the faery explorer Rajosh Gonewhiskers discovered the ancient and abandoned City of the Dragons called Winterfang first occupied in the early days of the Addanc whom TAL-NIK slew in The Old Time. Rajosh found its entrance, the city hidden in a mountain in western Darkfrost Peaks. In the city was a gaping hole that went straight down large enough to admit any size dragon.

1864 After Cataclysm: A large group of Silthani elves of Shannidar depart Sigils Arch and the Citadels in their migration to the floodplain of Feymark'ul to begin the building of a series of remarkable towers upon artificial hills later to be called the Tors of Hallows'gone. For the next thirty-two years a steady stream of elves would leave Shannidar for the floodplain.

1896 After Cataclysm: The Fall of Sigils Arch. The Mound Barons leads a vast host of scorpinids from the jungles into Shannidar again with the formions, cyprian bog giants and hordes of Kraxa'kin trolls from the swamps. The quick fall of the South Citadel prompted the other citadels to retreat to the Arch and as one large group the Silthani race of elves together departed Shannidar never to return. They passed through Dretchwold and settled in Feymark'ul during the dry season.

1917 After Cataclysm: In the Deep, across the caves and cavern expanses of Hollowrealm a religious war erupted between those factions worshipping the old god Oelth who dated from the Age of Shadowed Ice and the shadowy goddess Ashadula of the Xakkiun Oracle who first appeared at the end of the Shadowed Ice period. A third sect worshipped the Dark Tree, called the Limbs of Darkness that was first discovered at the Cataclysm which opened a new and anciently occupied series of caverns where stood a gigantic, black fungalwood tree. This sect served the Mrul and his Minions who tended the Black Tree and were known to have survived from The World Before. This underworld war resulted in the eradication of the religion of Oelth, the enslavement of his worshippers and the dividing of the spoils between those who honored Ashadula and they who served the Mrul.

The Ashadula Oracle became a place of pilgrimage and the Dark Tree became an object of veneration. Though the Deep spawned many cults and beliefs it was these two figures that all religions Below Dagothar regarded.

1919 After Cataclysm: The War of the Pillars of Everleaf. The Sporu'kin trolls of Drakeroost Peaks gathered the Bone Kingdom armies and with an incredibly massive horde, invaded Borderealm. In those days Borderealm was completely covered in trees, many areas being thick impassable woods. The faeries of Treehelm, Arborealm, Enchandrus, Feyknot-on-the-Water and Everleaf gathered their forces and numbered in the thousands beyond counting. They separated into four hosts led by the Pillars: Manax the warsloth, Ish'layyar the bear shapechanger, Lycrops the white werewolf and Afangus'Kar the sabertooth. It took the faeries three moons to bury the dead invaders.

1944 After Cataclysm: For years Druldosh the Draconarch, smarting from the loss of his troll forces in Dimwood, had gathered to him more and more monsters and warriors to his seat in the ruins of Talan Dathar. In this the 98th year from the Ambush of the Treants when he lost the trolls, King Thalleus of the centaurs and faeries and King Eganosh Faerymane the ariel with his seven races of Ayr assembled and attacked Talan Dathar with the trees called Elmlord Guardians. The combined forces of the fey slaughtered the host of Druldosh, put the dragons to flight and chased the Draconarch out of Dimwood back into Darkfrost Peaks, the Hama'kin trolls retreating with him.

2144 After Cataclysm: The Caedorians finish their new city, Caedathal East, named in commemoration as a New Talan Dathar, a large district within designed for the families of the Brard living among them. The central stone fortress of Haddons

Gate constructed of megalithic blocks is garrisoned with Caedorians but the Palace and the vast wooden city of Haddons Gate is given over to the population of the Pol'tr.

2160 After Cataclysm: In this the 16th year of the completion of Caedathal East in Arborealm on the coast of the Spanwsea the Caedorians finished their magnificent Temple of Eternal Lore. An ancient artifact was brought to Caedathal by a delegation of elementals called the Hollow Men, hundreds of hooded, robed figures, an archaic race of earthborn elemental people led by a gigantic elemental hulk called the Stratamental. They delivered an item of clear crystal, The Tablet, to the stewards of the Temple of Eternal Lore. Men were instructed to seek out Elderboughs concerning what was to be done about this relic. This was the first recorded appearance of the Oraclon Tablet in the histories of Men and the elementals stated it had been taken from below Mount Talisman.

In Everleaf at this time did appear The Old Man of the Woods in the Dome of Elderboughs. Before an assembly of faeries and the Great Cedar of A'DIN he uttered a prophecy known from of old that had been taken from the walls below Mount Talisman of *"...the birth of a Mighty One...a warrior like as one the world has never seen. Great signs shall herald his entry into the world."* Elderboughs nodded but said nothing as the faeries marveled, for in those days Manax was the Mighty One.

2195 After Cataclysm: [TAL 1, Year 35] After a series of incidents involving human incursions into what the faeries considered was their own sacred woodland domains, faeries from Arborealm, Treehelm and Feyknot-on-the-Water gathered in Everleaf and petitioned to the Queen of the Fey, De'nelia, sister of Dhishra, the two High Shars. The faeries were shocked and left with a feeling of betrayal when the Queen of the Faeries ruled that they had no cause, that Men had as much right to the woods as they, finding that only Everleaf Pines and Enchandrus Domain forests had the Protection of Elderboughs as strictly the realms of the fey. The ruling was very unpopular and further injury was caused when Ashrey the shar forbid any appeals to Elderboughs on this matter, for Ashrey and the fifty Jubilants were Keepers of the Barkwalk and had power to admit or deny all who came to petition the Ancient Tree.

2232 After Cataclysm: [TAL 1, Year 72] Early in the year the faeries noticed that the elementals across Dagothar were on the move. This much older race were mysterious to the fey, but regarded as friends. Reports came to Everleaf that the whole race of elemental beings with its myriads of families had all gathered around the treeline of Titan Oaks where the majority of the last Titans dwelt. Elderboughs received a petition from the alarmed Titans asking for His intervention for they knew not the intention of the elementals, the Titans reminding the Great Tree that they had obeyed His command regarding the dwarves delivered by Dhishra all those years earlier.

In the early summer Mount Talisman for the first time ever began billowing forth smoke, great white plumes filling the sky. Shortly after this was noticed the whole of Dagothar shook so that fruit fell from trees and Everleaf's forest floors became covered in pine cones and needles. Then the sun did not rise and in The Long Night the faeries delighted to find that munchroot grew to astonishing sizes that elderbread had not grown to before. The white and red mushrooms filled the forest floors.

In this year the dragons of the world grew restless, many an egg did not hatch in its time and the wyrms suffered nightmares. The Queen of the Fey announced that a Mighty One has been born in Dagothar. At Titan Oaks the news of this birth alarmed the Titans, for a giantess who was of partial elemental ancestry had given birth to a son belonging to a particularly old Titan who had captured and taken her from her clan in Deep Ore. Many Titans in those days took their females from among the giant stock. Fearing the countless masses of elementals that encircled their woods the Titans banished the giantess and her newborn son, sending them out to Deep Ore Peaks where the elementals gave her escort to a hidden cavern with a natural spring. They brought her food and materials and built her a home.

This year marked the birth of Craniax, last of those with elemental sky giant blood, his name in Old Gyant meaning *Head of the Giants.*

At the end of the year the fey in Everleaf received panicked warnings from Enchandrus that a host of strangers, very powerful were heading into Everleaf Pines. Two dozen figures, tall and robust, not of Dathari blood were led by a large bearded person of serene demeanor who carried an ancient whitish horn with two wells. The warsloth Dijix opposed the strange leader rudely and before astonished faery onlookers the warsloth warrior was shoved effortlessly aside. Instantly poliwogs, wickerworls, yelkai, warsloths and slap weasels charged only to be blasted backward through the air at the blowing of the amazing horn. Manax, spear in hand, began to charge but was stilled by the inner voice of Ashrey in his mind- *They are Ha'akathrals...the First People.*

The mysterious visitors were escorted into the Dome. Their leader stood before the face of the Great Tree.

"TAL'ANIN," boomed the horn-bearer looking up at Elderboughs.

"TAL-NIK." The Archaic Tree smiled and golden light bathed the visitors as they reverently bowed their beards to the ground. TAL-NIK continued.

"From Mount Talisman have we come. From the old archivist halls of Talan Dathar have we come. From the council of the Dragon-Chronicler who lives among Men have we come. From the unknown to the known have we come." As he spoke a swarm of large striped bees flew out of the horn and flitted about Elderboughs.

"WHAT NOW IS KNOWN?" The faeries listened with interest.

"The Mighty One, the child of prophecy...he is indeed born," spoke the bearded athak. "He is TAL'VARI of the Codex." Many faeries pressed in further.

"TAL'VARI...A SON OF TWO WORLDS."

"He is the fire of Olam...he shall lay low the height of the Titans. A soul divided, he shall reign over great and small till the Year of Reunion comes at the end of the sixth and final TAL." The athaks departed and Ashrey waited in silence for a moment to speak with Elderboughs, few hearing.

"Father," the shar spoke aloud softly, "what is a TAL?" Her curiosity burned within for she knew those older than faeries, the athaki and elementals, called Him by the title TAL'ANIN.

"A CALENDAR OF THE OLD TIME KEEPERS...EIGHT HUNDRED SIXTY AND FOUR YEARS." Encouraged by His openness, she ventured more.

"You and TAL-NIK spoke of Craniax in a prophecy. What is this Year of Reunion? What will happen? What is the sixth TAL?"

"AS THERE BE FOUR PILLARS OF EVERLEAF, THE TAL DYNASTY OF WORLD-BEARERS BE FOUR IN NUMBER WHEN TAL'ISSA COMES FORTH IN THE SECRET YEAR.

"DAUGHTER OF EVERLEAF, THE TIME COMES WHEN ALL THAT HAS BEEN LOST SHALL BE DRAWN BACK TOGETHER."

Unknown to Ashrey, the High Shar Dhishra was listening and took note that the title of TAL'ISSA was female.

2295 After Cataclysm: [TAL 1, Year 135] A group of Aelvani elves petitioned the Queen of the Faeries for leave to assemble a crew of elves and faeries for a voyage across the Spawnsea. These elves were long-sighted and feared the growing dissension among the fey concerning the humans, and the rapid multiplying of Men. Already there were whole races of the fey that had ceased reproducing. Foreseeing a conflict on the horizon they opted to seek out a far away new home, a haven and refuge for elves and fey. Their petition was heard in full and vehemently denied without explanation. Ashrey and the Jubilants took vote and decided for the elves, that they could appeal to Elderboughs and such action earned them the ire of Da'nelia, Queen of the Fey.

A huge assembly of faeries and elves filled the Dome of the Great Tree and listened to the appeal, Elderboughs shocking them with his approval of their plan. He dropped two of His massive goldenwood branches with instructions that the elves haul the wood to Yadel Lake and built with it a sea worthy vessel. Their god declared- "WHEN THE TIME COMES TO RETURN HOME, THE LIGHT FROM THIS VESSEL SHALL DIRECT YOUR PATH."

The Aelvani elves built the ship and named it *The Golden Bough,* each plank of goldenwood covered in the script of the elves preserving their traditions and the words of Elderboughs. In this way did 160 wood elves with a group of faeries disappear from Dagothar to become the mighty race of the Aelmari, or Silver Elves of Aroth Beyond. This incident deepened the division between the fey of those favoring the authority of the Queen and those in favor of the decision of Elderboughs.

2304 After Cataclysm: [TAL 1, Year 144] Faeries of Arborealm appeared in the Dome of Elderboughs reporting that the humans called the Pol'tr had been erecting fortified towns where no Men had ventured before and that over a thousand Men were now building docks and homes along the edges of Yadel Lake. Other faeries said that there were Men of a different type now wandering the timber reaches high in Drakeroost mountains, fierce Men who killed trolls and orcs. A council on Men is held with thousands of faeries before the Queen. Many elves with the fey demanded action and Manax announced that he and his warsloths were ready to push Men back toward the sea. The Queen ordered the warsloth general to hold his tongue and many of the elves raised their voices in protest against the Queen's reticence. Some began to call for her sister Dhishra to be Queen.

Before the serene face of Elderboughs a riot erupted as the Queen tried to explain that in the prophetic annals they were shown below Mount Talisman that there was a plan for the future that involved Men and that the world was big enough that faeries need not fear them. In the chaos of struggling, fears voiced and accusations uttered, Da'nelia was struck in the face and a flash of red bathed the inner Dome as Elderboughs' light darkened bringing silence to the fey. All realized that the Archaic Tree was angered over the smiting of his daughter. Instantly the fifty Jubilants, Ashrey and the shars, were empowered by Elderboughs in the Wrath of the Jubilants remembered by all the fey. These daughters of the sylvan god forced every single faery and elf out of the Dome, down the Barkwalk and sealed shut the entry. Dhishra, sister of the Queen, was amidst the arguing faeries and found herself also ushered out of the Dome. The suddeness and sheer power and violence of the shars stunned the faeries.

In this year after this event the Aelvani elves divided themselves into two groups and the faeries gained an enemy who would haunt them for millennia...a female who would become the dreaded Shadowitch.

In the Aelvani Civil War half the wood elf population vanished in m igration into the interior of Splinterdark. In the centuries that followed these elves would venture into the caverns of Darkfrost, travel down into the heart of the underworld at the beckoning and promises of the Minions and ultimately become the infamous and feared dark elven nation of the Aelvatchi of the black city of Sarthaldon. When they departed Everleaf they escorted Queen Da'nelia and many faeries who joined her into Splinterdark. The remaining fey and elves of Everleaf and Enchandrus were in disbelief that Da'nelia had given up her throne and chosen banishment.

These events began the *Rift of the Fey.*

2376 After Cataclysm: [TAL 1, Year 216] The *Great Shaking of A'DIN* happened in this year, being the first appearance of the Broken Moon as it had come to be known. The actual first appearance was as The Second Sun that was destroyed in The War of the Star People in 1824 AC. In the quaking the Caedorian city of Caedathal East was broken apart, its Temple Precinct damaged as was Haddons Gate of the Pol'tr. The destruction of forests, whole regions sunk into the earth, the appearance of new hills and ruinous seas occurred across Dagothar and Aroth Beyond.

After the defenses of Caedathal East were toppled in the quaking the Caedorians and Brard amassed their forces after receiving news of the approach of an army heading toward their domain. The rank-and-file soldiers of Men marched out in The Great War and fought against a Minion horde of Silapenti snake warriors from the jungles. The battles were fought on the South Illyriac Plain, the site ever since called Whispermoor. The Caedorians and Brard repelled the invaders but at terrific cost and a deep animosity developed between those who fought and the Polt'tr who did not, but stayed in their wooden city around Haddons Gate. The Gate fortress was little affected by the earthquakes. The Pol'tr had plenty of time to take to the field but did not and the Caedorians were expecting to be relieved but were not. From this year onward there was no more peace between Caedoria and the people of Pol'tr. It is said that the ghost shades of Whispermoor are of those Caedorians and Brard who died there calling for their Pol'tr allies for help. Caedathal East and the Temple are repaired.

2385 After Cataclysm: [TAL 1, Year 225] Craniax the sky-giant wrestles the Gargantulon, simple-minded son of the old Titans of the Mygok lineage who was innocent of their trespasses. The other Titans had run the dim-witted colossus off and Craniax, also an exile from Titan Oaks since his birth, sought the Gargantulon out. He befriended him at the foothills of Deep Ore where the forests of Splinterdark and Treehelm merge. For a whole day the woods shook and trees split as Craniax and the Gargantulon bellowed with laughter as they took turns throwing one another, smashing through the trees and foliage. The story of their friendship spread far and wide and the faeries watched Craniax from afar with interest.

2448 After Cataclysm: [TAL 1, Year 288] In this year the Rift of the Faeries was complete. The enchanted sylvan beings had become split into three distinct groups. The fey were those who remained in service to Everleaf, the shars and Elderboughs. Those who rebelled against the idea that faeries had to suffer at the encroachments of Men chose to depart Everleaf came to be called athradoc. The third group of faeries were indecisive, some neutral, but not wanting to rebel against Elderboughs by making Men their enemies and yet not wanting to make enemies of those faeries who did have issues with humans- the athradoc. This third group were regarded by the fey and athradoc as pathetic for they chose not to take sides and came to be called the exiles of Everleaf. Exiles and athradoc split into many groups and disappeared into the many woodlands and hill countries across Dagothar.

2464 After Cataclysm: [TAL 1, Year 304] A small army of Titans departed Titan Oaks and marched against the Silthani elves of Feymark'ul during the height of the flood season. The elves were terrified to see these gigantic figures waist deep in their waters amidst their fortified island tors throughout the floodplain. The Titans informed the elves that they would accept tribute in exchange for protection, for, as they could see, no invaders could attack even during the floods because the Titans were so tall. In this way were the Silthani elves fallen under the power of Titan Oaks.

2471 After cataclysm: TAL 1, Year 311] The Titans march against Grol-galdir and attempt to take Daggerhold, the fortress that guards the entrance to the city of the Deep Ore dwarves. The Titans succeed in taking the castle, gaining access to Chainway Bridge. A Titan ventured across the massive chains of the bridge that held in place huge slabs of stone for walking planks but dwarves hidden in a cliffside observatory pulled their levers and unhooked the tethers sending the hapless Titan to his death over a thousand feet below. Seeing this and knowing of no way to access the mountain, the Titans gave up their design against Grol-galdir.

2484 After Cataclysm: [TAL 1, Year 324] The Titans sought to take Ricanor Castle, justifying the aggression with fact it was they who constructed it. Already lording over the Druil'kin trolls of Deep Ore and the Bone Kingdom orcs and goblins as well as the ogres of Fingersdeep in the eastern range, the Titans instigated the Siege of Ricanor to oust the EM'M dwarves. Valiantly wielding Quakemaker the Hammerworn king led the dwarves in their defense but had to retreat to the most fortified areas of the keep.

Suddenly a new ally of the dwarves appeared and a troll giant among the Druil'kin tried to oppose him, but Craniax felled the troll giant and then hurled challenges and anger at the Titans, his dishonorable kin. His challenge was met by their mountainous leader and before both armies the last elemental sky giant fought Anyax the Titan Lord. Craniax took a blow to his shoulder while flattening the face of the bigger Titan with a boulder-packed fist. Anyax collapse like a tree before the host and laid still at the foot of Mount Talisman.

The Titans roared in rage and took up boulders, raining them on the smaller sky giant. To their astonishment Craniax sang loud a song and powerful winds issued from the mouth of the elemental giant that pushed aside the rocks in the air and delivered a blast of fear upon the Titans. They fled to their woods and the Bone Kingdoms dissolved to creep back into their caves.

Later in that same year the EM'M dwarves made their departure from Ricanor Keep, the place to immense to defend against gigantic adversaries, opting to migrate into Bone Kingdom caverns that they battled for. In the winter the Titans found Ricanor abandoned and many moved into the castle constructed in the days of Mygok the Titan.

2485 After Cataclysm: [TAL 1, Year 325] EM'M dwarves take by force a huge central cavern of the Bone Kingdoms located in Fingersdeep, those who participated in the siege the year before.

2514 After Cataclysm: [TAL 1, Year 354] the city of stone called Boldur Hill is built by the Men of Pol'tr from Arborealm in the lightly wooded area between Arborealm and Everleaf. This site would later be known as Barrowen. These were quiet years for mankind.

2530 After Cataclysm: [TAL 1, Year 370] the First Devilspire Invasion. The Bone Kingdoms of orcs, goblins, ogres, trolls and cave giants invaded the floodplain of Feymark'ul of the Silthani elves during the dry season. This first invasion saw great loss of life among the attackers who were not prepared for the archery skills of the elves and nor were they situated to assault fortified citadels surrounding great towers of extraordinary height. In this year the elves ceased all annual tribute payments to the Titans for their refusal to come to their aid when called for.

2538 After Cataclysm: [TAL 1, Year 378] a group of hunting Titans happened upon a cloud giant name Gruthmar who was using cord nets to fish salmon from a river in Deep Ore. The other giants knew Gruthmar as peace-loving. After he pulled up his nets the Titans seized his fish and one punched him when he protested. Gruthmar fell, tried to stand back up but lost his balance in dizziness and fell into the icy waters of the river from which he did not return. The Titans departed unaware that a cairn giant had witnessed the incident and had remained invisible because he had not moved, resembling a pile of rocks. The cairn giant reported the murder to Craniax who bellowed to the sky with the force of a divine horn in the *Call of the Giants*.

Across the face of Dagothar the mighty wind-empowered voice of Craniax the sky giant was heard by his gigantic kin from east to west. Giants of all kinds gathered in western Deep Ore from Treehelm, Everleaf, Drakeroost, Enchandrus, Splinterdark, Ettertooth Mountains, Devilspire, even Dimwood, Darkfrost Peaks and the southern jungles. They arrived singly and in groups- frost, cave, storm, cloud, fire, sandstone, cairn and hill giants, stone, tree and cyprian bog giants. For the first time the giants gathered in the thousands and held a council, listening to Craniax as he listed the trespasses of the Titans. Put to vote they together agreed and pronounced judgement upon the Titan race. The giants made Craniax the King of their kind and with a host of giants as the world had never seen before, Craniax led his army into the forest of Titan Oaks and effected a great slaughter among the Titans, the survivors suing for peace, which was granted. Craniax's eyes fell upon the beautiful young giantess captive named Heartha whom he took back from the Titans and made her his wife. The Titans until this event had ruled over many giants and had took from their communities the giantess maidens they coveted.

This episode was ever after remembered as the War of Giants and Titans. But the kingship of Craniax was not honored by all for there were other giants in the world who had not responded to the call. Among these were the dusk giants of Hollowrealm.

2544 After Cataclysm: [TAL 1, Year 384] Hunting giant aurochs in northern Deep Ore Peaks, Craniax happened upon a great alabaster wyrm guarding the entrance to a cavern he knew well. Inside the cave a female alabaster wyrm was laying an egg.

"Who are you?" asked Craniax after introducing himself.

"I am Barshak of Darkfrost...inside my consort labors hard and long. We are of the race of Winterfang." The alabaster dragon was huge and poised to defend himself against the elemental sky giant. But Craniax was wise and could read the hearts of strangers and knew these wyrms were to be no trouble in Deep Ore. This was the year Ishaak the Alabaster was born, later to be called Burnbreath...and the Draw of Craniax. Years later Craniax found the cave empty again, shards of yellow egg covered in dust.

2575 After Cataclysm: [TAL 1, Year 415] The Bone Kingdoms of Devilspire Mountains again attack the Silthani elves of Feymark'ul in the Second Devilspire Invasion effecting a great slaughter of elves. The orcs had grown smarter, bringing many cave giants and mountain ogres that hurled great rocks at the elven fortifications. After the invaders tired of their several sieges of the Tors and returned to their mountain haunts, a sizable portion of the Silthani migrated into the trees of Splinterdark. These elves disappeared for a while from the historical record. Some early chronographers declared them to have been captured by the Shadowitch much later, ending their days in her dungeons and buried under the foundations of her Keep. The rest of the Silthani continued in Feymark'ul.

2580 After Cataclysm: [TAL 1, Year 420] The Rape of Splinterdark occurred, also called the Rise of the Shadowitch. Almost three centuries after her departure from Everleaf as Queen of the Fey, Da'nelia was now a sorceress with an army of basks, evil half-formion faery insects very much like large spiders, the ancestors of the weavernbasks. The largest part of her army were the gnolls of Splinterdark, a wicked canine race. She secured most of Splinterdark by enslaving those races that would not join her. A great many unsuspecting fey and athradoc were captured in these early years before word about the Shadowitch spread throughout the world.

2593 After Cataclysm: [TAL 1, Year 433] Faeries in Everleaf leapt out of their burrows when suddenly a circle of fire appeared within Ti'el City of the wood elves. Nearby faeries watched as a tall shadowy form with glowing eyes emerged out of the ring of flames, followed by four scaled monsters with long toothed snouts that hissed and smelled of acrid sulfur. The shadow used a long-handled scepter of darkfire and beat the infernal beasts back into the ground just as the ring of fire closed the leave a smoking circle of burnt earth under the trees.

The imposing shadow entered the Barkwalk unopposed and strode into the Dome, the faeries watching closely as shadows swirled like armor about his form. The shars and faeries listened to Elderboughs and the shadow speak back and forth in a language none had heard before. Then the words of the dark visitor were made comprehensible when it began to speak in high sylvan.

"She travels the caveways of the Deep like a goddess. None defy her. Her entourage were once known among the Branchborn..." Hearing this the faeries were perplexed, for they were aware the shadow spoke of the underworld.

A pained expression passed over Elderboughs' face. The strange figure of darkness continued.

"An army of loyalists, vicious, they are greatly feared by all...the whole of Hollowrealm call them shadowfae."

"AND WHAT NAME DO THEY GIVE THE ONE I HAVE LOST..." A powerful sadness carried on the words of the Archaic Tree and the fey were stunned silent at His display of emotion.

"She is known as the Mycomaiden...Lady Death-Bringer. Three times the Minions have sought her out and three times their servants did not return."

When the shadow departed it was Ganeshu the Wise who informed others that they spoke of Sharassa, firstborn of Elderboughs. By the end of the day all of the fey knew this.

2609 After Cataclysm: [TAL 1, Year 449] Construction begins on the Keep of the Shadowitch. The foundations of her dungeon levels are deep below the forest and consecrated with vaults where captive faeries were chained inside and sealed shut. These enchanted beings lived for long periods of time even in captivity, some becoming mindless with rage and desperation, broken spirits that later haunted the dungeons and forest. Formerly the Queen of the Faeries, the Witch was now the greatest enemy of the fey and athradoc. In the centuries since the Rift her mind had broken like those frantic faeries she tortured in her Keep.

2628 After Cataclysm: [TAL 1, Year 468] The Keep of the Shadowitch is completed and the myriads of slaves that built it are decapitated and their skulls dipped in boiling pitch and mounted into niches along the walls of the castle. Hundreds of wickerworl faeries had been captured by Da'nelia's sister Dhishra who was loosely allied to her but often rebellious, going her own way. By this time Dhishra and her nymphs were known as the Thorns of the Shadowitch. To commemorate the completion of the Keep Dhishra brought her sister her greatest captive- the last living unicorn. In an elaborate ritual the Shadowitch chopped off the unicorn's horn and then slit the throat of the faery horse, forcing many of the wickerworls to drink the cursed life essence of the unicorn. In this manner she transformed them into the hideaous race of the shaghoths.

2641 After Cataclysm: [TAL 1, Year 481] The Third Devilspire Invasion of the Bone Kingdoms into Feymark'ul against the Silthani elves. The elves yielded several Tors and made their escape east into Splinterdark. Because the orcs and others did not want to range too far from the caves of their homes they broke off pursuit. These same Silthani elves would later grow strong again as the warlike Hadatchi, the Wild Elves of Splinterdark.

2644 After Cataclysm: [TAL 1, Year 484] The controversy of the fey and athradoc concerning mankind spreads to Dimwood among the kingdoms of Eganosh Faerymane and the Noble Ones as well as Thalleus the yak-centaur king. Of the Ayr only the Magrari Guardians departed the faery hosts, these bulldog shapechangers serving as the elite defense force of the ariel

Eganosh. Feeling that the Queen of the Fey had been wronged in Everleaf they decided to leave Dimwood. They passed through Devilspire mountains with little resistance and entered into the service of the Shadowitch in Splinterdark as the overlords of her thousands of gnolls.

2682 After Cataclysm: [TAL 1, Year 522] In this year the Shadowitch received a dark messenger inside her guarded throne room. Its appearance was sudden, startling the witch who instantly perceived her visitor to be much older than herself. With large, depthless eyes it looked down on her as she sat upon her chair. The bulbous eyes withheld vast intelligence and she saw that its body was hidden within folds of archaic skin.

"Who are you?" the Shadowitch hissed. It did not dignify her with a response. A moment passed and something appeared in its massive, cracked hand.

Melt your crown, witch, it conveyed to her with words appearing in her mind. *Pour this into the cauldron. Forge a sword and with it execute vengeance upon your enemies.*

"My crown is but little silver and gold," she stated, eyeing the vial of glowing purplish fluid in a vial in its hand.

It is enough...

The Shadowitch was about to say more but the Minion had vanished. It was two moons later that the witch in her dungeon forge below Splinterdark crafted the relic sword *Avengiclus*.

2691 After Cataclysm: [TAL 1, Year 531] While hunting giant brush hogs in the forest Craniax found himself surrounded by several timber giants, a race especially quiet in wooded areas. They demanded to know why he was hunting in their territory.

Craniax remembered that the timber giants had not answered his call a century and a half earlier when at war with the Titans.

"Why did you not answer my summons?" Craniax demanded, ignoring their own question.

"We did not hear your call," replied their leader. A lie. The sky giant slapped the timber giant leader off his feet swiftly. When the woodland giant hit the ground he withdrew a long flint knife and Craniax deftly ran him through with his hunting spear, pinning him to the earth. Craniax stood about fifteen feet higher than the timber giants, but they still advanced. Two of them went down quickly and the others, seeing this, took flight.

Seeking refuge from the mighty Craniax the timber giants entered the service of the Shadowitch.

Earlier in this same year Craniax has a daughter by his wife, Queen Heartha the giantess. His daughter is named Ishyxa, for in her veins was the blood of Titans, elementals, sky and stone giants. The archaic designation *ish* referred to one who was a part of four. At birth of Ishyxa many giants brought gifts of earth and fire to King Craniax in his cavern in Deep Ore. The Titans learned of the birth, still sore over the loss of the beautiful giantess for Heartha was considered their property, having been their slave.

2707 After Cataclysm: [TAL 1, Year 547] Druldosh the Draconarch of Darkfrost Peaks renews his kingship and builds his domain, spreading his wings over the hama'kin trolls, cave and storm giants, the Bone Kingdoms of goblins, orcs, minataurs and ogres, the frostlings and the wyrms of Darkfrost.

2730 After Cataclysm: [TAL 1, Year 570] Siege of Haddons Fortress. The Pol'tr of Haddons Gate had built a vast wooden city in Arborealm around the stone foretress that had remained occupied by Caedorians. In this year the Pol'tr sieged the citadel and the Caedorians surrendered and were escorted peacefully out of Haddons Gate to return safely to Caedathal East.

2736 After Cataclysm: [TAL 1, Year 576] Faeries in Dimwood report that unusual and dangerous monsters reeking of underworld scents appeared in the forest, concentrated around Blackmar Deeps. In this year the flesh-eating trees called dendrites first appeared in Dagothar.

2744 After Cataclysm: [TAL 1, Year 584] the scents of underworld molderonds and kiss-me-deadlies were found on the wind in Everleaf and very quickly the musk badger Hedgeguard and warsloths exploded from the trees to surround a group of deadly and ancient feylorn. Moonlost faeries from of old, Oathnayers too, called wayfaeries. These dark faeries surrounded the infamous Triarchy of Zephyr, Fogfiend and Darksilk nymphs of the Deep named Malinga Gale, Lillani Myst and Sedusha Shade. They were protected by hundreds of poisonous shrewnids, little hooded mushroom feylorn. With this group was Bythiok with his barbarian Jabbersnout halflings, the huge dire racoon shapechanger Nacruul the Fierce, a few arcan-solitar spider-fey Deep rangers, the famous Vulpinar Outlander who was a foxman underworld guide and explorer with his companion Jixie the jinx-pixie. The warsloths were surprised to see the mighty Ecrops, called the Hatchet-hoof and his auroch Ayr band called the Hurok Marauders. In the rear, blacker than shadows were a few hundred murderous minoshees, or ancient horned banshee elves of the Moonlost all standing behind their leader, Luasi the Terroress.

Faeries appeared from everywhere in Everleaf to see these visitors who had not been among them for thousands of years. Ashrey and the shars give them escort through the Barkwalk into the dome of Elderboughs. In the dome the host of feylorn bowed reverently to the Archaic Tree, astonishing the fey, except for Sedusha Shade. The darksilk nymph stood quietly staring, her depthless dark eyes taking in the golden tree with curiosity. Faeries of Everleaf press in through the Barkwalk and squeeze inside the dome in anticipation. Malinga Gale and Lillani Myst, both beautiful with dark hair and eyes and pale skin, approached Elderboughs.

"We have waited so long-" Malinga began.

"...in wandering high and low-" Lillani continued.

"We have found a home." -Malinga.

"Below the House of the Athak." -Lillani.

"I AM PLEASED." Elderboughs smiled, golden light flowing through them. Sedusha Shade's black eyes widened but she said nothing as her sisters continued.

"We come...were told to ask for your blessing." -Malinga.

"A place to plant...we have found a sanctuary." -Lillani.

"WHAT OF MY VIOLENT DAUGHTER?" Hearing this the fey listening to the exchange stiffened, for they understood that Elderboughs spoke of the true shadowfae. The Mycomaiden.

"Do not be angry with her!" -Malinga.

"She mourns each death..." -Lillani.

"Our Protectress-" -Malinga.

"...for her we would die." -Lillani.

"OLDEST COCOON...FIRST TO SENSE THE TIMES."

"Yes, Father. She knows-" -Malinga.

"She has seen a New Scattering." -Lillani.

"A darkness in Everleaf." Malinga.

"We must take your blessing." -Lillani. Hearing this exchange a worry gnawed at the heart of the fey.

"I WILL GO WITH YOU." In the following silence a golden, gigantic pine cone dropped from above to land on the dirt floor near Sedusha Shade. Four shrewnids ambled over and hoisted it up and instantly the gold glow changed to a brown light.

"We will hide the blessing-" -Malinga.

"Till the secret year." -Lillani.

As the feylorn departed the dome the darksilk nymph continued to stare at Elderboughs, seeing things very far away. Coming to her senses she shadowformed and slipped out through the Barkwalk. The crowds of Feylorn disappeared toward the woods of Yadel Lake.

Deep in the night three shars carried a nethering Dhishra back into Everleaf Pines and into the Barkwalk Court. The nymph was covered in pollens and scents of the underworld, her skin bruised and claw scrapes were criss-crossed over her body. One of her eyes was swollen shut and as the shars worked their healing magics on her Manax the warsloth general looked down on her with curiosity knowing that she had tried to enter Doorwood Hill Forest and had been driven off with violence.

2760 After Cataclysm: [TAL 1, Year 600] Druldosh the Draconarch sends forth waves of armies, Bone Kingdom mercenaries or orcs, ogres, cobble goblins, minataurs and hill giants against Sigils Arch in Shannidar where the Ayr lived under the rule of Eganosh Faerymane. Dragons of Darkfrost and trolls, lizard folk and Silapenti snake warriors join them. Two citadels are taken but the Noble Ones escape. Craniax, his giants and the dwarves of Grol'galdir march to their relief and the Draconarch's forces retreat.

2761 After Cataclysm: [TAL 1, Year 601] Shannidar is again invaded. Silapenti, lizard folk, kraxa'kin trolls and mantis people, formions, attack from the jungles. Days later the fields are flooded with frostlings come down from the mountains with many more Bone Kingdom mercenaries. The apanthoi, bruun and hawks deal valiantly with them and a lone hawk named Soaroch having espied the court of Druldosh from on high over the mountains of Darkfrost returned to Sigils Arch with the news that the war was a feint, that Druldosh was amassing a huge army in the mountains and that the Draconarch had received a strange visitor, a tall dark mass that burned the ground itself where it passed. In the Court of Eganosh Faerymane one of the seeryns visiting from Everleaf overheard this and informed Eganosh and the court that Soaroch described the appearance of a *Minion* from the Deep.

When the Ayr received word of the approach of Craniax and his Deep Ore Alliance the enemy retreated before the sky giant's host could reach Sigils Arch. More hawks were sent out and they confirmed that armies were camped in the mountains.

2762 After Cataclysm: [TAL 1, Year 602] Druldosh the Draconarch personally led his immense horde against Sigils Arch, armies of frostlings, trolls, Bone Kingdom forces and mercenaries, giants and dragons. From the jungles issued forth his allies of lizard folk, Silapenti snake people, formions and the kraxa'kin trolls of the swamplands. But the Ayr under Eganosh were prepared, and Thalleus with his centaurs and the Elmlord Guardians came quickly into the fray. Before the Draconarch's forces left the mountains the hawks took word to Craniax and the giants and dwarves of Deep Ore marched immediately. In *War of the Draconarch* the fey, giants and dwarves defeated the enemies after Craniax slew Druldosh in combat and then killed another dragon. The wyrms of Darkfrost grew afraid and fled, abandoning their armies as Thalleus, the centaurs and raging trees fell upon their flanks.

But there was still a darkness over Dagothar, for the war of the Draconarch was known far and wide. It had been rumored that the axemasters of Devilspire were allied to the Draconarch and were to participate in the attack against Sigils Arch, but the rumor was untrue. Never did the axemasters leave the domains of their temple in Devilspire mountains. But the Titans of Titan Oaks believed the rumor and thought this would be the end of Craniax and his host.

While the King of the Giants was away on the field of battle some of the disgruntled Titans left the security of their wood and visited Craniax wife and daughter, still smarting over the fact that Craniax had taken his wife from them. She had originally been their prize. After abusing her the Titans killed her and slew his young daughter.

When Craniax returned to Deep Ore Peaks and discovered his family murdered he fell to his knees and bellowed loudly. The echoing grew louder and louder and the scream of anguish was carried on the winds to be heard by all of Dagothar. Across the world the elementals stopped what they were doing and listened, for Craniax was an elemental sky giant. The Titans began to grow afraid and dragons across the face of the world refused to take flight.

When Craniax ceased his bellowing he took his dead wife and daughter into his arms and sat back against a wall of stone as more and more giants assembled, numb with shock and horror at the scene. In the silence Craniax opened his mighty throat and sang a song.

Over a thousand miles away the forest and dome of Everleaf was silent, all having heard the scream. A mournful expression darkened the face of Elderboughs and the faeries remained silent in alarm. Suddenly the sylvan god opened his great mouth and began to sing the very words of Craniax. Tens of thousands of voices belonging only to the elementals joined in the song and it was the first time the faeries ever heard the *Dirge of the Fallen.*

The song finished the fey understood something terrible had happened in the world. Far away from Everleaf the giants brought gigantic tablets of wood to Craniax and carver's tools. He spent a long time perfectly etching his messages to his wife and daughter in to the wood and all of the giants from hundreds of miles around gathered as Craniax wept openly watching the flames burn away the tablets that took his words to his loved ones on The Other Side.

Three days had passed since he found their bodies. Five more passed as he sat in silence refusing to eat or drink. On the morn of the ninth day he took earth and ashes and covered his body in mourning. He commanded all to leave him be, to go home and resume their normal lives. He would mourn one hundred more days. But he did not say what he would do about the trespass, for all knew these murders were the work of the Titans.

On the hundredth day of his mourning under earth and ash he swam in a river and ate salmon all day as he received visitors. The dwarves of Grol'galdir had made for him a gift and stone giants brought it- a full suit of white, gleaming dragonscale armor taken from the body of Druldosh the Draconarch, a mighty iron helm and huge armored boots. A large, menacing visitor emerged out of the ground and Craniax told his giants to stand down. The ancient catastromental, leader of many of the elementals, rose forth to its full height and Craniax knew of its destructive power. It was also called a stratamental, and it spoke these words-

"TAL'VARI...know that we hold the guilty in their wood...a necklace around Titan Oaks..."

Craniax accepted the gifts and sent them all home again. They perplexed, awaiting a summons for war that did not come. Rested, fed and seemingly at peace, Craniax casually walked to Titan Oaks and the elementals entrenched around it opened a way. The King of the Giants spent four days slaying Titans, Titanesses and ever Titan child he discovered. Elementals informed him that a few escaped into Devilspire and Craniax strode forth into those mountains and killed those he could catch. Then happened the turning of the year.

2763 After Cataclysm: [TAL 1, Year 603] Craniax methodically searched all the caverns and passes, caves and large tunnels for Titans. When he found one or a group in hiding he gave them battle and killed them. He stalked the mountains day and night convinced that more were concealed among the range. He strode around the perimeter of the mountains searching for Titan tracks and the King of the Giants spent an entire year wandering Devilspire mountains. When he came across giants who were not allied to him or under his kingdom he killed them quickly and word spread across Dagothar that Craniax had become drunk on blood-lust.

2764 After Cataclysm: [TAL 1, Year 604] Hunting a lone Titan who had evaded him in Devilspire Mountains, Craniax diligently followed his trail into Feymark'ul, across the plain and into Towerhenge. The primordial towers from The World Before were much higher in those days, enormous superconstructions that even baffled the oldest elementals. In Towerhenge the unexpected screams of the Titan drew Craniax to a secluded place between three towers where a an enormous cloud serpent, one of the Mistwyrms, devoured her kill.

Robbed of his quarry Craniax challenged the strange dragon and defeated her with his massive war maul. She flked to the top of a high tower where she had laid her nest. Craniax climbed the tower and the Mistwyrm fought him with renewed savagry, the sky giant marveling at her prowess as he steadily weakened her with blows and wrestling. In their struggle he glanced about a hundred feet into the roof of the tower to see two gigantic swirled eggs in a wide nest, the dragoness seeing that he had found her prizes.

"There be greater wyrms to fight than me, King Craniax," she offered, trying to entice him away from seeking her eggs. "Ask of me what you will and I shall speak the truth."

Craniax paused. It was known that whatever any cloud serpent had seen, *all* cloud serpents had seen. An idea formed in his mind.

"Tell me...where might I find any more of the race of Mygok?" The cloud serpent closed her eyes in relief, concentrating on the images of Titans. After a moment she replied.

"In the south...the cyprian bog giants of the jungle are scions of the Titans...the firbolgs too. Also those abominations that live below Mount Thokax in the Deep of the ancient Nimbolc dwellings, they are also of the blood of Titans. In the underworld you will find the last large colony of Titans. They have taken dusk giants as wives." Craniax knew then that he would be going into the underworld. He departed the wyrm in peace. Towerhenge was the last home of the Mistwyrms of Dagothar.

2766 After Cataclysm: [TAL 1, Year 606] In the far south Craniax fought and killed many of the cyprian bog giants, a couple troll giants and those kraxa'kin trolls stupid enough to challenge him in their swamp. He traveled through the jungles to an unknown plain, across a mountain range and looked out over an unknown sea suspecting that Aroth Beyond lied somewhere over the horizon.

2767 After Cataclysm: [TAL 1, Year 607] On his trek back north Craniax happened upon a meadow in the jungle surrounding a single stone tower of many different colored blocks. Peering into a high window he saw a pretty woman painting letters in a table-sized spellbook, who, upon seeing the spying giant, introduced herself as Yavanna Sylvanborn, an enchantress. At first Craniax was taken aback at the total lack of fear and surprise from the faery woman but his memory jolted him into paying closer attention for he suspected her to be the infamous Sorceress of Kyult Tower...known as the Venom Goddess of the Silapenti snake people who served and worshipped her.

Craniax recalled the old stories about her, that she was of the First Birthing from the cocoons of Elderboughs before the Shars and fey he knew so well. A younger sister of Sharassa the Mycomaiden who haunted the Deep. Knowing her to be evil, an agent of the Minions, the sky giant could not find it in his heart to challenge her. Her controversy was with a race that he had no dealings with. Men.

He departed after a brief conversation and found himself wandering through an old, abandoned stone metropolis built by humans. At its center was a gigantic stone block pyramid that rose above the jungle. Yavanna had told him that Men were the monument, not the apex, that each stone represented a soul of Men that together supported the topstone. Men in the city were ruined because they had placed the apex upon the monument before they were sanctioned to do so by the Builders, seeking their inheritances before the time. Craniax pondered this and climbed the pyramid. At the top he knocked the topstone off to slide down the other side. Perhaps he could free Men of this trespass, he reasoned.

2768 After Cataclysm: [TAL 1, Year 608] Craniax exited the jungles and sat to dine with Eganosh Faerymane, his brother Alaryel and the great ones of the seven races of Ayr at Sigils Arch. They told him of the violations and violence of the wyrms of Dimwood. Bereft of a Draconarch the dragons had become uncivilized, wild and unruly. Craniax set out and entered Dimwood, giving battle to several dragons and even killing a few. They scattered, some making promises to behave.

He then departed Dimwood and climbed into Darkfrost Peaks. At Mount Thokax on top of the world he fought and chased off and killed most of the firbolgs. By a stratagem some crafty firbolgs set a trap and succeeded in knocking Craniax off a cliff to roll down the side of a mountain unceremoniously crashing into the timberline below splintering trees and making a lot of embarrassing noise.

In a maddened rage the sky giant ran back up the mountain face and chased the terrified firbolgs into their strongholds and slew all those that could not reach the safety of the smaller tunnels Craniax could not enter. In Lower Thokax the King of the Giants explored the fabled ruins of ancient Nimbolc, ancestral home of all dwarvenkind. In the darkness he was attacked by a great beast he could little hurt. Twice he launched himself into a battle frenzy and twice he was thrown back powerfully to hit a cavern wall. Perceiving in the blackness a second great beast approaching Craniax fled Lower Thokax into the safety of the upper mountains.

He then visited Thrulmir-of-the-Cliffs, the giants sanctuary on Mount Nibengrul Icepeak in western Darkfrost. Before leaving the fellowship of his giant kin he got drunk twice.

2769 After Cataclysm: [TAL 1, Year 609] Craniax finds the funnelweb cave system in Darkfrost Mountains exactly where the cloud serpent of Towerhenge said it would be. He made his descent into the caverns of Darkfrost Peaks mindful of avoiding any that appeared to lead toward Lower Thokax. Craniax, the Mighty One of A'DIN, known in the scriptures as TAL'VARI, vanished into the depths of the underworld and did not resurface for ten years.

2772 After Cataclysm: [TAL 1, Year 612] King Craniax drank deeply from a cool spring and looked up to see several dark and shadowy figures regarding him silently. These shadowfae and moonlost faeries made way for a tall, slender mushroom-hooded feminine faery who touched Craniax and subdued him with her witchery. She visited in her mind the places he had traveled and saw the deeds he had done. Craniax swooned from pleasure as she saw the world through his eyes. When he woke up the King of the Giants did not remember the incident until long after he had departed Hollowrealm.

2779 After Cataclysm: [TAL 1, Year 619] The doings of Craniax in the Deep are wrought with mystery. It is said that only Laer'garoth the Dragon-Chronicler has ever been told all that transpired in the Deep. What is known is that in Hollowrealm the sky giant happened upon monsters and creatures from the Old World that had escaped the Shadowed Ice but never again resurfaced. PreCataclysm cities and ruins littered the underworld's many caverns and cave systems, some reoccupied over and again by migrating races. Other stories have surfaced about this ten year trek below Dagothar.

Craniax slew Inarix the Moltenwyrm of the race of wicked lavamanders, chief of the ember dragons of Wyrmrealm. He happened upon tens of thousands of elves in the dark building a colossal city of petrified fungalblocks next to a gigantic hard-as-stone Black Tree on a plateau in an immense cavern. Craniax attempted twice to knock apart this vile Tree but Minions appeared and chased him off with their powerful sorceries the elemental sky giant did not understand. Craniax wounded a Minion by slamming his maul into the side of its head before he ran out of the cavern. Far enough away he marveled while inspecting his burned-smooth maul head. The decorations of metalwork had disappeared from the intense heat of the Minion.

Craniax fought and killed King Wulfgrog of the dusk giants and then drowned Vyock the Titan in the Abysshicar Sea. He called underwater to the dragonturtles of the Deep and three nearby surfaced to listen to his words. Craniax told them of Imigorn the triton-whale, their friend of old, that Imigorn was alive and well swimming the Spawnsea above on the surface and that the way up was through the Bubbling Mountain south of the Harukku Isles. The ancient dracoturtles thanked him and rejoiced that their friend Imigorn was free of the Minions who had enslaved him.

Many were the adventures of Craniax in the ten years he explored the underworld. His visit with Sharassa and the shadowfae has been forbidden to write about; his fight with the warlock Omak and what transpired is a secret only the Mycomaiden, Laer'garoth the dragon and Elderboughs share. His breaking through a cavern wall to discover archaic ruins from a civilization that had thrived in The World Before is an account that has been mysteriously removed from every historical record detailing the life of Craniax except for one small note in the *Testimony of Laer'garoth the Old.* Nine months exploring these most fantastic structures filled with the untouched debris of a lost civilization reduced to a single almost uninformative sentence in the book of the Dragon-Chronicler.

After ten years traveling through Hollowrealm the sky giant emerges from the underworld and finds himself in Blackmar Deeps of Lake Mir Dol'hinnon in ancient Dimwood.

2780 After Cataclysm: [TAL 1, Year 620] Craniax attacked the Bholbash frostwyrms of Devilspire Mountains that had migrated out of Darkfrost Peaks. These were known as the shardlings, slender dragons with dark underbellies but icy white scales on their wings and backs by which they concealed themselves in snow and ice. Completely still, even Craniax could not tell if a shardling was near because they appeared like boulders covered in snow. These frostwyrms breathed streams of frozen air filled with razor-sharp ice cycles. Unable to catch a shardling, Craniax moved on. In Ettertooth Mountains he fought and killed a black dragon whose name goes unrecorded, before he vanished north in the endless waste of The Great Desert of Eternal Sands. An elemental giant, Craniax was unaffected by the heat and lack of water.

2782 After Cataclysm: [TAL 1, Year 622] Emerging from the Great Desert of Eternal Sands covered in dust Craniax leaves in his wake a trail of broken glass and smashed glassolisks. He enters the mountains of the north in eastern Dagothar inhabited by the races of the Cloudborn, happening unexpectedly upon Mount Icedorn, seeing Castle Kagg'nthrok, a giants redoubt. Storming the castle the sky giant slew four stone and rock giants that opposed his advance as well as a gigantic snowcat in the inner gate. The giants inside lowered the tower gate to keep him out and dropped boulders on Craniax, who took the large rocks and hurled them over and over at the gate. Above, atop the tower a giant yelled down.

"Mighty Craniax! We are kin. Kings do not kill their subjects!" The sky giant ignored this and broke the gate with a powerful throw of a boulder. Before he could enter another giant spoke.

"Go north, Mighty One! Give battle to them that killed your bairn." Craniax dropped another enormous stone he was about to throw and looked up.

"What?"

"In Mulgrir Vale, at the well of Mimag cavern where the Cloudborn Titans rule the races of the north." Hearing of Titans unknown he departed in haste.

In this year King Craniax slew the Cloudborn Titans, male, female and bairn- none of that race escaped his fury. But he departed the north leaving behind their scions, half-breeds, firbolgs, half-Titan giants and others they spawned in their rapine over the centuries.

2784 After Cataclysm: [TAL 1, Year 624] By this time the Madness of Craniax is well known, so when the faeries of Borderealm see him descending from Drakeroost mountains after passing over the range heading toward Everleaf there is a panic. Craniax is now forty-three feet tall, covered in dried blood and body fluids of the slain, dust, caked mud, his hands and face adorned in scars, hair wild and tangled, armor beaten, tattered and hanging loosely. His gigantic maul is burned smooth, riddled with scrapes and dents and his mighty helm is bashed in with impact craters. Manax, Lycrops, Ish'layyar and Dhishra assemble large groups of faeries prepared to oppose the sky giant but Elderboughs forbids it and Craniax, alone, walks into and through the Barkwalk into the dome of Everleaf. The faeries remain still, staring at the shocking visage of the Mighty One of A'DIN as he stops before the Archaic Tree. In the silence of the dome he drops his 900 pound maul to thud on the floor. He removes his massive iron helm and drops it with a crash as he falls to his knees amidst the quiet assembly.

"My Lord..." his voice deep like thunder in a long cave. The serene face of Elderboughs regarded him compassionately.

"WHERE HAVE YOU BEEN, MY SON?" Still bowing his heavy head, the giant replied.

"To and fro, above and below...paying debts, Ageless One."

"BE THERE MORE TO PAY?" Craniax inhaled deeply.

"Nay, my Lord. There be none left who owe."

The gathering of fey, all more ancient than the young Craniax, stared dumbfounded at the ragged giant encased in ruined white dragonscale armor, the skin of the dead Druldosh the Draconarch, for they understood his words to mean that he had slain the whole race of Mygok the Titan. Many remembered the words of TAL-NIK several centuries before- *He shall lay low the height of the Titans...*

Craniax collapsed into a deep slumber and slept an entire month for each year of his sojourn.

2786 After Cataclysm: [TAL 1, Year 626] Craniax awakens completely revived in this the 24th year since his family was murdered by the Titans. He spends time with the fey in Everleaf and talks with Elderboughs. There is celebration and laughter with many faeries bringing gifts of munchroot, muscameed brew, ciders, branchweaving, leaf wreaths of gooseberries and the gigantic enchanted produce from the Moonfurrow Gardens of Enchandrus. At seeing so many among the fey bringing presents a tiny sylph separated herself from the company of her sisters and began searching for something to offer but distressed. And Elderboughs noticed.

"WHAT TROUBLES YOU, LITTLE YAHLRA?" Many of the faeries looked at the tiny white-haired sylph. Her eyes were wide and she reddened, embarrassed.

"I...I have nothing to give," her eyes watered and the dome stilled. The Great Tree looked down on her with all seriousness.

"YOU BEAR A GIFT PRECIOUS EVEN TO IMMORTALS... THE SPARROWS AND LARKS YOU HAVE STILLED, THE SERENADING OF THE FORESTS HAVE PAUSED AT YOUR VOICE IN THE MOONSETS." Yahlra's wings straightened and she perked up.

"A song? Can I sing a song?" Elderboughs smiled and she was bathed in His golden light as more and more faeries began regarding her in a new way. The Great Tree looked at Craniax and Yahlra turned to stare up to the King of the Giants. She looked quietly at him as more faeries spilled in from the Barkwalk feeling the air of something important in passage.

When Yahlra began to sing to Craniax every faery in the dome remained still. Dhishra stared, buried between nymphs and dryads all cuddling along the eastern tree wall. The melody of so powerful a voice from so small a being astonished the fey and suddenly all the other sylphs joined in the Song of the Sylph. Those burning munchroot journeyed in their minds and hearts back to those peaceful times Yahlra and her sisters sang about.

Tears dripping down his face, Craniax deep voice joined in the song and when it was over the sky giant told Yahlra that hers' was the best gift of all. And in the back of the dome, lying tangled with her younger sylvan sisters, Dhishra felt a flash of envy and anger at the sylphs.

Before taking his leave, Craniax learns from Elderboughs where he must go to have his deeds recorded for posterity.

2804 After Cataclysm: [TAL 1, Year 644] In Arborealm humans make a clearing and roast many cows, providing many barrels of fine wine in stacks for the meeting of Craniax the giant with the dragon sage and historian, Laer'garoth the Old, the Hornbreaker, wyrm of Caedoria. Talking to the Dragon-Chronicler, Craniax learns the histories of the elementals, the Ha'akathrals called athaki, of the First Birthings of pre-faery antiquity, the Titans, of the fey, athradoc, moonlost, shadowfae, of the giants, the Minions and denizens of The World Before now residing in Hollowrealm. In return Craniax tells Laer'garoth of all his adventures and experiences after he discovered the dead bodies of his wife and daughter, his travels, conversations, battles. The life of Craniax was preserved later in the authoritative record, *Testimony of Laer'garoth the Old.* Hearing of the meeting of Craniax and the Caedorian dragon in an affair hosted with hospitality by Men, many of the fey began appearing more frequently among humans.

2844 After Cataclysm: [TAL 1, Year 684] Craniax visits Mount Talisman, remembering his episode in the jungles at the pyramid and meeting the Sorceress of Kyult Tower. He discovers that Ricanor Castle built by the Titans is now infested with thousands of the foul druil'kin trolls so he sets about cleaning the vermin out, chasing them to death like rats seeking crevasses. He moves into Ricanor Castle and several giants of Deep Ore Peaks join him in the vast halls of the castle overlooking Mount Talisman.

2880 After Cataclysm: [TAL 1, Year 720] the Magrar of Splinterdark in league with the Shadowitch are now in control of the gnolls in her service and have through much intercourse with the lesser, evil canine breed now fathered the gnollocks. With consent of the Shadowitch the Magrar lead the gnolls against the city of Boldur Hill in Borderealm, a city of the Men of Pol'tr. Faeries inform Everleaf of the invasion and it is quickly understood that this is an attack against Men, not sylvankind. On the field Men are defeated and driven back to the safety of their walls in the city, which the gnolls siege.

In the forest of Everleaf the faeries suffer controversy over the plight of Men. It is argued that an invasion into Borderealm is an insult to them as well while others think it is not their affair. Begrudgingly, Manax accepts a vote to lead the charge against the gnolls and fights valiantly in battle. The Magrar inherit the title of Ignoble Ones in this contest for in battle they slew a great many faeries, their ancient kin. Manax the warsloth killed four of the Magrar stunning the others into a retreat back to Splinterdark once the gnolls lost the Battle of Boldur Hill. It is said that this incident turned the Shadowitch against the Magrar for their fleeing the might of Manax.

Boldur Hill's master weapon smiths melted down a Dathari relic in the possession of the Men of Pol'tr since their beginnings in Talan Dathar. This old, huge tower shield was made of a rare silvery iron found only in trace amounts in Darkfrost Peaks, a metal that became enchanted when heated molten and forged. It was a secret of the Nimbolc dwarves from antiquity. In appreciation for raising the siege of their city the master smiths melted the tower shield and forged a unique, silver-iron swordaxe of appropriate size for an eight foot tall warsloth. It was the first weapon of its kind- a longsword tapered at its end into a war axe.

This new magical blade, indestructible when contacting other weapons and armors, was delivered to Everleaf in a solemn procession and given to Manax in a display of human humility that startled the faeries and humbled the prideful warsloth general. Manax would still be holding that sword over 44 centuries later when he met his death at the ruins of Boldur Hill in the tragic Battle of Barrowen.

2904 After Cataclysm: [TAL 1, Year 744] Blue-skinned star people came down from the sky and flew over the ruins of Talan Dathar in winged chariots that rained a mist over the ancient metropolis that killed the plants and trees throughout the ruins. Foliage withered away in days and trees dried out to ash to blow apart in the breezes. Faeries in Dimwood watched in amazement as hundreds of star people came out of their flying chariots and labored throughout the vast ruins. They had odd tools and weapons. They all had nose horns and rode on floating platforms leading many of the fey to believe that these were some unknown race of star faeries. They spent a few weeks digging in the earth and removing wreckage and debris left behind from the War of the Star People that the faeries remembered had occurred in the Year of the Second Sun. They departed as quietly as they came and it is said that the trees had never grown back among the ruins of Talan Dathar.

2928 After Cataclysm: [TAL 1, Year 768] a scholar of Caedathal East among the Caedorians studied the records of the past and spent long hours discussing history with the great Laer'garoth the Old, the dragon-chronicler of the Protectorate and realized that this year was 552 years after The Shaking of A'DIN when Caedathal East was broken apart and rebuilt, which was itself a disaster that happened exactly 552 years after the War of the Star People in the Year of the Second Sun. This scholar was named Chanoch and he prophesied to the people that a terrible destruction of Men would occur in this year with the return of the Broken Moon.

He was ignored in Caedoria. Then a massive invasion poured forth out of the hot Great Desert of Eternal Sands, a host of tall, horned ogres, a race of darkish dwarves, a second race of dwarves of heroic size and reddish skin, many dusk giants, bloodborn orcs, hobgoblin mercenaries and a countless tide of the underworld's uluk'kin trolls. These armies were led by draconian warsorcers and cave minataurs who in turn were led by one of the anacient Abominids. A Minion.

Passing over the Illyriac Plain unopposed they fell upon the city of Boldur Hill of the Men of Pol'tr. The Whisperstriders of Arborealm in these days ranged wide and rode astride the dragons of Caedoria, Brard and Pol'tr. As an army of Caedorians and Brard marched to the aid of Boldur Hill so too did an army of Pol'tr advance from Haddons Gate and Arborealm when suddenly the Broken Moon appeared as a red star of brilliance casting a growing tail across the sky. The army of Boldur Hill retreated into their city at the sight of the immense underworld host, far greater than that of the Magrar 48 years earlier.

For seven days the battle raged as the underworlders cut down more and more of the Men of Boldur Hill, Caedathal East and Haddons Gate. As the war raged and the Broken Moon appeared to darken the sun, the faeries of Enchandrus and Everleaf again quarreled among themselves over the decision to help Men or not. Their bone of contention was that humans were becoming too populous, that their villages were encroaching closer and closer. Many did not join the relief force but others did follow Manax and his warsloths to Boldur Hill.

Manax and the Five Thousand, not even a twentieth of the number of fey within two days' march, assaulted the Minion army and turned the battle. After killing two dragons and wounding a third, seeing its forces in disarray fighting on four fronts, the Minion vanished.

The Men of Caedoria and Haddons Gate departed the field of battle as if they had lost, so many of their own among the fallen. Their armies had been reduced to a third. The Men of Boldur Hill had fallen in defending their old, wives and young. The walls were ruined, streets filled with the dead and dying. The Pol'tr stayed long enough to collect the population of survivers, their kin, all families now without fathers, uncles, brothers and sons and took them back to Haddons Gate. The Men of Caedoria filled the abandoned buildings with the bodies of the dead and with fifteen hundred armored warsloths, quietly buried the city of Boldur Hill creating a vast necropolis. Since this year was Boldur Hill known as Barrowen, when the Broken Moon passed across the vault of the sky.

The Rift of the Fey deepened as arguments and accusations increased among the woods inside the dome and Barkwalk and outside in Ti'el City of the Aelvani elves. Some faeries defended their position that Men were not their concern while others were shamed into silence at their hesitancy when learning that over a hundred thousand humans had died. They also learned that when the Caedorians returned to their city they found it damaged by a quake when the Broken Moon had blocked out the sun's light.

Men repaired their city and buried the dead that the earthquake killed. But the loss of life and power of the Pol'tr was catastrophic. In southern Arborealm was the Southwoods where the Pol'tr had built hundreds of towns since the days of the fall of the horned wyrms of Southwoods. But in the quaking the entire coast sank beneath the Spanwsea within the space of a moment drowning a population of 50,000 men, women and children spread throughout the settlements that went under. Sailors ever after claim that on a clear day they could see tree tops in the deep waters off the new coast which came all the way up to Caedathal East now. Much of Caedathal East's outer areas sank below the new coastline and after rebuilding the city the engineers and architects gave the Caedorian city a new name- Daethalon, meaning, WE BUILT AGAIN.

Chanoch became known as the Chronicler and is credited with the founding of the Order of the Broken Moon. Having lost their northernmost city, Boldur Hill, and their southernmost frontier, the Southwoods, unable to expand westward into Caedorian territory, the Men of Pol'tr expanded eastward into the Yadel Lake region of Borderealm and the lands that would one day be called Hinterealm. This year began a separation of ties between the Pol'tr and Caedorians.

2943 After Cataclysm: [TAL 1, Year 783] the EM'M dwarves of Fingersdeep lead by the Hammerworn Kings depart Deep Ore Peaks and are met by a Whisperstrider and dragon of Caedoria west of Arborealm. The dwarves are granted permission to pass through Caedoria and given rights over water and earth as long as they continue to move and have no plans to settle in their realm. As the EM'M pass through Caedoria ever under the watch of Men a delegation of dwarves are taken into the vast stone metropolis of Daethalon where they are amazed at the architectural feats of humans. This was the first and only time a dwarf was ever admitted into the Temple of Eternal Lore.

2944 After Cataclysm: [TAL 1, Year 784] the EM'M are escorted through northern Arborealm around the domain of the Pol'tr who refused to grant the dwarves water and earth rights in their migration. The EM'M approach Yadel Lake in bad need of water and again are denied by the Pol'tr. The Caedorians having returned to Arborealm proper, the EM'M were left with no course other than pushing through into northern Yadel Lake area to replenish their water stores.

Camped at the lake's northern edge the dwarves await the return of their prospectors. Several teams of dwarves had set out to explore Drakeroost Mountains. While the EM'M camps waited a host of Pol'tr descended upon them but Theogon Hammerworn with Quakemaker led his warriors in repelling the humans in the Battle of Yadel Lake. The dwarven prospectors returned with news of an excellent site to camp on a natural plateau high in the range as word arrives of the coming of another army of Men. The EM'M relocate under cover of darkness into the mountains taking refuge in the timberline finding natural caves and caverns at a site later to be known as Meadowlair. The Pol'tr do not pursue.

2952 After Cataclysm: [TAL 1, Year 792] in the 8th year since the EM'M settled the caverns in Drakeroost they were again attacked by the Pol'tr. This force was five times larger than that of the Battle of Yadel Lake. But the humans were no match for the dwarves in their own environment. A mountain race, the EM'M slaughtered the Pol'tr in the Battle of Timbershelf, less than half of the humans escaping back into the woods below.

2970 After Cataclysm: [TAL 1, Year 810] The Shadowitch
Wars begin with the Invasion of Borderealm. From
Splinterdark forest the Shadowitch sent her army across the plain
to attack Enchandrus with a horde of shaghoths, basks, Magrar
and gnolls, timber giants as her great host of Silapenti snake
warriors descended from those who had attacked Men in 2376
AC invaded Treehelm. Many faeries of Treehelm and
Enchandrus were captured and dragged back to vanish into the
dungeons of the witch. The Magrar sought vengeance against
Manax and tried to cut him down but the godlike fury of the
warsloth general prvented this. Hakkix slew a Magrar and three
more fell dead and dying to the sloth general's swordaxe. Eight
Magrar who survived lost fingers, limbs, were maimed or lost an
eye in the battle.

The Pillars of Everleaf lead in the defense of Enchandrus and
pushed back the horde of the Shadowitch, they never reaching
the sacred ground of Everleaf. Treehelm did not fare well and
the Silapenti took everything back to the witch's keep they could
find, alive or not. Manax proposed an invasion of Splinterdark
but other faeries having escaped from the witch's domain
informed the warsloths that an invasion is what the witch
expected and wanted, for a third army of monsters was in the
wood for this purpose.

Back in the Keep the Shadowitch spent four days cutting off the
heads of terrified faeries with her accursed longsword
Avengiclus. Faery skulls were mounted in the walls of the
castle.

2997 After Cataclysm: [TAL 1, Year 837] Craniax in Deep Ore
Peaks caught Webol the Evil with a stratagem, but Webol
perplexed the King of the Giants with a question he was unable
to answer. Webol told Craniax that a true king only punishes the
unjust, those who have done him ill or a disservice.

"Why, O King, have you expended yourself with the capture of one who has never done you ill nor could ever be a threat?" Craniax paused. He has heard tales of Webol, been told that he was evil, but could not recollect any evil he had ever done. The giant was unable to come up with an answer and Webol continued.

"A wise king would have no trouble catching me again should I prove to be deceitful to the king." Craniax let Webol go, unaware that Webol was like Sharassa and Necralissa, of the First Birthing before the coming of the fey...and very powerful indeed.

3024 After Cataclysm: [TAL 1, Year 864] the dark elves called the Aelvatchi in the underworld near the Black Tree complete their wonderfully engineered city, Sarthaldon, built beside the primordial Keep of the Mrul, prehistoric steward of the Limbs of Darkness. Sarthaldon in the Aelvatchi elven dialect means *through darkness we see.* In service to the Mrul and his Minions the dark elves multiply exceedingly and become a major power in the Deep.

On the surface world Craniax looked up from snatching a fist full of salmon out an icy river in Deep Ore. He had not heard nor perceived their approach, but a dozen bearded figures bigger than humans stood motionless on the other bank looking at him. They wore the hides and skins of animals from Aroth Beyond and the underworld and strapped to their thighs, arms and backs were weapons from the Old World before the Shadowed Ice. Craniax knew he was in the presence of Ha'akathrals. Before he could speak one raised his right hand in salutation.

"TAL'VARI...I am called Athadur. Shield of TAL-NIK. Join us at our camp. My lord need unveil many things to you."

Craniax followed the athaki to the camp of TAL-NIK where the leader of the First People ate and drank long into the night with him and told him secrets not even Laer'garoth had revealed.

3096 After Cataclysm: [TAL 2, Year 72] a foreign dragon, of alabaster hue, descended upon Daethalon out of a low cloud bank and looked about the city with curiosity, watching the activity of Men who appeared to him like ants among the fabulous buildings and water parks spread across the city. The dragons of Caedoria, having been flying about, return to find this alabaster wyrm and set upon him instantly with violence, led by Laer'garoth the Old.

Five dragons against one turned quickly into four wyrms when the foreign intruder blasted Sraejik Darkscaled with searing lightning boltsthat stunned the other dragons in to halting their assault.

"Who are you," asked Laer'garoth, as leader of the Protectorate of Daethalon while tens of thousands of Caedorians and Brard watched on.

"I am Ishaak the White of Deep Ore, but of the blood of Winterfang." Laer'garoth knew of the ancient dragon families of Darkfrost but had never seen one. The electricity breath had surprised them all.

"Why have you attacked us, Ishaak?" Hearing this the alabaster wyrm stood to his full height while standing in Goat Market Square. A colossal dragon of white shimmering scales.

"It was you who attacked me while I was peacefully admiring the wonders before me." Laer'garoth bowed his head, knowing then that Ishaak was a noble dragon, realizing also that Sraejik was only unconscious and not dead. From this day onward Ishaak was called Burnbreath and his name was remembered by Men. From time to time the alabaster wyrm would visit

Caedoria and the wyrms of Pol'tr as well. Ishaak grew rather fond of Men and at the Court of Elderboughs he gave frequent reports of their activities abroad, for Ishaak Burnbreath was a free spirit and roamed the world unimpeded by attachments.

3132 After Cataclysm: [TAL 2, Year 108] The Shadowitch Wars continue with the second unexpected invasion of Enchandrus. As one of her armies engages the defending faeries before relief can come from Everleaf and the hated Manax and other Pillars, another force of the witch attacks the Moonfurrow Gardens and steals much of the produce of magical vegetables and fruits that are spirited back to the Keep in Splinterdark. It is believed the invasion was merely to secure the enchanted produce for more ingredients for her sinister concoctions. Having valiantly defended the gardens against a superior host the yelkai elk-centaurs are given the title of Moonfurrow Guardians.

3150 After Cataclysm: [TAL 2, Year 126] Craniax returns to Splinterdark and finds his old friend, the simple-minded Gargantulon of Titan descent. They wrestle through the woods splintering whole sections of trees, throwing one another through the air and laughing uproariously. Until the silence around them is noticeable. Looking around Craniax sees that he and the Gargantulon are surrounded by angry trees of all kinds with all sorts of faces, bitter and full of wrath.

"Go away King of the Giants! What you mistook for kindling was one of my kin...smashed to bits in your idiot's dance. A king who kills his subjects is not a king at all." Shocked that a race of treants lived in Splinterdark and apalled that he had accidentally killed one, Craniax said nothing. He bowed his head, humbled and returned home.

3180 After Cataclysm: [TAL 2, Year 156] in this year happened an event famous in faery history. The pythoness Shea, a witch of the wood, was captured by monsters of the Shadowitch when she ventured too close to Treehelm. Shea was thrown into the dungeons of the witch. After refusing to join the mad witch's ranks when asked in the throne room of the Shadowitch, Shea severed off one of the witch's horns before she fought her way out of the tower. In the lower casemate Shea was touched by the slender fingers of a darksilk nymph that instantly paralyzed her. She was dragged to a dungeon cell and kept till the injured witch could personally see to her.

But the darksilk nymph relinquished her hold once they were in the cell and Shea blinded the nymph with venom-spittle as she morphed into a snake and slithered out of the Keep and through the forest undetected as hundreds of patrols were sent out in search of her.

Months later, after whispers of the tale reached Everleaf Pines, messengers of the Shadowitch arrived in the Court of Elderboughs just days after Shea reappeared among the faeries there. They demanded the return of Shea to Splinterdark to answer for her crime of assaulting the Queen of Splinterdark. In return the Shadowitch would release two freshly captured sylphs, eleven bantams from Enchandrus and one of the last known pegasi. Shea was summoned and hearing of the proposed exchange she told Elderboughs defiantly that she will fight, not willingly concede to go back and face such a slow and terrible death that awaited her. The faeries marveled at her courage in talking to the Great Tree in this manner but Elderboughs forbade Shea to return to Splinterdark until after the Shadowitch is dead.

At hearing that the witch would some time die the fey again wondered.

3193 After Cataclysm: [TAL 2, Year 169] for many years the Shadowitch watched the former Silthani elves from Feymark'ul who had migrated into western Splinterdark. In this year she received more than a few reports of how mighty these elves had become, thus the Shadowitch Wars now focused on them. After several strikes followed by a full invasion the witch was mystified for she knew these elves and their ways when they occupied Sigils Arch, but now she learned that as the Hadatchi they had adapted to the forest in unforseen ways, had become wild elves, unpredictable. In several skirmishes with the evasive elves her forces were thwarted and even defeated by walking trees.

3204 After Cataclysm: [TAL 2, Year 180] perceiving the several lost battles and failed invasion attempt of the Shadowitch against the wild elves, the Magrar lead the gnolls and their own gnollock offspring out of Splinterdark and into the Illyriac Plain, building Callorock Keep in what would one day be the center of a sprawling gnoll city. Unable to oppose their departure without losing much more of her forces, the witch remained silent, plotting vengeance.

3234 After Cataclysm: [TAL 2, Year 210] in an elaborate three day long ritual the Shadowitch cuts off the wings of the last pegasus in the world, the magical creature full of enchanted energy that the witch draws out through pain. Chained by the neck to a post the pegasus bears the Shadowitch like a steed forced to trot in a circle of symbols seven hundred times until, exhausted, the cursed Minion-forged longsword Avengiclus is thrust through its neck. She removes the woodland beings hearts, blood and innards and cooks them in a stew for four days that she feeds to captive elves, faeries and halflings in her dungeons. These unfortunately beings suffer for hours before dying only to raise back alive again as undead servants of the witch. Over six hundred in number, this small army was known as the Husks of Splinterdark.

3241 After Cataclysm: [TAL 2, Year 217] after bringing all of the denizens of Southern Devilspire Mountains under the rule of the Great Mother, the axemasters, a rugged, large breed of cave orcs, had only the giants of the mountains left to bring into the fold. All others had sent their envoys to the underground temple complex. The giants balked and in a series of campaigns the axemasters brought down Malbolg the Stormbringer, followed by his cave, stone and rock giants. Giants of Ettertooth, Titan Oaks, Deep Ore and Splinterdark came to avenge Malbolg but were also driven back and the unbealable valor of the orcan axemasters became known throughout Dagothar. When Malbolg was killed the hill giant tribe joined the Cult of the Great Mother of the axemasters and the Fall of the Giants was ever after known in this region as the Rise of the Disciples of Devilspire. By this date the axemaster cult was already ancient, its origin lost in the antiquity of The Age of Forgotten Years.

3248 After Cataclysm: [TAL 2, Year 224] During a time of great expansion and building a fleet of ships departed Daethalon and sailed for an eastern coast where they built the city of Hinterport near the mouth of the Yadel river. The Pol'tr were already occupying much of the interior all the way north to Yadel Lake and were not pleased that a Caedorian port city was built blocking their way into the sea to the south. This same city would in the future be known as Kings Bane.

3259 After Cataclysm: [TAL 2, Year 235] the druil'kin trolls of Drakeroost Peaks roust the Bone Kingdoms of goblins, orcs, ogres and minataurs attacking the EM'M dwarves at their main cavern, later known as Meadowlair. Though the invaders were beaten and scattered the EM'M knew their location made them vulnerable within and without so the Hammerworn kings sent out dwarven war parties with prospectors to search for a better place to build their home on the western side of Drakeroost mountains.

3265 After Cataclysm: [TAL 2, Year 242] a party of dwarves happened upon one of the mysterious human mountain men of Drakeroost, who signaled them to follow him into a narrow pass. They carefully pursued and found themselves in a cave that suddenly opened up in to an immense and very defensible cavern that led into a cave system with an underground river. Amazed, the dwarves were in awe of finding a mountain home for their people and humbled that this home was revealed to them by a human vagabond. For centuries afterward relations between the hardy mountain men and the dwarves of Drakeroost was good.

3274 After Cataclysm: [TAL 2, Year 250] Arborealm is a forest now filled with thousands of hamlets, villages and towns of Caedorians, Brard and Pol'tr. At the end of an eight month period of tension the Pol'tr suddenly amass two secretly prepared armies and march from Haddons Gate to Daethalon attacking the Caedorians. At the same time the Pol'tr attacked the Caedorian coastal city of Hinterport using hundreds of hastily constructed vessels built in secret along the western coast of Yadel Lake.

The unexpected assault on Daethalon was a feint that kept the Caedorians from sending aid to Hinterport as the Pol'tr overran the city and captured it, known as the Theft of Hinterport. This was the beginning of the First Arbor War. The Caedorians lost a city and many were killed in its defense. The Pol'tr attacking Daethalon retreated back into the woods before accruing any serious casualties.

3277 After Cataclysm: [TAL 2, Year 253] Emim'gard is completed, made habitable by the dwarven populace and fortified. The entire population of EM'M dwarves in southern Drakeroost migrate under military escort to Emim'gard leaving behind dwarven structures later to be called Meadowlair.

In this year a tiny delegation of warsloths led by sylph sent from Everleaf visited Thelic Hammerworn, extending the friendship of Elderboughs, the Ancient Cedar of A'DIN. The Emim dwarves remembered in their stories how Elderboughs had interceded on their behalf through his daughter Dhishra against the Titans in the days of their fathers. Their first ally in their new homeland of Borderealm, the Hammerworn rulers sent a delegation of dwarves to Everleaf Pines.

3282 After Cataclysm: [TAL 2, Year 258] the Pol'tr again assault Daethalon, a three tier attack by soldiers, sailors aboard ships and by dragons. The wyrms of Pol'tr joined humans in their fight earning the enmity of the dragons of the Caedorians and those of the Brard. Until this date wyrms did not take sides in the disputes of Men. The Brard joined in the defense of Daethalon as did thousands of Caedorians who lived in Treehelm. The fighting spread to the villages of Arborealm, Caedorian and Brard against those of the Pol'tr. Caedorian readiness saw to a quick defeat of the Pol'tr in this the Second Arbor War.

The Caedorians exacted both tribute and securities from the Pol'tr, which had never been done before. The first born sons and daughters of leading Pol'tr families were taken as hostages, furthering the Pol'trian animosity for the Caedorians. Hinterport is taken back from the Pol'tr and three fortified garrisons of Caedorians soldiers are placed around Yadel Lake.

When news of the Pol'tr defeat reached Hinterport and Yadel Lake many thousands of Pol'trians families who had not participated in the war escaped by ship to the islands known to be a few days sail off the coast toward the heart of the Spawnsea. These islands had been known in antiquity because they were once in sight of Southwoods before it sank below the sea. These Pol'trian escapees became a nation of privateers and pirates first known as Raiders of the Spawnsea. Later they would become the pirates of Rivensail.

3283 After Cataclysm: [TAL 2, Year 259] the Raiders of the Spawnsea in a new fleet of ships began attacking both Caedorian and Brard shipping along the coast, accompanied by brown-scaled horned wyrms of the isles, a colony of dragons that had earlier lived in Southwoods who had been defeated by Laer'garoth the Old. The dragons of the isles joined the Men of Pol'tr who had become pirates, seeking adventure and food. Men were able to pull up the tasty treasures of the sea in wide nets, slippers things of the depths that the dragons found delicious.

3284 After Cataclysm: [TAL 2, Year 260) engineers in Daethalon digging up prior foundations of the old city when it was called Caedathal East discovered a sealed vault full of pre-Caedorian tablets full of records. No men were able to translate the texts, which numbered in the thousands, a library of spell texts, stone tables and stelae. Laer'garoth the Old was shown the writings of the buried library for he alone was able to read the Old Dathari script.

In this year the dragon carefully dictated the Odagathus yith Omalacrul , or ancient *Book of Mind and Mage Lore,* from Talan Dathar, to the scribal mage named Nikkolo Ord Magi. Later in the year it was found that another collection of tablets in the same vault contained draconic script and was the same text, the Omalacrul, but much older and signed by the talon of Garoth Dracomancer, a dragon, who had studied under the early MageLords of House Malacrul in Talan Dathar *before* The Cataclysm. Copies of the Book of Mind and Mage Lore were made.

3285 After Cataclysm: [TAL 2, Year 261] to the far west along the coast of the Spawnsea the Raiders of the isles built a new city, calling it Edgehaven. It was their plan to have a base of operations on the mainland but far enough away from the Caedorians that they would not be marched on. These Men were the ancestors of those who would later come to be known as the slavers of the Edgehaven.

3288 After Cataclysm: [TAL 2, Year 264] the Pol'tr attack Daethalon in the Third Arbor War. Armies and navies from Haddons Gate, Yadel Lake with the mountain men of southern Drakeroost, mercenaries from the western regions now called Hinterealm and fleets from the isles of the Raiders and Edgehaven converge of Caedoria...met by fully prepared fleets of Brard and Caedorian warships and armies already in position.

The Pol'tr never reached the city walls but during the battle another army worried the Pol'tr, a host of Caedorians from Treehelm who marched swiftly not to the defense of Daethalon but straight into Arborealm where thousands of undefended Pol'trian settlements and villages were spread around the wooden city of Haddons Gate. Ten thousand torches lit burned Haddons Gate to the ground and almost a thousand hamlets and villages were put to the torch.

Countless black columns of smoke rising from distant Arborealm set the Pol'tr in a panic as they retreated to their homes and wood. Weapons were dropped, provisions left on the field. Caedorian soldiers escorted over fifty-five thousand men, women and children out of Arborealm and into the Yadel Lake forest. Arborealm was completely searched and emptied of all Pol'trians, who were forbidden to return.

Many among the Pol'tr escaped into the sea, hundreds of ships joining the Raiders of the isles. Several ships went to Edgehaven and their crews sold out the other vessels full of unarmed refugees, gaining their own station among the pirates of Edgehaven by selling the men, women and children of the ships they escorted. This is the beginning of the slave trade along the Spawnsea.

Hinterealm all the way to Harrowood was now thickly populated with Pol'tr and Hinterport was strengthened by the Caedorians as a boundary between the two people, the Pol'tr even forbidden access to the sea by way of Yadel river. It is said that in this year a large group of Pol'tr traveled through Harrowood and into the unknown lands beyond Drakeroost.

The burning of Haddons Gate had the city reduced to the largely unaffected megalithic structure of the fortress that would remain there for thousands of years.

3312 After Cataclysm: [TAL 2, Year 288] In the dark of night they appeared silently, a massive gathering of elementals had traveled to Deep Ore Peaks, many thousands from near and far. The giants of the region were alarmed and Craniax was told. The sky giant, perplexed, was visited by these elementals who informed him that he was that very day one thousand and eighty years old. Confused all the more, Craniax asked them why they had not told him when he was a thousand years old, why did they wait eighty years? Their leader, a catastromental, replied,

"Do not be foolish, TAL'VARI...in one thousand and eighty years is a Great Year accomplished."

Craniax thanked them, but decided he would take this matter to someone more knowledgeable about such things.

3336 After Cataclysm: [TAL 2, Year 312] Craniax visited Laer'garoth the Old of Daethalon, frightening the wits out of the Caedorians who had not seen the forty-three foot tall giant in living memory. The sky giant marveled over the expansive architectural feats of Daethalon and drank deeply of the warm mead barrels the humans brought to him in wagon loads as he and the dragon sat in Sacral Court.

He related his experience with the elementals that had gathered to honor his birthday twenty-four years earlier, explaining to the wise dragon that it somehow marked a period of import to them, this one thousand and eighty year duration. Laer'garoth explained that the elementals were very ancient and closer to the Builders than any other races in Dagothar and that in their memory were secrets of Time that no others fathomed because they had not lived as long. The dragon attempted to explain the architecture of the Ages of the Gods but the giant grew more and more confused.

Craniax departed none the wiser, though he had a good time. But Laer'garoth mused over the timing of this visit, for it marked Craniax's one thousand and one hundred and fourth year alive, the period of two visits of the Broken Moon. The Dragon-Chroniclers knew what Craniax did not...that his life was intertwined with that of Men.

3344 After Cataclysm: [TAL 2, Year 320] This year is noted for three significant events. Among the Pol'tr of Yadel Lake are some families descended from Caedorians who had long served as mercenary knights. These men founded the Order of the Shadow Knights and they are easily marked among the Pol'tr for their very pale green eyes so uncommon among the blue, hazel and brown-eyed Pol'tr. The Order of the Shadow Knights would one day be known as the Knightshades.

In Caedoria in this year was founded the Rangers of Borderealm from the earlier Whisperstriders. Their first Conclave was held in secret at the ruins of Haddons Gate in Arborealm.

The third event was the summoning of the Rangers of Borderealm to the Court of Elderboughs in Everleaf where they stood before the Archaic Tree to learn that their fraternity was foretold in the elder prophecies, that they were destined to be protectors of all races throughout Borderealm even after He was gone...a statement that astonished the attending faeries.

Elderboughs informed these rangers that in the Days of Reunion their descendants would provide mankind its greatest blessing and aid. At this meeting among the Shars and Jubilants the number of Borderealm rangers was forever sealed at seven.

3348 After Cataclysm: [TAL 2, Year 324] the Shadowitch receives her estranged sister, Dhishra, in the Keep in Splinterdark and accolades her with the cursed longsword *Avengiclus*. De'nelia gives her the title Thorn Maiden. Dhishra swears allegiance to her sister and becomes her greatest ally. All the wood nymphs who follow the High Shar Dhishra become the thorn maidens.

3349 After Cataclysm: [TAL 2, Year 325] the Emim dwarves begin the carving of Battle Rock, a natural granite rock of enormous size hundreds of feet out from the entrance to Emim'gard. Hollowed, with underground tunnel leading into Emim'gard, Battle Rock is a marvel of defensive dwarven engineering.

3357 After Cataclysm: [TAL 2, Year 333] dark elf dominance in the underworld centered at Sarthaldon City in the cavern of the Limbs of Darkness saw attempts made by these Aelvatchi elves to control the Oracle of Ashadula at the ancient Xakkiun Temple. This holy precinct in Hollowrealm was a major place of pilgrimage long occupied by the draconians, a lizardlike, dragonoid people. The dark elves tried to exert their authority over the complex confident that they were allied to the Minions but they met great resistance in the foreign sorceries of the draconian bloodmancers.

The Aelvatchi, losing hundreds of soldiers, then sent five thousand to secure the Temple but these too were driven back in the Revolt of the Bloodmancers. The draconians then fortified the precinct and in this year began the Tithe,all who entered the Oracle had to pay an offering and all were informed that this tax would continue as long as Sarthaldon contained sinners.

The Aelvatchi convened for war but were forbidden it by the Mrul.

3360 After Cataclysm: [TAL 2, Year 336] at Il-Makkabor of Red Anvil the Haddarim dwarves complete the Pillar of Macewise in the center of their ten level mountain city, also finishing their deep tower crypts. These sepulchers are immense towers that were built downward deeper into the earth. Also in this year the Haddarim dwarves began sending Captains-of-a-Thousand into the mountains of Devilspire to battle the Bone Kingdom cavern coonies wherever they found them while being careful to stay clear of southern Devilspire and the domain of the axemasters. This tradition would last for centuries allowing unblooded young warriors the opportunity to partake in Red Anvil ceremonies when they dragged their captives back to Il-Makkabor.

3367 After Cataclysm: [TAL 2, Year 343] by this time the lizard folk had spread throughout Feymark'ul occupying the abandoned ruins of the Silthani elves who departed for Splinterdark. The Tors of Hallows'gone were megalithic constructions, now dank and dark and suitable for the lizard folk's birth warrens. For years their hatcheries were undisturbed and the lizard folk population grew so rapidly the axemasters of southern Devilspire sent their Bone Kingdom vassals out on expeditions to reduce their numbers yearly.

Also in this year in Drakeroost Peaks occurred *The Seven Against Umiok the Burner,* when the seven Whisperstrider rangers of Borderealm from Caedoria fought and killed the wicked giant Umiok who amused himself by dipping human captives confined in iron cages into fire pits. Umiok was mad, playing a three-holed pipe loudly to the screams of his victims.

A single ranger of House Ehrluft of Arborealm visited the Court of Elderboughs and shocked the assembly of faeries as he spoke forwardly with Elderboughs. Ranger Hedrold, surrounded by warsloths, nymphs, dryads, yelkai, halflings, bantams, some treants, stump gnomes and wood elves said-

"Had one faery been cast into the fires of Umiok all of Everleaf would have brought down this giant. We rangers are few in number and overspread across a vast territory...we do not have time to clean your house while tending ours." Several faeries took offense, for they were ancient and Men's lives were but a very short time. The warsloth Dijix laughed.

"What is the time of a flea to the dog?" Hearing this insult many of the fey were embarrassed, but the human spoke in his own defense.

"Very old and very many you are, so choose which sin you fall prey to- disregard for human life or cowardice. Seven men did what seven thousand fey did not." Some faeries were offended, others shamed. And there was a third group that began to admire Men. House Ehrluft would later be known as the Caerean House of Arrowloft.

3385 After Cataclysm: [TAL 2, Year 361] a lone warsloth using hammer and chisel was decorating a megalithic pylon when the woods all around him silenced. The aura of the trees bespoke danger and he stopped his work to look about.

His eyes fell upon a tall figure armored in shadows standing between two trees.

"You are Gano'tax." The warsloth nodded at the Dark Reliquar, recognizing the large scepter he had seen thousands of years ago on the back of this strange visitor to the Court of Elderboughs. Gano'tax perceived this shadowy figure to be of divine antiquity. Alone in the forest with this intruder, the warsloth listened.

"Go now to the Pilot...tell Him my steps are haunted, I can not come. Tell Him there will be no war in ninety-five turnings...the Pass will be insignificant. The Deep is divided with powers, unrest, civil war. The shadows of Lady Death-Bringer conspire throughout the caverns below bringing discord to the Minion empire."

Gano'tax blinked and the powerful visitor was gone. It took several moments before the first bird chirped that the wood was clear.

3401 After Cataclysm: [TAL 2, Year 377] With new invasion of Bone Kingdoms at their border of Feymark'ul the lizard folk retreat into Splinterdark and through negotiations join their population to the forces of the Shadowitch.

3405 After Cataclysm: [TAL 2, Year 381] the swelling lizard folk populations of Dretchwold join a massive lizard folk horde from the southern jungles in their attack on Shannidar which is occupied by the Ayr. Eganosh Faerymane and his brother Alaryel lead the faery race of shapechangers in the defense of the citadels and Sigils Arch beating away the lizard folk.

3437 After Cataclysm: [TAL 2, Year 413] a Shadow Knight of the Pol'tr slew the Hynomancer of Yadel Lake, earning the title of *Mageslayer*. It is said that the Hynomancer grew too powerful in his slumber magics and ability to make people do things they did not remember by studying a copy of the Odagathus yith Omalacrul texts. Because of similar reports of unusual advances of power uncontrollable, the Omalacrul texts were forbidden and all known copies were sought and destroyed. A single copy was placed in a lead box and sealed in a hollow beneath a corner stone of the new wall of the temple in Daethalon.

The Shadow Knights would one day be called Knightshades and this particular knight, named Pleor, had his longsword preserved by the order for it maintained unusual properties since killing the wizard. Years later the Knightshade weapon smiths melted it down and reforged a new blade with the same metal, calling it Mageslayer. Again the blade exhibited enchanted properties.

3448 After Cataclysm: [TAL 2, Year 424] a series of terrifying hauntings transpired throughout Arborealm, the incident now known as the Ghosts of Malacrul. There were sightings of demonic-looking visitors that murdered men horribly at five different locations in this year. One in Daethalon, one in a village in Arborealm, one at Haddons Gate where a thriving tent city had emerged, one at southern edge of Yadel Lake and a fifth was discovered dead out at the isles of the Raiders. The only link these five dead men had with another is that a copy of the Odagathus yith Omalacrul text was found among their belongings.

Those among the wise were aware that this evil was executed by demons who feared the knowledge contained in the book.

3480 After Cataclysm: [TAL 2, Year 456] the scholars of the Order of the Broken Moon knew that the Broken Moon would return in this year and they published widely their knowledge and calculations. When the Broken Moon did appear as a red star that grew in size they expected the worst but it did not happen. A minor earthquake felled several older structures but the city and civilization of Caedoria continued uninterrupted. The alarmist warnings of invasion and mass death went unfulfilled. The Caedorians, finding stress fractures throughout the old Temple of Eternal Lore repaired the structure and then buried it, laid a new foundation over the buried temple precinct and built the new Temple of the Broken Moon, which was not as prestigious. The Order lost a lot of popularity for it seemed to be of little relevance, a relic of the past. The Broken Moon was no longer to be feared.

Many of those in the upper hierarchy of the order left it and became politicians while those that remained used a secret tunnel access to enter the underground and older temple. For many years they made a copy of the Codex Caerea which was taken from the walls of the inner sanctum using enchanted light rods on the wall texts.

Also in this year began the *Feyfolk War* in Everleaf. As the quaking shook the trees of Everleaf Pines the faeries called the fey assembled against those they called athradoc, expelling them from the woods and forbidding them to access the Barkwalk and Pool of Solace.

3481 After Cataclysm: [TAL 2, Year 457] Hinterport of the Caedorians was suddenly attacked by a huge fleet of strange ships hoisting red sails manned by a red-skinned race of men from the east using vessels with a bank of oars along its flanks. Hinterport of the Caedorians was sacked with only the Pol'tr near enough to aid them but they did not come and were not considered allies.

3502 After Cataclysm: [TAL 2, Year 478] the Emim dwarves finish their fortress of Battle Rock, a marvel of engineering, and the outer fortification of Emim'gard's inner gate keep.

3504 After Cataclysm: [TAL 2, Year 480] the Feyfolk Wars continue. Dhishra the Thorn Maiden and her athradoc followers in Splinterdark and Treehelm invade Enchandrus forest but they are met with a larger force of fey who drive them out. Manax the warsloth general sets upon Dhishra and in an epic combat between the thorn maiden and warsloth Dhishra passed her blade across Manax's chest, opening it. In a fit of rage the warsloth general nearly decapitates the thorn maiden three times as she fended off his assaults and retreated with the athradoc. Manax was forced down by Hakkix and Mithix as other faeries shoved munchroot in his mouth and open wound, over a dozen fey laying hands on him as they worked their healing magics.

The athradoc melt into Arborealm and Treehelm and are pursued, then into Splinterdark but many of the fey do not venture into the forest's interior. For the next two years warsloth parties scoured Splinterdark seeking the thorn maiden leader.

3535 After Cataclysm: [TAL 2, Year 511] The Raiders of the Spawnsea of the isles attack Hinterport of the Caedorians, forcing the Caedorians to yield the harbor while unable to take the fortified city. The pirates took all the vessels in the port and harbor, burned those they did not and sailed off loaded with stolen provisions and people who would live their days out as slaves.

3552 After Cataclysm: TAL 2, Year 528] the Feyfolk Wars continue as the athradoc assemble for war. Most of those athradoc not joined to the Shadowitch are by this time chased out of Splinterdark and residing in Treehelm. The host of athradoc, even more numerous than before, again led by Dhishra the thorn maiden, met the host of the Pillars of Everleaf at the northern edge of Arborealm and clashed in a day-long battle that left the entire plain strewn with nethering, wounded and dead faeries. Near sun down both sides retreated with those of their allies still alive they could gather up, shocked at the unexpected loss of life on both fronts. Both fey and athradoc that evening held heated councils about continuing a conflict that that so utterly depleted their numbers.

It was at this time that the fey realized that there were many faeries spread across Borderealm who had not taken sides in the conflict of fey and athradoc. At a council in Everleaf at the Barkwalk entrance and not in the dome of Elderboughs these faeries were summoned to give answer for their negligence in helping the others against the athradoc. Many thousands of faeries chose not to participate in this civil war, what was being termed The Rift. Arguments broke out and the violence of the offended drove the peace-seekers out of Everleaf and their banishment was imposed. This was thence known as the *Banishment of the Exiles.*

3564 After Cataclysm: [TAL 2, Year 540] the three-eyed draergnomes occupy the desert ruins of Gotsduin, ancient capital of the Sand Kings in the Eternal Sands desert. But weird happenings in the ruins disturbed the draer and compelled them to abandoned Gotsduin. They found Mount Ogrori and its caves and began building their new home.

3575 After Cataclysm: [TAL 2, Year 551] a Pillar of Everleaf who counted himself among the exiles named Ish'layyar, a great black bear changling, with the nymph Vanica sought audience with Elderboughs but were refused admittance into the

Barkwalk. They tried to enter and Ashrey and two other shars set upon Vanica but were distressed that the nymph so easily overcame them. The wood giant Thigg opposed Ish'layyar and was dropped to the ground instantly before he then scattered the wickerworls, knocked out a warsloth and threw a pine titan. Then Manax appeared and with his entourage beat back Vanica and Ish'layyar.

Then exiles who had come with the two and a whole crowd of fey who lived in Everleaf interposed and stopped the fighting. These had much reverence for Ish'layyar and Vanica and many protested to Ashrey and Manax that they had overstepped their authority- that banishment was not imposed by the will of Elderboughs but by the will of faeries *outside* the dome.

In her wrath at being beaten down by Vanica, Ashrey of the shars spat- "*Never!* I vow on my life you shall never walk the Barkwalk till I am on The Other Side!"

Ish'layyar, Vanica and Thornlok with their gathering of exiles were escorted out of Everleaf by fey and Aelvani elves and the shars were stunned as they watched many of their fey allies willingly go into banishment, joining Vanica and the others as they disappeared into the night of Borderealm. This group of exiles sought to dig their burrows in northern Arborealm but at good distance from the habitats of Men.

3588 After Cataclysm: [TAL 2, Year 564] Dhishra the thorn maiden against leads an attack of athradoc in the Invasion of Arborealm, also remembered as The War of the Exiles. The athradoc attack by moonlight and set upon all four groups of exiles, those led by Thornlok the dragon, Vanica the nymph, Ish'layyar the bear and Ganeshu the Wise. Ganeshu, a faery elephant changling had spent decades sharing and learning with the dragons of Caedoria, Brard and Pol'tr as well as a colony of green dragons that lived among the willow weirds in Enchandrus.

When attacked the horn of Ganeshu still the athradoc for they knew not its significance nor were they prepared for the power of the noise. Ganeshu led his exiled faeries into the meadows and Vanica, Thornlok and Ish'layyar followed his example. As the fighting increased as more and more athradoc left the dark of the trees and advanced into the meadows many were silently snatched into the air and never seen again.

Great black shadows in the air swooped down with talons and tails that killed dark faeries with ease. Dhishra looked and saw the many dragons, white, brown, green and black, Laer'garoth the Old among them. The athradoc flee and Ganeshu with Lycrops and many other faeries depart into the wilds of Treehelm while Thornlok travels to the ruins of the dwarves in southern Drakeroost and makes his home in Meadowlair with the faeries under his guidance. Some exiles move on to Harrowood.

Ish'layyar and Vanica with their host stay in northern Arborealm but are again attacked by the athradoc who chase them to the gates of Winnowyn-Under-the-Mountain, a primordial ghost from The World Before known to the elementals. The faeries are allowed to pass under the mountains into the lands to the east but the The Gates are shut behind them.

3607 After Cataclysm: [TAL 2, Year 583] because of excursions into their domain, over thirty servants of the Great Mother, the Disciples of Devilspire, attacked and slaughtered thousands of the orcs of Ebrog Pass in what is called The Revenge of the Axemasters.

3618 After Cataclysm: [TAL 2, Year 594] the Shadowitch, never forgetting those who did her injury, attacks the Magrar and their gnolls in the Illyriac plain with a large host, intent to take Callorock Keep. The Ignoble Ones, having built enchanted sleds pulled by the labor of their chained captives are by this time called Muzzle Lords and they allow none of the army of Splinterdark to return to the witch. It is said that in this campaign the Shadowitch lost over half of her military power for many years.

3624 After Cataclysm: {TAL 2, Year 600] the rangers of Borderealm, still known as Whisperstriders, begin their training astride mountaindrakes from Drakeroost as opposed to dragons. The drakes were lighter, smaller, equal to horses in intelligence and easier to feed, maintain and hide. As the duties of the Whisperstriders took them more farther afield the dragons of Caedoria and the Brard were needed at home.

3641 After Cataclysm: [TAL 2, Year 617] after a rapid population explosion of the Bone Kingdoms of Deep Ore Peaks the orcs, cobble goblins, minataurs and ogres gather under the call of an ogre chief named Targrak, King of the Shardlings. By feeding the shardling dragons the ogre chieftain gained their allegiance and in this year Targrak assaulted Daggerhold of the Galdirim dwarves with a host so massive it stunned the dwarves of Grol-galdir. Known as both the Battle of Daggerhold and the Chainway Bridge Massacre, the dwarves lost Daggerhold and almost lost Chainway Bridge. The massive pulleys and levers had frozen solid and they were unable to collapse their chain bridge at the onslaught of the Bone Kingdoms. Galdirim barely held the bridge and won the battle only because the Bone Kingdoms feared the giants and knew a prolonged siege would draw the attention of Craniax.

3662 After Cataclysm: [TAL 2, Year 638] at the break of dawn a fleet of Raiders of the Spawnsea from the isles attack Hinterport again, and again the pirates steal oof with the ships in the harbor, loaded and empty and capture more slaves.

3672 After Cataclysm: [TAL 2, Year 648] In this year the Pol'tr royally recognize the Order of the Shadow Knights as sworn servants of their people. For a long time they were regarded with distrust because they were descended from the green eyed Caedorians. The Shadow Knights were known to possess tyhe relic longsword Mageslayer and in this year of acceptance among the Pol'tr they formerly become the *Knightshades*.

Some among the Knightshades were also members of the elite Order of the Arcanum, also called The Craft by the Caedorian scholars, a fraternity of learned men spread through the ranks of the Pol'tr, the Caedorians and the Brard. Sometimes known as the Society of Mancers these wizard wise men in Caedorian by now were known as the Societas Arcanum. Among the Brard elite they were the Order of Seers, later to be revered as the Council of Sages and Seers. Among the Pol'tr these men were of the Craft Arcanumus, later to become the famous *Arcanacrafts*.

In Treehelm the faery leader Ganeshu of the Exiles of Everleaf encounters a mystir, a very old air elemental enchantress who takes him far through the woodlands to a deeply hidden sanctuary with ruins of early human occupation dated from The Scattering Years where he sees a ghostly golden pillar apparition. In this the Cavern of the Fey in Splinterdark the faery elephant changling is instructed to bring his exiles to this place of refuge, a secret retreat not even the Shadowitch knew of.

3674 After Cataclysm: [TAL 2, Year 650] a great fleet of corsairs from the Raiders of the Isles attack Daethalon harbor and the coasts of Arborealm, vanishing over the horizon before the Caedorians can assemble a response and leaving in their wake burning and pillaged ships.

3690 After Cataclysm: [TAL 2, Year 666] Theod Rikkic Hammerworn slew the troll giant chieftain Grurj of the sporu'kin trolls of Drakeroost with the relic war hammer Quakemaker when the troll giant visited Emim'gard with his delegation. Grurj appeared before Theod and demanded the Emim pay tribute to the cavern city of Baavr. The burned skull of Grurj was dipped in silver, padded and worn as a helm by Theod Hammerworn.

3691 After Cataclysm: [TAL 2, Year 667] led by the outraged sporu'kin trolls of Drakeroost, the Bone Kingdoms attack Emim'gard. The horde of goblins, trolls, ogres and minataurs are surprised when movable slabs open on Battle Rock and large rocks are launched at them upon the open field. In the press many of those in the horde were smashed, crushed, maimed and the host dispersed in each and every way to their corners of the mountain range, thus beginning The Bone Kingdom Wars of Drakeroost.

3697 After Cataclysm: [TAL 2, Year 675] The Second Battle of Battle Rock continued the Bone Kingdom Wars as five armies of sporu'kin trolls, orcs, cobble goblins, ogres and minataurs concentrated not on Emim'gard proper but only on trying to take Battle Rock, which stood alone on the open plain next to the mountain. They broke themselves in wave after wave never entering or breaking through its hard granite rock. Again they scatter in retreat.

3710 After Cataclysm: [TAL 2, Year 686] Emim dwarves discover cave entrance to the tradevein below Drakeroost, these veins being corridors that connected the settlements and strongholds of the Bone Kingdoms whereby they conducted their marches, trade and slave labor. An army of Emim dwarves invade the tradevein and attack the deep cavernhold of Khu'urg of the sporu'kin trolls, killing many as the others scatter into the crevasses and tunnels of the range.

3711 After Cataclysm: [TAL 2, Year 687] the Emim dwarves invade through the tradevein system and kill the trolls of the underground city of Baavr just northwest of the mountain later known as Cairnstone.

3712 After Cataclysm: [TAL 2, Year 688] the Bone Kingdom Wars continue as the Emim dwarves march up the tradevein and attack the orc city of Givrul in a large cavern. In this year on the surface of the mountain range under the sky the Emim war parties put an end to the marauding of the cave giants oppressing the mountain folk. The giants hotly contended with some rock elementals and the Emim entered the fray and slew the giants. This began a friendship between the elemental leader Crysmar, a crystalline elemental, and his rock people.

3742 After Cataclysm: [TAL 2, Year 718] The last of the four explorer group expeditions of the Pol'tr returned through Harrowood safely back into Hinterealm. In four large groups the Pol'trian population of Yadel Lake and Hinterealm under military escort migrated through Harrowood to vanish into the east. It was done quickly and quietly and news of their disappearance through Harrowood stunned the Caedorians and Brard, for none knew what lied beyond the Drakeroost mountains.

The Whisperstriders and dragonriders of Caedoria flew over the abandoned towns and settlements and confirmed that the Pol'tr were gone. The Hinterfolk and the mountain men were still in the land and now many Caedorian families resettled in the land.

3744 After Cataclysm: [TAL 2, Year 720] in the second year of their migration after departing through Harrowood the Pol'tr settled in a garden land of large lakes, tall timbers, mineal wealth and rich soil. They settled around Nectar Lakes, later to be called Three-Bridges Lake Garrison. The Pol'tr were amazed to find evidence that humans had passed through the same area long before they had.

3756 After Cataclysm: [TAL 2, Year 732] the Magrar of the Gnolldom Plain (formerly the Illyriac Plain) amass a hundred thousand gnolls and many gnollocks besides and attack Il-Makkabor of Red Anvil in the First Ettertooth War. But the Haddarim were mighty and the Magrar were upset by the ferocity of the Tunnel Kings. Not since Manax the warsloth had the Magrar suffered any of their own to die in battle. But in this series of battles the discipline and training of the armored dwarves saw to the quick defeat of many times as many gnolls, the slaughter of gnollock knights and the killing of a Muzzle Lord. The invaders departed but the Magrar vowed to return.

3762 After Cataclysm: [TAL 2, Year 738] Dhishra the thorn maiden walked the halls of the Keep of the Shadowitch concealed powerfully under a masking spell that made her appear like one of the witch's vile stewards. Dhishra was caught in the act of attempting to steal the powerful artifact longsword Avengiclus but she escaped into the haunts of Splinterdark. Some believe that the witch only allowed her to escape.

3773 After Cataclysm: [TAL 2, Year 749] the Muzzle Lords of Callorock Keep in the Gnolldom Plains returned to Il-Makkabor with over a hundred thousand gnolls and ten thousand gnollock knights. Again, the Tunnel Kings, known of old as giant-killers, routed the gnolls, effected a great slaughter spreading the bodies of dead and dying dogmen in a long train from the mountains to the city of Gnosh where they had come.

The alien fighting style, changing front lines, alternating tactics and use of unfamiliar weapons designed to take down large opponents worried the Magrar. A third of the entire host of Gnosh city was killed in the mountains and on the plain and more than half of the Magrar had to walk home because the dwarves had broken their slave-sleds or killed the slaves moving them.

The Second Ettertooth War ended and this time the Magrar vowed to never again attack the Haddarim.

3805 After Cataclysm: [TAL 2, Year 781] the Sylnadorians of the south advance through Dathom Peaks and attack the Pol'tr at Nectar Lakes initiating the First Dathom War. The Sylnadorian cavalry was more numerous than their footmen and was supported by reddish, leathery hill and mountaindrake riders in the sky. This was the first contact between the Pol'tr and the red-skinned Sylnadorians. The Pol'tr held their positions and the enemy retreated back through the pass.

3819 After Cataclysm: [TAL 2, Year 795] an army of well-organized insect warriors called formions in the jungles of the Silapenti had multiplied into countless colonies. They flooded into Shannidar and attack the Ayr settlements, citadels and Sigils Arch. But the formions were unfamiliar with the power, cunning and magics of the faeries and especially the ferocity of the bruun, ariels, hawks and apanthoi. As formions advanced toward Sigils Arch they crawled more and more over the pieces of dead formions and their leaders, seeing the tens of thousands of dead kin, ripped apart, burnt, bitten in half and crushed, ordered their bands to halt.

The formions held council in the fields amidst the strewn bodies of their dead kin finding no faeries among those killed. As one hive-minded body they turned and marched back into their jungle.

3825 After Cataclysm: [TAL 2, Year 801] the Pol'tr plan out and begin building Dor'Ath-by-the-Sea, a major city on the scale of old Haddons Gate but located on coast of the Athean sea, even to rival Daethalon of the Caedorians. Along the coast is found much evidence of prior human occupation.

3888 After Cataclysm: [TAL 2, Year 864] Craniax was thrilled to receive visitors at Ricanor Castle. TAL-NIK of the Beasthorn and many of his ha'akathrals visited for eight days, drank the mead, smoked the pipe and the King of the Giants did learn many things about The Old World.

3912 After Cataclysm: [TAL 3, Year 24] A spectacle appeared in the night sky above Dagothar seen by all living things. An object, a great black darkness blocked out the stars, a shadow with distant tiny lights of its own. Across the face of Dagothar the voices of the elementals sang in a powerful song in words unknown even to the oldest faeries. As one the elementals raised their voices and many witnesses claim that elementals they were watching were lifted up into the night sky.

It is said that the ghosts of the many thousands of dead elementals raised from their places and climbed into the sky, that elementals still standing yielded their ghosts and left behind statues of themselves, odd pillars, strange rocks and crystals, curious formations in nature. Many of the spirits of elementals frozen to death in the Shadowed Ice were now rejoined with their kin.

The great black object moved lazily across the dome of the sky taking away most of the elementals, living and dead, for a few of them remained in the world. Those who had made vows to the Golden One, who promised to see his will fulfilled.

3942 After Cataclysm: [TAL 3, Year 54] the hama'kin trolls migrate to Mount Thokax in Darkfrost Peaks and encounter an unknown race of dwarves, an anciently lost race that formerly occupied the mountains in the days of Nimbolc. These dwarves had returned from the west, weakened and few in number. In the First Hama'kin War the dwarves barely beat back the trolls.

Dhishra the thorn maiden convinces Rajosh Gonewhiskers that he must steal the relic longsword Avengiclus from the Keep of the Shadowitch, for it is the source of the witch's power and a threat to all the faeries, fey and athradoc. Rajosh, lightning quick, steals the sword and the Shadowitch appears instantly but Rajosh leaves behind only a single whisker in the air as he hurtles forward through time and space faster than a blink.

Finding the whisker the witch cast a necromantic spell and like a zombie Rajosh stopped, turned around and took the sword back to her throneroom before he even got a mile away from Dhishra's hiding place outside the Keep. Retrieving her sword the witch lets him go and he vanishes in haste, again, as always, leaving behind a single whisker that she places in a vial for the future when she might have need of the speedy faery.

3944 After Cataclysm: [TAL 3, Year 56] the hama'kin trolls with goblin vassals attack Mount Thokax and the dwarves are unable to defend the vast fortifications. They are slaughtered and the entire lost tribe of dwarves who returned to Mount Thokax are eaten by the trolls. Upper Thokax is turned into a troll den, but none ventured into Lower Thokax sensing the dangerous things that lurked there among the ruins of ancient Nimbolc.

4014 After Cataclysm: [TAL 3, Year 126] the Shadowitch holds an omen vigil attempting to divine the secret location of the hiding place of the faery exiles who are with Ganeshu that she knows are somewhere in her domain of Splinterdark. She is met with a powerful magic that obscures all of her searching so she sends out hundreds of her husks, the undead faery abominations, to search them out. On her throne the witch spent two years meditating, seeing through the eyes of her husks and caught not a single glance of faeries in hiding.

Angry at being slighted, unable to find the sanctuary, she executes all the prisoners, mostly faeries, wasting away in her dungeons with Avengiclus.

4032 After Cataclysm: [TAL 3, Year 144] as Daethalon grows old, so does its memory. Few remember the histories of the Broken Moon and when it returns in this year it is little regarded. The quakes are mild and it does not pass directly over the sun to darken the world. The sky turns reddish but the coloring is faint and passing.

In this year happened the War of the Exiles in Splinterdark as several Shadowitch armies scoured the woods in search of the faery sanctuary. Ganeshu led the exiled faeries in a series of battles against her forces and they learned the secret of the husks, which the faeries later called the Eyes of the Dark Queen. Seeking her sister's favor, Dhishra and the thorn maidens attack Ganeshu but are horrified when the faery elephant leader goes into a blood rage killing two thorn maidens and nearly crushing Dhishra to death.

At seeing the might of Ganeshu and the white werewolf Lycrops through her husks, the Shadowitch sets her shaghoths on them but the faeries disappear and can not be found. In wrath the witch turns her armies on Dhishra and her athradoc host who then flee Splinterdark for the safety of Treehelm.

The quakes in this year destroyed the interior of Mount Forknost, the ancient home of the Silverbeard and Silveraxe dwarves then living among the Galdirim. This quake sealed the entrance to the dungeon mines.

Among the Pol'tr the scholars of the Craft Arcanamus recorded the passing of the Broken Moon in their annals but in Caedoria the Societas Arcanum began taking on the form of a cult, a pseudo-scientific religious group dedicated to the study of history and prophecy.

4097 After Cataclysm: [TAL 3, Year 209] the Winter Years began, eight years of extreme cold and overcast with little sunlight throughout the year. Summers were mild with cool spells that were unnatural. Crop failures, starvation, erratic animal behavior and cannibalism widely reported.

In this year a seer of the Brard is expelled from the Society of Mancers. He preaches a message of coming darkness, the return of the Age of Shadowed Ice and many people listen to him. The prophet Zadk, as he is named, tells the people that life, warmth, water and food in abundance is found in the underworld and that all races had once been there to survive the Shadowed Ice.

4101 After Cataclysm: [TAL 3, Year 213] the prophet Zadk among the Brard is strongly opposed by the prophet Erythuil of the Caedorian Societas Arcanum, who accuses Zadk of being a false prophet, an agent of the Minions in the Deep. But the common people have never been explosed to the libraries of The

Craft and its societies so hearing of these Minions never before mentioned fell on deaf ears. Further, the threat of enemies they never heard of before meant little to a people who hungered during the Winter Years. The world had grown cold and the message of Zadk seemed to gain favor with the people of Brard.

Late in this year the prophet Erythuil was found dead in his study, door bolted locked from within, his body burned badly from the crown of his head to his waist, though his chair was curiously unburnt. An old copy of *The Lost Scriptures of Achuzan* lying open on his desk.

4104 After Cataclysm: [TAL 3, Year 216] with so many Caedorians flooding into the city fleeing the violence of monsters and armies of strange creatures in Treehelm, all of Old Caedoria became overcrowded and the message of the false prophet Zadk became more appealing. With the food shortage critical the Caedorians did not concern themselves overly with the decision of the people of Brard to depart Caedoria.

The Brard were now convinced the Winter Years were really the beginning of a New Shadowed Ice, that they must relocate now or soon be frozen out of the underworld where there was food and water. Zadk and his trusted disciples led the Brard with their green dragons and three Whisperstriders out of Caedoria.

4105 After Cataclysm: [TAL 3, Year 217] the Brard marvel that their leader Zadk knows the exact location of massive caves that lead to a huge watered cavern under the Mountains of Drakeroost. An abandoned orc city under the mountain range is where they rested three days and made camp before resuming their journey into the Deep. That Zadk knew how to get them there safely was taken by all as a sign that he had found favor with the gods. In this year the Brard vanish from off the face of Dagothar to reappear in the underworld.

4177 After Cataclysm: [TAL 3, Year 289] in Everleaf Pines a thick quiet fell upon the woods. The faeries grew alarmed for it was apparent to all that Elderboughs was troubled. Many animals fled to other nearby forests as the Archaic Tree brooded in silence. This carried on many days and the entire city of Ti'el around the dome and Barkwalk made so sound. At the soft inquiry of a sylph, Elderboughs' great eyes opened. She stood alone at the edge of the white stone ring around His massive trunk as morose faeries listened.

"The wood is silent...birds won't leave their nests. No songs in the sunlight. Stags have led their deer away. When you are dark we grow fearful."

Elderboughs smiled and the entire dome was filled with golden light.

"EVEN IN THE DEEP THERE IS LIGHT, LITTLE YAHLRA." His mood vanished and laughter was heard again in Everleaf, for He knew they were unmindful of the times. A visitor was expected who did not come.

4219 After Cataclysm: [TAL 3, Year 331] the Poltyrians of Dor'Ath-by-the-Sea are attacked by a large Sylnadorian fleet of red-sailed warships as a Sylnadorian army passes through Dathom Peaks and attacks the city of Nectar Lakes in this the Second Dathom War. Nectar Lakes falls to Sylnador and the survivors are taken as slaves back into the unknown south but the fleet of the Sylnadorians is destroyed by the Poltyrian war vessels that do not allow a single Sylnadorian ship to return home.

4296 After Cataclysm: [TAL 3, Year 408] in the years since the Sylnadorian sack of Nectar Lakes, the city was rebuilt with massive fortifications and well-garrisoned. The Poltyrians in this year remove their capitol from Nectar Lakes to Dor'Ath City on the coast of the Athean Sea.

4344 After Cataclysm: [TAL 3, Year 456] the first bowmaster of House Arrowloft is put through the trials and accepted into the training of the Rangers of Borderealm. By this time the title Whisperstrider was only made in reference to rangers of centuries before when the Brard and Caedorians were living together in Daethalon and environs.

4357 After Cataclysm: [TAL 3, Year 469] the Third Dathom War is fought between Sylnador and Poltyria. Three Sylnadorian armies ascended through the Dathom pass and all three were repelled by the army of the fortress-city of Nectar Lakes, later to be called Three-Bridges Lake Garrison. It is said that over four hundred thousand Sylnadorian soldiers lost their lives to the organized military discipline of the Poltyrians. Three-Bridges cemetery on east side of the Old Fortress today is on a series of high artificial hills. It is said that these hills are the displaced dirt from the digging of deep trenches wherein the dead bodies of the Sylnadorians were cast in and burned.

4381 After Cataclysm: [TAL 3, Year 493] after a period of starvation, disease and unfavorable living conditions the Brard people had secured for themselves a series of off-the-cave caverns watered by natural springs, one being half-flooded and swamplike with fungal plants and game. By this time the newer generations of Brard born in the underworld were adapted to see in the dark and their senses of hearing and smell had sharpened. They harvested lichens that ate stone and gave off luminescent gases they made for glowing tea, ate molderond stalks ground into powder for bread and caught fish and slippery things for meat and bones that they ground for pastes, caulking, glue and meal.

Their cavern was hollowed further into hundreds of residential recesses containing whole families eash some as many as four hundred people, a virtual city of carved stone they called Zaddiki after its long-dead founder, Zadk. It was believed by the Brard that the world above they had come from was gone, buried under mountains of ice and dark, that a New Shadowed Ice had come.

In this year their cavern city was attacked by hornback orcs of the Deep but they repelled them. The Brard presence in Hollowrealm was known to the other races of the underworld who at this time did not feel threatened by them. They were called by others as the Barad-ai, or Deep Men.

4440 After Cataclysm: [TAL 3, Year 552] the Shiver Scale Blight affects the whole world of dragons. Everywhere across Dagothar and Aroth Beyond the dragons and dragonkind creatures are afflicted with a cold, fevers and uncontrollable shivering that causes their whole hide of scales to shudder in violent spasms. Dragons of all kinds, all ages and in every region above and below the world die off from this bizarre malady.

It is said that from this year onward no Scarlet Wyrms were seen on the surface again, the royalty of dragon kind. The Blight killed off the copper dragons and most of the shardlings. Laer'garoth the Old, the other Caedorian and Poltyrian dragons fell sick but none died as they were carefully tended by humans.

Craniax chose eleven giants from Deep Ore and told the rest to stay on guard lest the Bone Kingdoms attempt mischief knowing they were gone. These twelve giants travelled widely around the whole of Dagothar from Darkfrost mountains to Drakeroost Peaks burying all of those dragons where they were found. Visiting Towerhenge the King of the Giants was saddened to find it empty. No trace of the cloud serpents that once occupied the strange and dateless ruins.

Word spread among the giants that the Blight had afflicted the underworld too and the wise in those days estimated that only one out of every thirty dragons in the world survived the disease.

4519 After Cataclysm: [TAL 3, Year 631] a horde of about nine thousand hornback orcs, badly equipped, unarmored and with crude old battlefield-stripped weapons try to invade Zaddiki city of the Deep Men and over a period of two days they are slaughtered. Far back in the shadows Aelvatchi dark elf spies studied the underworld humans and their defenses.

In this year the Barad-ai formed the Shieldguard, elite warriors trained only to defend the home front.

4577 After Cataclysm: [TAL 3, Year 689] after two back-to-back battles with a passing horde of migrating goblins the Shieldguard of the Deep Men became formerly known as the Sons of the Shield, the oldest military order of the Barad-ai, highly trained in defensive warfare only. The Barad-ai began training men and women as an expeditionary force as well, called the Sons of the Sword, the second recognized order. These soldiers would leave the others in the hands of the Sons of the Shiled as they explored the tunnels and waycaverns of the Deep.

4580 After Cataclysm: [TAL 3, Year 692] a wild wyrm, a black dragon having no knowledge of Men, happened upon Daethalon by way of flying over Treehelm from Splinterdark but ultimately having departed Devilspire Mountains. The dragon stopped to state at the sprawling city of the Caedorians. Laer'garoth of the Protectorate appeared and warned the strange wyrm off but the black dragon fought Laer'garoth viciously instead. After a hot contest Laer'garoth tore out the younger dragon's throat but not before its talons had ripped deep into his bowels. Event recorded in the annals as the Maiming of Laer'garoth the Old.

The Caedorians ceremoniously and sadly built a vast crypt for their hero dragon. As Laer'garoth lie wounded many months he was thrilled to receive Craniax the sky giant who had come in haste at the news of his friend's fate. The forty-three foot tall giant scared the wits out of the people but they soon received him with much honor and mead barrels. Scholars declared that it was written in the records that the King of the Giants had visited Laer'garoth before in this very city.

For many weeks did Craniax and Laer'gaorth enjoy long conversations as the old wyrm weakened. Navaniz the Black listened with interest and even befriended the legendary sky giant, vowing to visit him one day at Ricanor Castle. It is written that Laer'garoth shared many secret things with both Craniax and Navaniz, that it took many years for Laer'garoth to die.

4584 After Cataclysm: [TAL 3, Year 696] from out of the jungles of the Silapenti appear two separate armies led by a Minion each. Each army contained hordes of Silapenti snake warriors, formion insent people, cyprian bog giants, lizard folk and kraxa'kin trolls. Both armies marched around Deep Ore Peaks and invaded Caedoria. The Minion armies were separated, taking different routes, but Craniax, his giants, and the dwarves of Grol-galdir descended upon one of the armies and destroyed it with the help of local faeries from Treehelm and Titan Oaks. Craniax attempted to slay the Abominid over and over but gets knocked down each time. The Minion, without its army, vanished.

The second Minion with its vast horde fell upon Caedoria, attacking Daethalon in Arborealm at the exact time when Ishaak

Burnbreath the Alabaster Wyrm was visiting the dying Laer'garoth. Navaniz the Black with the dragons of the Protectorate joined by the Alabaster Wyrm with the army of Caedorians met the host of the Minion on the field of battle at Ghul-Run. Ishaak's fantastic breath weapon of searing electricity worried the Minion and when it was about to retaliate against the white dragon, Navaniz bit the Abominid and it screeched powerfully knocking the young dragon unconscious. The other dragons noticed that the Minion was wounded and they took turned swooping down on it, slashing, biting and spitting their weapons. It disappeared amid the battle and Men drove the enemy snake warriors, bog giants, formions, lizard folk and trolls into Treehelm and Splinterdark.

In celebration of their victory Men granted the title of Bold to Navaniz for his fearlessness in biting the Abominid, for all knew the old tales of Talan Dathar, that Minions easily slew dragons in the past. Navaniz is chosen to be leader of The Protectorate of wyrms of Daethalon for he was also of the brood of Laer'garoth the Old who was no more fit to lead the dragons, this dated in the 1104th year of the laying of the Temple of the Broken Moon.

In this year, thirty-three days after the battle with the Minion host, the Broken Moon appeared in the night sky, grew very large in the weeks to follow but never darkened the sun. It disappeared as quietly as it came and no quakes were reported anywhere in Dagothar.

4599 After Cataclysm: [TAL 3, Year 711] Laer'garoth the Old died at Daethalon laying atop the massive slab of his open-air crypt chamber, the sun on his scales. Many dragons came to pay their respects and the dragons of The Protectorate watched them warily. The huge burned skull of the black wyrm that maimed him was placed in the crypt as was a copy of the histories of the world of Men, the *Testimony of Laer'garoth the Old,* a book that had long been famous among the Craft societies.

Over three thousand years of treasures were not sealed in his crypt with him by his own order, but were passed down to Navaniz the Bold. The sightless eyes of death had looked at Navaniz as Laer'garoth had breathed his last- "take these possessions for your journey, my son, for the gods have willed it in the years to come."

The wyrms of Caedoria were shocked when four white dragons of the Poltyrians arrived and quietly stared down at the lifeless body of Laer'garoth as the engineers slid the megalithic crypt walls and door into place, creating a massive new building in Daethalon covered in sculptures and reliefs of the service and valor of dragons from Talan Dathar to Daethalon. They did not speak, but reverence and a sadness was seen on them all and they ascended into the sky without a sound and disappeared into the sky.

4606 After Cataclysm: [TAL 3, Year 718] the Poltyrians of Nectar Lakes discover the Drakepeak Mines and build a cliff face settlement that penetrates the mountain of the Drakeroost range deeply, all the way down to a series of veins rich in iron ore. This same town would later be called Rogues Eyrie.

4617 After Cataclysm: [TAL 3, Year 729] a large population from Dor'Ath City relocated and built Cedar Post citadel, a stop between Nectar Lakes and Dor'Ath on the coast. This would later develop into a booming town and city with a huge fortress called Harpshire Castle.

4625 After Cataclysm: [TAL 3, Year 737] The Deep Men send an exploratory expedition out that six days out from home discovered another large cavern, a swamp wherein lived stykk'iun trolls, ancient counsins of the nasty uluk'kin trolls.

They reported the find and the expeditionary force now called the Sons of the Sword invaded the swamp cavern and slew the trolls, securing the swamp for food and resources. Aside from many species of edible insects, reptiles and amphibians, the swamp yielded an abundance of darklotus, a very strong paralytic poison.

4632 After Cataclysm: [TAL 3, 744] in this year it was reported that many groups of athradoc were again occupying northern Arborealm and some were rumored to have visited faeries in Feyknot-on-the-Water and Enchandrus. Many among the fey of Everleaf loyal to Manax amassed in their own groups to hunt them for they felt that the athradoc had no entitlement to the Moonfurrow Garden produce in Enchandrus, or access to Everleaf Pines nor Arborealm. But none care if the athradoc lived in Treehelm or Splinterdark for normal faeries did not venture into those parts. Much violence occurred in this year between fey and athradoc, the latter retreating deeper into Arborealm and Treehelm.

4633 After Cataclysm: [TAL 3, Year 745] the Poltyrians built Barristan Keep, another stop between Nectar Lakes and Dor'Ath City. Later it would be called Castle Waycross and even much later the fortress would be known as Castle Redshield.

4657 After Cataclysm: [TAL 3, Year 769] the uluk'kin trolls gained a new tribal chief who led them to assault the Deep Men in Zaddiki city. The trolls knew that the Baradi-ai Expeditionary Force was abroad in waycaverns to the west. the trolls fell upon the fortifications but were met with the vicious and organized defenses of the Sons of the Shield who slew half of their numbers in the first hour. The trolls fled and the defenders were forbidden by Barad-ai law to pursue, sworn defenders they were and they could not defend if they were gone while a second assault occurred. Far back in the shadows the Aelvatchi dark elf scouts watched the contest, studying Men.

4658 After Cataclysm: [TAL 3, Year 770] the Sons of the Sword of the Deep Men attacked the uluk-kin trolls of Murklbog caverns, slaughtered their defenders but did not make an end of the race for many trolls during the fighting grabbed their food and younglings and slipped away into the hundreds of vassal tunnels and caves escaping to places where the Deep Men would not follow.

4668 After Cataclysm: [TAL 3, Year 780] until this time the exiled faeries from Everleaf who followed Ish'layyar the black bear shapechanger, one of the former Pillars of Everleaf, lived quietly together in Greenvale forest, which in those days stretched from Barristan Keep (Castle Redshield) to the far north. For years they watched as Men multiplied filling the land.

Several villages appeared in southern Greenvale and the faeries took council among themselves on what to do. They were not athradoc and had agreed long ago that Men were not their enemies, but nor did that have any love for them, seeing mankind being the reason they were exiled.

It was known that Thornlok the faery dragon king resided in the old dwarven halls and ruins of Meadowlair in southern Drakeroost and that Fanglar Draketeeth with his timber wolves stayed in the mountains too. It was also discovered that many faeries had left Thornlok with Queen Nuala the termite-nymph and her subjects to haunt the ravines and shadows of Harrowood.

At this time Edek Rockrager and all his gnome scouts returned with reports on the lay of the land all around. Natalia the Vineweaver, a name infamously called in later times the

Shadeleaf Strangler, opted to make Grichmere her forest and with her went a cyclops moss giant named Beast and another powerful faery named Hawthorp, a dark dryadoc male who wielded a lethal wraithblade.

The Great Paw and his hounds took to the open plains that came to be called Houndsland and the very powerful nymph Vanica disappeared into the north in Applewood. Ish'layyar led all the others and made it to Lake Fellstar in Sunkenwood. To the exiled faeries who had passed beneath Wynnowyn-Under-the-Mountain, this separation was known to them as The Second Rift.

4669 After Cataclysm: [TAL 3, Year 781] the newest settlers of the Deep, the Barad-ai, had no knowledge of what a terraskan aberration was. The other races all knew that when such a gigantic, immortal beast neared their caverns or strongholds they were to set out piles of dead beasts or bodies so that the colossus would follow the scent and feast while being cleverly led away so that it would not trample one's civilization.

This was recorded as The Year of Sorrow. There was nothing the Sons of the Shield could do as the behemoth, impervious to weapons, trampled through Zaddiki city as if it was not there, collapsing structures, burying people alive or crushing them to death. A dragon tried over and over to assault it but was so injured that the Deep Men had to give it a merciful end.

Having successfully led the aberration to Zaddiki city over a period of weeks with chopped up pieces of cave buffulo, the dark elves of Sarthaldon city watched the destruction the terrascan monster made. An entire division of dark elves numbering in the many thousands, prepared to assault the Deep Men in their weakened state, stood for a long time, baffled. Every single leader and horn blower was dead, killed silently and many elves claimed to see shadows along the walls, mushroom people who could disappear and a very tall female who breathed death upon those she looked upon. In haste the dark elves retreated to their city.

4692 After Cataclysm: [TAL 3, Year 804] a man was thrown from his horse while hunting boar near the edge of Grichmere. His horse reappeared at Candlewick where he was from and a search party was sent out. They found him camped with a fire and plenty of fresh vegetables and fruits, and they were astonished. His right leg, broken, was wrapped in tight vines and long leaves but when they unwrapped it the bone had already mended. The lost hunter was sincere, claiming that dogs spoke to him, that a woman lived in the wood of a beauty stolen from goddesses, that *faeries* lived in this forest.

As the man was no commoner, but greatly respected, his tale was heeded and for many years a delegation of people from Candlewick brought a wagon full of gifts and food to the site. They would leave the wagon and return a week later to find that it had been emptied.

The people of Candlewick were a mystery to other humans, for they were a people who had migrated into the land long before the coming of the Poltyrians, before the arrival of the faeries.

4710 After Cataclysm: [TAL 3, Year 822] a large population of Poltyrians splinter off from Nectar Lakes and settle to the east establishing the kingdom of Southern Gates. These people would begin construction on the megalithic fortified wall-castles called The Shield, now known as the Old Warfront remains built to keep the Sylnadorians out.

4752 After Cataclysm: [TAL 3, Year 864] an exploration party of the Deep Men happened upon a waterfall in a low-ceiling wide cavern filled with a strange prickly plant with luminescent yellow and green blossoms. When reaching the falls they stilled, seeing large, bearded dark eyed figures that resembled men but were bigger, thicker...older.

"Come. Sit. No harm can come to the camp of Ha'akathrals."

For many hours did Baphomans of the Kindread teach the Barad-ai the ways of the Deep, of its races and secrets. The Deep Men listened and took note of the stories, accounts, of knowledge on Hollowrealm politics and edible plants. They were shown how to make a nourishing milk from the bublar blossoms of the cavern and a pain-deadening medicine from its petals.

Quietly listening and observing from the back of the athaki camp sat TAL-NIK silently regarding Men.

4767 After Cataclysm: [TAL 4, Year 15] in this year the Deep Men change their military policy. Until this time, not wanting to incur unnecessary enemies the Barad-ai maintained a position of only attacking those who threatened their own civilization. But at this time Barad-ai prospectors brought home the news of the existence of a docile species of reptile beasts that could be used for labor, pack animals and even food. Till then they had relied heavily on their herds of cave buffalo.

The reptaurs were owned by the race of draconiacs, fanged cousins of the more civilized draconians. The Deep Men invaded their conical shaped cavern which was perpetually full of warm steam fed by an underworld river. The draconiacs fled and the Barad-ai acquired the reptaurs.

4801 After Cataclysm [TAL 4, Year 49] prospectors of the Deep Men happened upon an immense, easily protected cavern with an entrance too small for a terranscan aberration, an amazing cavern that opened up to whole underworld ocean. The discovery of a sea in the underworld shocked the Barad-ai and plans were immediately put into action to occupy the cavern. The underworld sea would be a constant source of salt and nourishment. This was the origin of the Barad-ai city of Arud-Run on the Abysshicar Sea.

4822 After Cataclysm: [TAL 4, Year 70] the Poltyrians founded the kingdom of Cedar End, much of the domain being the Cyrus Forest at the time.

4824 After Cataclysm: [TAL 4, Year 72] in Caedoria a bowmaster of House Arrowloft for the first time became First Ranger. Called Javan Far-Eyes, it is said that he was summoned before Elderboughs in Everleaf where he was told many things in private council with the sylvan god.

In the underworld, after 23 years of labor, the cavern city of Ardu-Run was finished and the entire population of the Barad-ai migrate from Zaddiki.

4845 After Cataclysm: [TAL 4, Year 93] out of the river Eastering and into Sunkenwood invaded hundreds of water trolls that sought Lake Fellstar as a new home. The quara'kin trolls attacked the faery exiles of Everleaf in a series of battles after receiving reinforcement from Eastering river. After ten months Ish'layyar and the others drove the trolls out of the lake with great slaughter.

4848 After Cataclysm: [TAL 4. Year 96] the Poltyrians, ever expanding and multiplying, founded the kingdom of Westford, taking Cedar Post Citadel as their capitol and renaming it Harpshire Castle.

4885 After Cataclysm: [TAL 4, Year 133] the Poltyrians founded the kingdom of Westerness, taking Barristan Keep as their capitol, calling it Waycross Castle. The Kingdom of Westerness would later be known as the Barony of West Barrister.

4896 After Cataclysm: [TAL 4, Year 144] in the Year 72 *Arud-Run* the Deep Men completed the Academy of the Black Death. Over a thousand Barad-ai warriors in 20 groups set out into the underworld's caves and waycaverns in 54-man units to capture males and females of every Hollowrealm species they could find. Using the darklotus poison to capture their prey the Deep Men filled the Academy training dungeons where their captives would be well fed and exercised. This was the beginning of the lethal knights called Sons of the Black Death.

4905 After Cataclysm: [TAL 4, Year 153] during the storm season the city of Dor'Ath was flooded twice within weeks of the other, high winds felling towersand destroying ships in the harbor. By the end of this year the people began the construction of a mighty one hundred and ten foot high sea wall that was two hundred and fifty feet thick at the base that tapered at the top where was situated a fifty foot wide top, with inner galleries and chambers for storage and garrisons.

4909 After Cataclysm: [TAL 4, Year 159] the Poltyrians founded the kingdom of Haringdown, later to be called Harington barony. In this same year an expedition of hunters did not return from Grichmere forest. Two large parties of searchers went into the largely unknown wood and found no evidence of the lost hunters but reported that they felt watched and threatened the entire time they were among the trees.

4933 After Cataclysm: [TAL 4, Year 181] due to boasts made by Grimh pilgrims visiting the Oracle of Ashadula overheard by visiting titan ogres of the Taran Waste, the uni-horned ogres as a horde attacked the home caverns of the giant dwarves in the Horn-Helm War. The huge dwarves defended themselves mightily against the larger titan ogres and both hosts wore down the other in a mutual slaughter, though the ogres attacked with superior numbers.

The Taran ogres departed having taken nothing and the Grimh counted themselves as victors of the war, while the titan ogres realized that their adversaries were much tougher than anticipated. The other underworld race, the Aelvatchi dark elves and even Deep Men (Year 193 *Arud-Run*), understood by this war that the Grimh could not be defeated if attacked but had to be drawn out. Only while attacking could a successful counter-offensive be employed to defeat the Grimh. Many searched their earliest records for the beginning of this odd race of dwarves in the underworld who had grown huge, as tall as men and brawn as ogres. It was learned that these red-skinned dwarves had long ago wandered down through the funnelweb caves from called themselves the Nimbok.

4962 After Cataclysm: [TAL 4, Year 210] Poltyrian explorers mapping out the Outlands far from Dor'Ath City happened upon a road beyond Grichmere forest, a wood shunned by all. A road well-beaten implied it was well-traveled but none knew any race of men that lived in this alien country. Camping on the road for several days these Poltyrians came upon two of the Hollow Men, an ancient elemental people. The Poltyrians asked of them questions but the strange, robed figures only paused, then continued without answering which prompted one of the humans to grab a robe. At its touch the man fell to the ground, wet earth oozing from his eye sockets, ears and mouth. Arrows had no effect on the Hollow Men and the other Poltyrians went back and reported the affair.

For thousands of years the Hollow Men, hundreds of them, walked the road which disappeared into the far northern mountains. They mystified the Poltyrians but were regarded as nonthreatening.

4968 After Cataclysm: [TAL 4, Year 216] overpopulation in the Ekkan Caves led to the departure of whole immense armies of dark-skinned warlike dwarves gathered in their tribes with their gigantic reptilian siege-beasts called warthigs. In this year the Ekkan dwarf armies conquered the uluk'kin trolls, the Minatrorcs, four different cavern civilizations of hornback orcs and three Ekkan armies converged on Sarthaldon City of the dark elves till a shadowy Abominid appeared before their clan leaders. The Minion convinced the Ekkan dwarves to turn around or incur the anger of the Steward of the Dark Tree, to go forth onto the surface world and make war against those who had enslaved whole races of dwarves...a race who came down to Hollowrealm and built a city. The Ekkan were bewildered having not known such an enemy until the Minion described the Deep Men, called Barad'ai and told them how to locate Arud-Run. The Ekkan then forgot about the dark elves.

4969 After Cataclysm: [TAL 4, Year 217] the three armies of the Ekkan who met the Abominid marched to Arud-Run, joined half way there by a fourth army. As they neared the city of the humans they were joined by a fifth Ekkan army that had just won a battle against the Grimh. The five armies found the city of Arud-Run (Year 145 *Arud-Run*) very well fortified with blackades, dangerously-trapped walls and open tunnels that many dwarves entered only to find themselves ushered into the dungeon holds below the Barad-ai Academy. Over a thousand Ekkan dwarves pressed into a false entry before a megalithic portal shut them inside. Human engineers pulled levers that quickly flooded the trapped dwarves with sea water drowning them as they stood in their armor.

But the greatest surprise was the disciplined ferocity and valor of the Sons of the Shield and Sons of the Black Death that worried down the numbers of the dwarves faster than any other enemy had done to them. Remembering the words of the Minion the Ekkan dwarves now feared that these humans would defeat and enslave them too so they retreated in haste back to their tribal caves and spent years constructing emplacements and castles, walls and ditches waiting for an invasion that never came.

On the surface world in Everleaf Pines a solid circle of frost suddenly appears on the turf in the dome before Elderboughs surprising many faeries who scatter out of the way. A frigid air wafts through those assembled as a tall, black-enshrouded figure appears in the frost ring standing in front of the Archaic Tree. There are faeries standing there who remember the shadowy visitor from over fifteen centuries before. But only few recalled the Dark Reliquar's visits in the distant past.

"The Enemy have driven us from the Deep," rasped the shadowy guardian's metallic voice. "We have returned and grow mighty among the Cloudborn." The faeries heard this, knowing that the Cloudborn kingdoms in the far north were of giants and monsters amidst ice mountains.

"YOU WERE MISSED," said the sylvan god quietly, but the power of his displeasure was felt by all.

"I sojourned beyond the Deep...in Goriok Maw under the world. The source of their rising power, I sought. But it has evaded me. The Enemy and the goddess ended my search. Drove us back to the surface."

"WHAT OF MY CHILDREN IN THE DARK?" The faeries present tried to imagine what it would be like to be a faery in the underworld but Elderboughs was not asking about the fey.

Images of Barad-ai valor flashed through the Reliquar's mindscape.

"Many have fled their shield-walls and mighty ones have bathed their blades...only the Grimh do not fear them."

"BUT NOW THEY ARE ALONE."

"No. They have allies...the feylorn teach them secrets. " Hisses and gasps escaped the mouths of some of the faeries listening at hearing of their shadowy cousins. Moonlost, Oathnayers, shadowfae...feylorn. The Throne-Bane ignored them all.

"They are led by the Mycomaiden...a host of Moonlost." But both the Dark Reliquar and Elderboughs knew that the Minions were now free to concentrate their efforts against the Deep Men.

"WILL YOU KEEP TO THE TIMES, GUARDIAN?"

"I will. To the year the guardianship is renewed." The faeries saw the pained expression on Elderboughs' face at hearing these words but understood not what they signified. The cold visitor disappeared.

5011 After Cataclysm: [TAL 4, Year 259] the Poltyrians built the fortified settlement of Guilding Hall, later to be called Gildington.

5023 After Cataclysm: [TAL 4, Year 271] Poltyrian prospectors discover a wealth of iron ore veins in eastern Drakeroost Mountains, calling the peak Cairntop, for these men also discovered a sepulcher of a giant that had stood twenty-one feet high in a cave at the summit. This is the origin of Cairnstone Prison Mines.

5028 After Cataclysm: [TAL 4, Year 276] in this year a blue dragon, a young bull, flew down into Sunkenwood and explored the rich forests around the beautiful paradise Lake Fellstar, deciding that the hidden forest world would be his new home. The dragon was asked to leave by the faery exiles of Everleaf but the wyrm, Murtosh the Azuris, ignored them.

After biting a stumpgnome in half and laughing as the dead gnome's severed legs twitched in a dance on the ground, Edek Rockrager attacked the dragon. Then did Golon Treespear, a halfelf ogre and these two were then joined by Hash'gakkan, a cypress giant. The three of them battled the young dragon until Dungar and his bullfrog barbarian army arrived with Ish'layyar the black bear shapechanger leader. Murtosh was driven off but little hurt as he took to the sky, knowing that he would never get any sleep in Sunkenwood while angry faeries were about. He flew off in search of another home.

5040 After Cataclysm: [TAL 4, Year 288] for forty-nine years the Caedorians had been holding their Autumn Twilight Festivals in Arborealm's Twilight Meadows. Here the people enjoys arts and crafts booths, puppet shows, poetry reading, choirs of young girls and boys, bardic tales, candle light vigils, kissing booths, arm wrestling, foot races, tournaments and games, horseback rides for children on knight's war horses, knife-throwing and archery, barrel fishing, the exchanging of gifts, omens by candle-flickers and shadow boards, a market, dancing and music.

But in this year the celebrating Caedorians were astonished and thrilled when about twenty and timid and shy faeries with round eyes looking at all the activities came out of the dark forest. Seeing them the people sent young children to go out and beckon them forth, and for four days the faeries laughed and played with humans, surprising the Caedorians with how rapidly they learned their speech.

In the following years, and every year after until the Autumn Twilight Festivals were ended in Caedoria, more and more faeries gathered to join the humans in their festivities, exchanging gifts, singing songs, dancing and learning games. As time passed the Caedorians changed the name of the Twiling Festival to that of The Fair because it was the only time of the year that men entertained faeries.

5052 After Cataclysm: [TAL 4, Year 300] in the Year 228 *Arud-Run* a Whisperstrider of the Deep Men and his dragon steed disappeared in the underworld. Reports filter to Arud-Run of off four-armed dark elf warriors, assassins that fight like demons prowling the darkest corners of the Deep. This was the first year that the Barad-ai had any contact with the Aelvatchi headhunters, the sons of the six maralich cultists of Sarthaldon.

At this time the Barad-ai army was divided formerly into the Sons of the Shield for defense, of the Sword for expeditions, of the Abyss for the sea and the Sons of the Black Death, a knight order. Each division was given its own commander and ranking officers. Though the army of the Deep Men had one general, the highest ranking leader under him was the Death Commander.

By this date the dungeons below the Barad-ai Academy were full of uluk'kin trolls, draconiacs, slaathi, deep gnomes, Ekkan dwarves, hornback orcs, harukku from the Abysshicar sea isles, cavartaurs (giant rock minataurs), minatrorcs, draconians, Grimh, a few titan ogres from the Taran Plains, some dark elves and even one large five-head hydra.

Already the Knights of the Black Death were known throughout the underworld as perfect killers.

Also in this year Murtosh the Azuris slew a hill giant woman bathing in a spring in Deep Ore Peaks and ate her. Craniax was informed and the ancient sky giant tried to leap upon the blue wyrm but the young bull took flight, having had its full, laughing from the sky. But his laughter turned to a shriek when the 900 pound war maul of the elemental sky giant came hurling at him high above the mountain face. The immense weapon flew by him and he watched how rapidly the King of the Giants raced across the mountain to retrieve the weapon.

Murtosh flew out of Deep Ore Peaks but Craniax never forgot him. In Shannidar Murtosh dove out of the sky to feast on a faery bruun, one of the bear shapechangers of the Ayr. Alaryel sent the hawkmen at the dragon who fled to the haunts of Dimwood.

5088 After Cataclysm: [TAL 4, Year 336] Poltyrian explorers are astonished to discover a large city of humans hidden in the lands to the east, called Candlewick, with a population of many thousands who spoke a strange accent but still understood their speech. The walled settlement was small and the Poltyrians realized so large a population meant that the city was underground. They learned that Candlewick had been built about thirteen centuries earlier.

Later in the year a train of Poltyrians approached but the gates were barred and guarded, no entry allowed and the Poltyrians were warned away.

5118 After Cataclysm: [TAL 4, Year 366] enjoying a restful trance, Ish'layyar in Sunkenwood, black bear changling, had a vision. He came to and traveled out of the wood, over Wilderealm to the coast where he found a strange race of elves struggling to push their beached ship off the shore. When he advanced he understood instantly what he saw.

In huge bear form he ambled forth as the elves got out of his way regarding him with suspicion. Ish'layyar had been in Everleaf when Elderboughs gave the wood elves the piece of himself, the goldenwood branch with which they were to build a ship. He knew these were of the race of Aelmari, the builders of The Golden Bough, a their flagship with keep constructed of Elderboughs' wood. The Silver Elves across the sea living in Aroth Beyond.

How the unfortunate elves had come to be beach on the shores of Dagothar was not known, but with a mighty heave the black bear shoved the vessel back into the water. In Aroth Beyond the story of the Black Bear of Dagothar became famous among the Aelmari the faeries among them, none knowing this was the former Pillar of Everleaf, Ish'layyar.

5130 After Cataclysm: [TAL 4, Year 378] Tarq the Blind, the last Hammerworn king, died. On his deathbed he ordered the Emim dwarves to put the kingship of the people to a vote, to elect any king of any clan, knowing that he had no son and that the hero of the people was Kheol Brazenheart. Brazenheart was elected and after the sealing of Hammerworn's sarcophagus, Brazenheart laid the relic war hammer, Quakemaker, atop the lid before the crypt of King Tarq Hammerworn was sealed. A fabulous monument dedicated to his memory and the Hammerworn Dynasty from ancestral times was constructed over the crypt.

5136 After Cataclysm: [TAL 4, Year 384] the early warnings of scholars of the Society of Mancers were ignored concerning their predictions of the return of the Broken Moon, and for this reason the Caedorians were unprepared for both the return of the Broken Moon and the sudden invasion of Silapenti snake people from the jungles lead by asn Abominid. No Caedorian army went forth to challenge the invaders as in the past, but the Silapenti, a countless horde beyond numbering, in the dead of night flooded into Arborealm and were passing through the walls and gates of Daethalon by midmorning.

The dragons fought back but were driven off by the sorceries of the Minion. The Caedorians were shocked, many dying in their bedrooms, awakening to the chaos. No organized defense was made. Tens of thousands of Caedorians fled into the woods, many cut down by the serpentine creatures that had no yet reached the city.

While the people of Daethalon were butchered and scattered the sky darkened just before noon. For months the heavens had been obscured in thick clouds and no sun was seen, but now the whole sky blackened as an earthquake trembled the buildings of Caedoria. Portions of the city toward the coast sank and the sea seemed to rise up to the tops of structures. By the end of the day Daethalon was barren of the living, the dead filling its streets.

By nightfall many thousands of armed Caedorians amassed and began killing the Silapenti, people having come from the hundreds of towns and villages in Arborealm. The Minion vanished and the snake people scattered, were killed, some fleeing into Treehelm. Navaniz the Bold had been out at sea scouting when the attack came. The dragons returned and only a fifth of Daethalon was rebuilt and reoccupied.

The quaking and tidal surge also damaged Dor'Ath City and several Poltyrian settlements. In this year the Poltyrians laid the foundation to Poltus City in Northgrove forest, declaring the Kingdom of Poltyria.

In autumn a couple thousand faeries gathered quietly at the Twilight Meadows fair grounds in Arborealm with heavy hearts. The festival grounds were empty. No humans played, gathered or sang. None danced and no gifts were brought. Laughter among the leaves was not heard. The Fair had been the greatest anticipated event of every year to the faeries of Enchandrus and Everleaf Pines, even many Aelvani elves having begun to attend.

For ninety-five years the Fair had grown. As the woodland beings silently departed they each put down their gifts in the grass of the meadow until piles of prizes and gifts littered the area. All knew that the Minions had come. The last to leave the meadow was a teary-eyed sylph.

5144 After Cataclysm: [TAL 4, Year 392] the pirate ship Tombnaga is captured, an infamous vessel of the Raiders of the Spawnsea captained by a demon-possessed man called Teurgon the Bleeder, who cut open his victim's skin and then dragged them in the salty sea until sharks or others monsters ate the living victim. The last of the Caedorian Mancers of Societas Arcanum, all clerics of the Order of the Broken Moon who possessed the secrets of the buried Temple of Eternal Lore and the Oraclon Tablet, conducted an elaborate spell ritual. They roasted alive Teurgon and his pirates in ovens that were very slowly heated as the wizards cast their protective spells. Cooked alive for a long period of time through magics designed to allow them to stay conscious during the excruciating pain, a series of enchantments was woven onto the pirates souls. Teurgon expired and became the Tome Warden the locals would later refer to as the Dask. His pirates became the dangerous guardian ember shades. The mancers cast the same spells of the vessel Tombnaga. The burning pirates while still alive and suffering were promised that they're guardianship would only endure 22 centuries.

5149 After Cataclysm: [TAL 4, Year 397] the Poltyrians discover the Crystal Lake cavern in which they promptly built in a large underground town that faced the open lake.

5160 After Cataclysm: [TAL 4, Year 408] the Caedorians of Societas Arcanum gave the faithful black dragon of The Protectorate, Navaniz the Bold, the ancient Oraclon Tablet that had been given to Men by the elementals in the year 2160 AC by instruction of Elderboughs.

"Fly, honorable Navaniz, make your home far away. Guard well this treasure of the gods, O seed of Laer'garoth Hornbreaker. In that far off year that you pass on to The Other Side shall appear one who is worthy to lift your burden."

The venerable sage of Caedoria spoke of a descendant of The Craft at a far future time but Navaniz did not know this. In this year did Men abandon the ancient city of Daethalon, already half overtaken by the sea. The Caedorians spread out through Arborealm with many going to increase the population of Hinterport (Kings Bane) with their last two dragons. Hinterport was already a thriving metropolis of Caedorians, hinterfolk, mountain men people and people descended from the Pol'tr who had remained in the land after their exodus to the east through Harrowood.

Navaniz flew to Deep Ore Peaks, to Mount Talisman where the Oraclon Tablet had been taken from, descended to Ricanor Castle and for a while he took up residence with Craniax his old friend and lived in the ancient titan halls with him and some giants. Navaniz carried with him a large harness full of bags containing the archaic treasures Laer'garoth had given him and more bestowed upon him by the Societas of Mancers. With all these he would eventually make his way to Darkfrost and spread out his bed.

5181 After Cataclysm: [TAL 4, Year 429] the Alabaster Wyrm, Ishaak Burnbreath, descends into Sunkenwood and talks at length with Hash'gakkan, Edek Rockrager and Ish'layyar, sharing news of other faeries, exiles, fey and athradoc he had encountered in his wanderings. They deeply appreciate his visit and news and the knowledge of other world events transpiring across Dagothar. They provide the huge white dragon a feast. Dungar the bullfrog barbarian leader summoned thousands of lake trout to a shallow in Lake Fellstar where Burnbreath breathed lighting bolts into the water broiling the fish before scooping them up.

5184 After Cataclysm: [TAL 4, Year 432] several Barad-ai scouts vanished, then a whole prospector party. Third a Whisperstrider who strayed too far from his dragon went missing. The Council of Sages and Seers convened and divined that the source of the disappearances was coming from the ancient keep known as Nethyroth, believed to have been abandoned centuries before. The cavern had been avoided because other Hollowrealm travelers coming into contact with the Deep Men had warned them the area was still haunted.

Thus began the *War of the Dreamslayer* (Year 360 *Arud-Run*), when the Sons of the Sword and Black Death assembled and traveled to the cavern where they found the twisted, needle-like tower. It rose high on a single island amid a creature-filled dark lake. The Deep Men were met with a hideous army in the cavern of ghastly four-legged orcs that had a single great eye for a face over a narrow slit for a mouth with no teeth. Among the mutant orc host were other that had been mutated, all on four legs like beasts, lizard folk, minatrorcs, a dark elf and humans were seen among them.

The Barad-ai began their assault and began hacking into the monstersbut were caught by surprise by two things that induced them to retreat from the cavern. As they gave the beasts battle some of the Deep Men fell asleep looking into the great eyes of the mutants. When they collapsed in slumber mutants around them quit fighting and hastily snatched them up and dragged them away. Just as the Barad-ai realized some dark enchantment was at work the black air above them exploded with mutated winged goblins, one-eyed pteragaunts that also employed this sleep power at those who made direct eye contact with them.

Over a hundred and fifty Barad-ai were left behind in the retreat, victim of the beholderkin magics as the great eyes of the orgs overcame them. The Deep Men in turn captured a few of the beholderkin mutants but were dismayed when these magical aberrations melted away at being separated from the others.

Seers of the council learned that the Dreamslayer of Nethyroth was of an archaic race that almost died out during the Shadowed Ice, called illithids, or mindflayers. This one knew the secrets of necrology on how to create orgs, or beholderkin mutants.

Later in this year the Sages and Seers received word from a merchant caravan of gnomes that the Dreamslayer had subdued the cavartaurs, huge cave minataurs, and the draconiacs. It had also gathered thousands of slaathi and a tribe of humpback umber trolls. The gnomes, traders of wares and information sold the Barad-ai maps of caveways yet unknown to them, and secrets that other racers would not want them to know. When questioned as to why they would sell these things the gnomes declared that the Deep is our home, though we are homeless, wanderers. They said they were Ogoki gnomes and gave the Deep Men an amulet boasting the symbol of their race, that when other Ogaki pass by Arud-Run they will know there is business here. As a parting gift the Ogaki informed them that the slaver of Nethyroth was soon to direct his attentions toward Arud-Run.

5185 After Cataclysm: [TAL 4, Year 433] In the War of the Dreamslayer (Year 361 *Arud-Run*) the Barad-ai city of Arud-Run is attacked by a large host of mutated orgs of pteragaunts, or winged goblinoids, cavartaurs, orcs, humans, draconiacs, slaathi and huge umber trolls all crawling on four legs like beasts having a single magical eye. The battle was fierce but the defense planned, for the Sons of the Shield had been training how to fight opponents without looking at their faces.

The departure of the Sons of the Sword and Sons of the Black Death nine days earlier was a feint to draw the Dreamslayer into assaulting Arud-Run, a plan concocted by the Death Commander himself. Once the host of the slaver was away from Nethyroth the Barad-ai army infiltrated the cavern, crossed the lake, slew all the mutants left behind, broke into the twisted tower, many gagging and horrified at the things they saw and smelled within. They destroyed everything but found no trace of the Dreamslayer, who had escaped.

Also in this year, on the surface world, *The Raider War* began as House Rivensail reigned prominent among the Raiders of the Isles in the Spawnsea. They exacted tribute from the Edgehaven Raiders . A series of violent naval battles ensued that saw the ruination and sinking of over five hundred corsairs and ships, both sides losing over half of their navies. From this date onward the pirates of the Isles were called Rivensail while those of the west were called Edgehaven.

5189 After Cataclysm: [TAL 4, Year 437] in this year happened the *Theft of Opal Mines.* Two days walk from Grol'galdir in Deep Ore Peaks lies Mount Vlashi'nor, an old retreat of the elementals now abandoned but seasonally mined by the Galdirim dwarves. As miners worked ore veins elsewhere in the mountain range, an unknown race of dwarves, dark and brawny with thick beards, traveled up from the world below. They discovered the mines from underneath and with pick and hammer they mined so much mineral wealth and semi=precious stones that as they labored they sent news back home for help transporting the lode. As kin in armed wagon trains took away the treasure the unknown dwarves found a few crystalmorph elemental artifacts of great value and uncovered a rich vein of pure silver. All of this was mined, loaded and transported back into the Deep.

Later in the year, back in season, the dwarves of Grol'galdir visited Mount Vlashi'nor only to discover that they had been robbed. The surface opals were all gone. They clearly saw the crude box-runic markings of a race who left signs on the walls marking worked areas. New cairns were found and exhumed and the Galdirim discovered a dark, unknown race of dwarf with very dark skin and large, malicious eyes. A race that tattooed their skin with light green luminescent ink. A tunnel leading downward was located and Mount Vlashi'nor was sealed shut, thence called Stolen Shaft Mountain.

5192 After Cataclysm: [TAL 4, Year 440] news sweeps across Hinterealm and Arborealm forests, village to village, that the Hinterfolk have been disappearing. Whole cottages found empty, belongings of those who lived there still intact. One entire hamlet full of homes was abandoned, but none who departed took their tools, weapons or animals.

Also in this year the faeries of northern Arborealm departed for Feyknot-on-the-Water, for Everleaf and some went to Enchandrus, all sensing a great evil spreading in Borderealm. Faeries arrived in Everleaf from the Yadel Lake area bringing the news that something vile now lurked in the ruins along the old lakefront structures left behind by the Pol'tr.

5195 After Cataclysm: [TAL 4, Year 443] news spread across Borderealm that Caerean hunters ran down a four-legged freak of nature, a *human*, with a single enormous eye that covered his whole face save for a slit for his mouth. The hounds and horses shunned the creature and with a single blink of its enormous eye the beast put a hunter's son to sleep.

5196 After Cataclysm: [TAL 4, Year 444] an entire Caerean village of over three hundred men, women and children was found totally empty, with all their possessions intact, by a postal courier in northeastern Arborealm. Over a thousand Caereans gathered with dogs and tracked the prints they found to Yadel Lake, to a ruined buildings' cellar where they found a chasm that led into a deep tunnel that the dogs refused to approach, even gnashing at their masters. Five men went down into the tunnel and did not return. A sixth attached to a rope was sent and after a while the rope tightened, eight men struggling to hold on until it snapped. Frightened, the Caereans waited three days and when a Borderealm ranger arrived he instructed them to help his dragon bury the cellar in rock and fill the buildings' entrances with rubble. For four more days they gathered stone from the lakefront ruins and also buried the building.

5197 After Cataclysm: [TAL 4, Year 445] a ranger of Borderealm investigated the ruins of Yadel Lake and did not return. Four other rangers then flew over the ruins of the Pol'tr and saw thousands of small groups of strange creatures converging into an immense host. A ranger went to Emim'gard, another to the Court of Elderboughs, one flew to Arborealm to the Caereans and the fourth went to Hinterport.

Hearing of the happenings in Arborealm the oldest among the faeries in Everleaf told the ranger they were dealing with a *Dreamlock* from The World Before, a race that was once numerous until the Shadowed Ice. Long before the coming of the branchborn the Dreamlocks had lost out in a series of wars with the Minions.

Manax, Hakkix and Dijix led the warsloths and many other faeries besides and intercepted the host of orgs as they made their way toward inner Arborealm. The host of the Dreamlock began to retreat at the faery onslought but the Emim dwarves formed up a shield wall slaughtered all orgs that came too close to it as the warsloths and poliwogs cut them down. The orgs were of humans, orcs and goblins of Drakeroost, long-bearded mountain men and even a group of hill giant orgs. The Dreamlock was searched for but could not be found in the Yadel Lake ruins.

5198 After Cataclysm: [TAL 4, Year 446] halflings and bantams in Treehelm began disappearing. The very few human villages at the edge of the forest were found empty. Treehelm, already a monster-ridden wood, becomes shunned by other faeries that sought refuge there and the small residents of this old forest began making the tall ribwood trees their home, the forest floor too dangerous to traverse. The cohabitation of wood halflings and barbarian bantams living in the ribwoods together gave rise to the race of clubbertots.

5199 After Cataclysm: [TAL 4, Year 447] Treehelm is now regarded as a haunt of evil, of unnatural monsters, faeries telling stories of horror in the Court of Elderboughs. But the wise among the fey are not fooled for they recognize the work of the Dreamlock. In this year Dhishra, the thorn maidens and athradoc who follow her, depart Treehelm, unable to battle with oppressive forces they perceived were encircling them. Dhishra leads the athradoc host into Splinterdark.

5201 After Cataclysm: {TAL 4, Year 449] eastern Splinterdark is invaded by a horde of four-legged mutants- halflings, bantams, tree trolls, toggl'ids (tree frog people) snake and lizard folk descendants of the Silapenti jungle hosts that attacked Caedoria, all having a single large eye covering most of their face. Along the outskirts of Splinterdark whole colonies of more toggl'ids are caught by surprise, put to sleep and dragged back into Treehelm along with a capture shaghoth.

Enraged at this bold encroachment into her domain the Shadowitch leaves her Keep for the first time in centuries leading a vast army of Silapenti, husks, shaghoths, lizard folk, formions and loyal athradoc faeries with timber giants and leaves Splinterdark to invade Treehelm. The horde of mutants is slaughtered freeing her toggl'id vassals and with Avengiclus she personally hunts down and captures the Dreamlock. She drags the mindflayer back to her Keep in Splinterdark and imprisons him in a special dungeon with a lab, forcing him to make her a whole new army of mutants.

News of the Shadowitch leaving Splinterdark to catch the Dreamlock renews the terror the faeries felt for the witch, none feeling safe in Enchandrus and Everleaf. It was well known that since the building of her Keep she had seldom left its walls.

5202 After Cataclysm: [TAL 4, Year 450] having made the Shadowitch a powerful host of orgs from the captives in her dungeon holds, the Dreamlock is decapitated by the witch using Avengiclus . Never did the Shadowitch realize that she had executed an ancient enemy of the Minions with a Minion blade. She boils the illithid's brains crushing it into a soup in his own foul blood and drinks it to acquire his power.

But the mindflayer was devious and a master of poisons that were woven into his own mind and when she drank the Shadowitch soon found that her legs no longer worked and she totally lost the memory of who she had been before becoming the witch. She developed a fear of the Minions, that she was a daughter of Elderboughs and once Queen of the Fey was forgotten. It is said that in slaying the Dreamlock the Shadowitch was killed.

From this year onward she became one with her throne, never to leave it again. As the Shadowitch struggled to combat what was happening to her, Dhishra snuck into the Keep and stole Avengiclus from the shrine that kept it. She escaped into the woods outside the Keep with her prize, exulting in her victory of obtaining the long-cherished relic when suddenly the sword vanished and the thorn maiden stood alone, holding nothing. Perplexed, Dhishra looked around and saw a single floating whisker still hovering toward the ground.

5207 After Cataclysm: [TAL 4, Year 455] The Ogoki high-gnomes, or High-Goks, were a scattered race of underworld traders, merchants, tinkerers, inventors, explorers, prospectors and engineers. For a few decades until this time the idea of an Ogaki city made its way through all the traveling bands as they came in contact and all were on the look out for a suitable cavern to build this city.

In this year a perfect cavern was located, fortified and a city planned out with fortresses carved into the rock around its three tunnel accesses. This was the founding of the famous underworld city of Jahargok.

5208 After Cataclysm: [TAL 4, Year 456] at instruction of Elderboughs the Aelvani elves construct the magical Ark of Isin, a container empowered by many spells of the Aelvani enchantresses. The faeries were not permitted to interfere and cast their own enchantments upon the Ark for it would be detected by the Shadowitch. The Ark was constructed to hold the artifact sword Avengiclus, to hide the Minion-cursed blade as the witch desperately searched for it through her own agents, allies, servants and husks. Rajosh Gone'whiskers had stolen the blade from the grasp of Dhishra the thorn maiden and delivered it to Manax, but the warsloth general took it to Ashrey and the shars.

5209 After Cataclysm: [TAL 4, Year 457] the Barad-ai military build Din'Arud (Year 385 *Arud-Run*), a fortress outpost in a small cavern that would protect the approach to Arud-Run from most of the other Hollowrealm civilizations, principally the Grimh. But this new place quickly became a settlement of its own, a city with civilians that boosted the garrison. Din'Arud means *The Second Arud.*

5238 After Cataclysm: [TAL 4, Year 486] the minatrorcs with their garbolg siege beasts attacked the Qaa, a nonagressive race of amphibianoids, a green-skinned people who hunted the ragrels and other rodents of the Deep. The Barad-ai receive a delegation in this the Year 414 *Arud-Run* of Qaa representatives and are in awe when these strangers ask for military assistance. The Qaa declare that they have heard of the bravery and fairness of the Deep Men and have never treated with any humans as enemies.

The Council of Sages and Seers convene immediately seeing great opportunity in forming their very first political alliance. The Sons of the Sword and Black Death are sent out with Whisperstriders and they run off the garbolgs and trorcs from the Qaa marsh cavern domain.

Almost instantly Qaa guides and hunters took up residence in Din'Arud and taught Men many of the secrets of Hollowrealm's many tunnels and marsh cavern systems. The Qaa were not offended that they were not permitted to live in Arud-Run city.

5244 After Cataclysm: [TAL 4, Year 492] two hundred soldiers from Guilding Hall entered Grichmere forest in search of a missing hunting party. Over eighty men, without their weapons and armor, ambled deliriously out of the wood in different directions. Some had lost their minds, others became mute. Those that recovered did so slowly and told stories of changing creeks, moving trees, shadowy stalkers, things that entered your mind and talking rocks. About a hundred and twenty soldiers never came back out of the forest. The survivors swore that the forest ate people and Grichmere was shunned for centuries. After this the exiled faeries from Everleaf living there maintained a careful vigil to ward away curious humans.

5326 After Cataclysm: [TAL 4, Year 574] the Kingdom of Opal Lakes is founded. Its first king, Vintner the Wise is the origin of the later very affluent Vintnerwise family.

5335 After Cataclysm: [TAL 4, Year 583] the Battle of the Shield Wall fought when Sylnadorian army attacked the Poltyrians garrisons along the wall. The Poltyrians noticed that it was the first time the Sylnadorians fought as organized hosts rather than collections of war bands. The Kingdom of Southern Gates is victorious against the Sylnadorian attackers.

5364 After Cataclysm: [TAL 4, Year 612] a race of mountain gnomes living at Snowtop made war against a wild tribe of people occupying ancient ruins called Bak-Yanus, a very large collection of buildings obviously in antiquity built to house very tall figures of about ten foot in height. The humans of Bak-Yanus yielded the ruins and moved south, seeking refuge in the upper reaches of Sunkenwood far above Lake Fellstar much higher than where the faeries dwelt. The exiles of Everleaf under Ish'layyar, their hero leader, watched them warily.

5376 After Cataclysm: [TAL 4, Year 624] a Whisperstrider and his dragon in Hollowrealm lowered to a wide cavern floor ending their flight, both having sensed something unusual. They suddenly found themselves *between worlds,* their own and another that was unknown to them. They were surprised when a stranger appeared, the Wanderer, also known of old as The Haarg, shambling forth between planes in her eons-long quest to cross-contaminate worlds with her sorcerous wares. They exchanged knowledge for gifts, and when done the hag told them-

"...when next we speaks...yous ssshall be free o' the Deep..."
She ambled off and took the rift between worlds with her leaving
them back in their own, neither understanding that the Realm
Walker spoke of the Deep Men in the far future and not of them
personally. This happened in Year 552 *Arud-Rud.*

5397 After Cataclysm: [TAL 4, Year 645] after several
attempts of the wild Men in the woods above Sunkenwood to
enter the steep valley to access Lake Fellstar, Ish'layyar led the
other faeries of his colony on a fear and terror campaign
harassing the humans every night, scaring them witless but
vanishing during the day. After a couple weeks of this the
humans departed but the faeries did not know where they had
gone.

5414 After Cataclysm: [TAL 4, Year 662] in the 207th year
from the founding of the city of Jahargok in Hollowrealm the
High Gnomes, or High-Goks, known to other races as the Ogoki,
sought to redirect what was perceived by their engineers to be a
spring, wanting to direct its flow into a series of sculpted
fountains. Unfortunately, the gnomes accidentally tunneled into
a wall that fractured like glass from the tremendous pressure of a
vast subterranean reservoir of sweetwater slightly angled and
higher than the level of the city. The cavernful of water emptied
into the city of the gnomes in the tragic *Deluge of Jahargok.*

Thousands drowned and hundreds vanished in the run-off waters
still clinging to floating debris and calling for help as they
disappeared forever in the canal works, drains and run-offs that
emptied into a spidery network of caves.

The buildings half submerged and the lower city washed away,
the surviving Ogaki salvaged what they needed, organized
themselves in to new groups, divided up families to equally
distribute women and children. A race of inventive tinkerers and

travelers, they reordered their whole society. Jahargok lost to them, they vowed to never again build a city. Three powerful groups emerged from this tragedy.

Ogaki Trade Lords would continue spreading across all of Hollowrealm as they did in the days before Jahargok networking all of the cavern economies through a series of outposts and embassies.

Templum Jahari and the *Stone Circle Gnomes* were considered as one group, priests and wizards. The Stone Circle gnomes were themselves further divided up into magecraft guilds of House Emerald, Sapphire Hall, Ruby Throne and those of the feared Iron Pillar. Templum Jahari and the Stone Circle gnomes wandered the underworld in enormous great wagons with rooms and balconies, amazing vehicles of differential geared wheels that rolled effortlessly using levers activating heavy lead weights hanging from pendulums. Both Jahari and Stone Circle were popular emissaries used by races of the Deep to communicate with other races.

Henchgnomes were the most famous group of the Ogoki, a military mercenary order widely respected. There were fifty-five bands of henchgnomes, each having three hundred soldiers each, with their wives, children and slaves in armored wagon trains. Many henchgnome outfits traveled with the Stone Circle and Templum Jahari gnomes as escorts and protectors.

After the Deluge of Jahargok the underworld races began seeing members of these three groups traveling everywhere throughout the underworld. Deluge dated to Year 590 *Arud-Run*. A very widespread colloquial in Hollowrealm after this event was- "...as wet as Jahargok!"

5433 After Cataclysm: [TAL 4, Year 681] a race of half-giants called fur'druuns were known as the Skull Drinkers because of their making of bone cups out of the skulls of their slain enemies. In this year the fur'druuns with their uluk'kin troll vassals attacked Arud-Run. The Sons of the Shield gave them no quarter and aid arrived from Din-Arud chasing off the vile attackers that were still alive. Dated Year 609 *Arud-Run.*

5448 After Cataclysm: [TAL 4, Year 692] Ish'layyar and a few of the faeries of Sunkenwood traveled to Snowtop to visit their gnome neighbors, but upon arriving their were warned off and then attacked. The faeries stayed away but had a look around the ruins of Bak-Yanus before returning to Lake Fellstar.

5461 After Cataclysm: [TAL 4, Year 709] a large host of Sylnadorians advanced upon Nectar Lakes to attack the Poltyrian city but as they passed through Dathom Peaks valley an even mightier horde of cobble goblins, orcs, minataurs, ogres and cave giants of the Bone Kingdoms descended upon them. The Sylnadorians, defeated, having lost a significant portion of their numbers, fled back south.

5466 After Cataclysm: [TAL 4, Year 714] the Aelvatchi maraliches, six female dark elves each having six arms, powerful sorceresses, give birth to the first four-armed headhunters, the assassins and dark elf killers of the Deep. Every eleventh birth of the maraliches is a two-armed black elf with scaly skin...the warlocks of Sarthaldon. The birth warren is a hatchery, for the maraliches grow long abdomens and give birth to one or two egg sacks every three or four days.

Unrelated to the Mrul designer-elf warrior birthing scheme, in this year the Aelvatchi dark elves extend their domain over the minatrorcs who surrender in two battles.

5467 After Cataclysm: [TAL 4, Year 715] the henchgnomes, a widespread military order in the Deep, establish a single citadel called Ogokiar, near the caveways that led toward the Ekkan domain. During construction they are suddenly attacked by Ekkan troops. This was surprising as the Ekkan had not ventured from their regions in a very long time. Equally astonishing was the instant intervention of a tall, mushroom-hooded female of great power and a host of shadows that followed her. They opposed the black dwarves and discomfitted them. The dwarves flee in terror of the feral Moonlost host of feylorn and the gnomes are awed that they had been saved by the one known for millennia in the underworld as the Death-Bringer.

Both dwarves and dark faeries are gone in a flash and the gnomes spread word far and wide about this unusual intervention. The Templum Jahari decree her to be a goddess ancient and dangerous. From this year onward the henchgnomes adopted a mushroom sigil as their emblem on their shields and armor.

5499 After Cataclysm: [TAL 4, Year 747] the ancient and powerful dryad exile of Everleaf named Vanica takes up residence in disguise among the Poltans. This year begins her empire building among the human civilization. Later she would develop a vast network of trade and habitations beneath Old Poltyria City in its lower galleries, vaults, catacombs, abandonments and tunnels. A small community of elven outcasts adapted to the dark sewers attach themselves to her, the gutter elves. In this way she becomes Lady Underground.

5518 After Cataclysm: [TAL 4, Year 766] the Bone Kingdoms of orcs, goblins, minataurs and ogres with scattered hill and stone giants leave the mountains and invade the Kingdom of Southern Gates, taking many away captive into Dathom Peaks before the people can mount a defense.

5520 After Cataclysm: [TAL 4, Year 768] using darklotus cultured to extreme potency, the Deep Men successfully capture a few live Aelvatchi headhunters, this being Year 696 *Arud-Run*. These special captives are placed in their training dungeons at the Academy so that the Sons of the Black Death can learn how to fight the four-armed dark elf assassins. Two headhunters are put on display in chains and tens of thousands of people come and see what they look like.

5581 After Cataclysm: [TAL 4, Year 829] Poltyrian scouts from the kingdoms of Southern Gates and Cedar End report that large hosts of Sylnadorians have scoured Dathom Peaks rooting out the Bone Kingdoms from their caves and tunnels. The mountains are littered with the dead, both red-skinned Sylnadorians and orcs, goblins, minataurs and ogres.

5601 After Cataclysm: [TAL 4, Year 849] a band of quara'kin water trolls from the Eastering river above Lake Fellstar infiltrated Sunkenwood undetected and killed a beautiful water nymph named Lilina, eating her. The blood in the water of the lake alerted the faeries and Ish'layyar was shown the remains of the beauty. The black bear shapechanger in rage climbed out of Sunkenwood with others who came with him following the scent of the water trolls till they found their grotto beneath a large hill in the Brinklands half-filled with river water. Ish'layyar and the mighty exiles among Sunkenwood fell upon the quara'kin trolls and slew all they could find- males, females and young.

5604 After Cataclysm: [TAL 4, Year 852] a maralich aberration gives birth to a female among the egg-sacks of headhunters and warlocks. This female is the first Blood Duchess of the

Aelvatchi dark elf race. More will be born and unlike their maternal counterparts, this type of maralich also gives birth to more headhunters and warlocks.

Also in this year, dated Year 780 *Arud-Run,* the headhunter assassins and warlock offspring of the maraliches of Sarthaldon attack Arud-Run of the Deep Men. In two days the dark elves were defeated and driven back. But in the contest a powerful Aelvatchi warlock rumored to have been a disciple of the Mrul killed two Knights of the Black Death, a Barad-ai warmage and then in one-on-one combat the warlock slew the Death Commander, Radis, to the disbelief of those watching. Ragis escaped with his inner circle back to Sarthaldon.

5616 After Cataclysm: [TAL 4, Year 864] In this year the Grimh send an army against Din-Arud of the Deep Men, dated Year 792 *Arud-Run.* As the fortified settlement was occupied by the Sons of the Sword and some of the Black Death, neither specially trained in defense, they took more losses than usual. Further, the Grimh were unmatched in siege tactics. Black Death reinforcements with Whisperstriders came and the Grimh departed, satisfied with the bloodletting and knowledge that they could take the Barad-ai when they wanted to.

Din-Arud was refortified, built stronger and from this day on it was garrisoned with the Sons of the Shield for a better defense.

An old, mysterious castle constructed of cyclopean rocks like giant puzzle pieces on the slope of Mount Icedorn north of Poltyria is home to a few hundred Kindread trappers, hunters and prospectors. Castle Kagg'nthrok was of old a giant's retreat back during The Madness of Craniax. Under cover of a heavy snow the Cloudborn horde attacked killing the Kindread mountainfolk inside, but at terrific cost for the Kindread were athaki, of the blood of Ha'akathrals and a very aged race.

The Cloudborn host of monsters and enemies out of the north at rest after the battle, drunk off their victory, camp along the slope of the mountain and inside the keep. In the dark of the night the heroes TAL-NIK, Waldomar Cragly and Athadur the Ruthless lead the full might of the Kindread on their beardhorns in the *Siege of the Hecklers*. The Cloudborn leaders are shocked to see the gigantic ram steeds, dark forms of Kindread, Dreadreavers, Baphomans, Hecklers, their followers called the Stoneskins, the five clans of the Kindread with their spearwives, mastogriff war dogs and the terrible Night Matrons.

Inside the castle an infernal howl pierced the night air and the Cloudborn realized that the giant ghost hound called the Hill Haunt had been summoned, a legendary help to TAL-NIK of the Two Horns. The Cloudborn begin to scatter as the Dreadreaver Mirthblade stormed the gates.

By night's end all the treasures were laid before the tent of Ayssula, the Night Matron, before equally distributed to the people. A pyramid of skulls and spears is erected as a monumental warning to the Cloudborn.

5628 After Cataclysm: [TAL 5, Year 12] the Poltyrians of Dor'Ath City lose four ships off the coast to a huge krakenlike beast. Reports told that the monster was singing and laughing as it broke apart the ships. But the kraken was never again seen in the Athean Sea along the Poltyrian coasts.

5679 After Cataclysm: [TAL 5, Year 63] the Sylnadorians attack Nectar Lakes again passing through an emptied Dathom Peaks, or one wherein the Bone Kingdom survivors do not attack Sylnadorians again for fear of retribution. This is the Fourth Dathom War and it would last nine years with the Sylnadorians being driven back despite the fact that they were far better organized than ever before.

5682 After Cataclysm: [TAL 5, Year 66] the Emim dwarves spent considerable resources and time refurbishing the tombs of their kings and crypt complexes, paying particular attention to the crypt of Tarq the Blind, last of the ancient Hammerworn Kings. It was considered hallowed as inside rested the relic war hammer, *Quakemaker*.

5688 After Cataclysm: [TAL 5, Year 72] in the 9th year of the Fourth Dathom War the Poltyrians defeated the Sylnadorians with the combined armies of all the Poltyrians kingdoms. At this time the largest Poltyrian kingdom was that of Poltus but Poltus City was ruined in the north in the final hours of the battle as the Broken Moon darkened the sky and caused earthquakes across Dagothar, even shaking the trees of Everleaf. Some live in the ruins trying to rebuild but the majority relocate and build Poltyria City.

Later in the year spies bring word that civil and political unrest in Sylnadoria to the south due to their loss of so many men not returning home from the Fourth Dathom War had cities fighting one another, kingdoms fragmenting into dictatorships, royal families were gathered and paraded to public executions, treasuries plundered and old tribal wounds were reopened resulting in bloodshed.

Toward the end of the year a great fleet of navy warships escorting trawlers, shrimp boats, log barges, longships, skiffs and even corsairs arrived in the Athean Sea packed with Sylnadorians. They landed on the coast south of Candlewick in a region no Poltyrians had yet tried to claim. The political losers who escaped are of the family called Ba'Dashan and they pay a large tribute of rare Sylnadorian treasures for the rights to settle the land, swearing fealty to the Kingdom of Southern Gates. The Ba'Dashan began building their first exilic city, Dar Gathis.

In the Deep the Barad-ai humans of the underworld involved themselves in an intrigue. The prophets of the Council of Sages and Seers learned that the draconians were moving a magical artifact that would be of great utility to the Deep Men. The Sons of the Black Death and a Whisperstrider were sent to retrieve it. They located the traveling draconians and were surprised that their escort was a large contingent of Ashadulim, an elite order of draconian knight-clerics of the Xakkiun Temple. One hundred draconian spearmen and eight warsorcers. The Barad-ai Council was at odds with itself, many dissenting, claiming that this act was criminal and may come with consequences.

The draconians were defeated, only a few fighting to the death even after realizing that the Barad-ai were not trying to kill them. They surrendered the relics to the dragon-riding Whisperstrider and in this way did the Deep Men obtain the Holy Plates of Arud, a fantastic set of clear crystal tablets that when held over unknown scripts the viewer could translate them easily. For many years the Sages and Seers had collected a vast archive of scripts, signs, graffiti, warnings, writings found all over the cave and cavern walls of the Hollowrealm. The Holy Plates of Arud from that year onward increased the Barad-ai's knowledge of the underworld and its races a hundredfold, this prize secured in Year 864 *Arud-Run.*

5689 After Cataclysm: [TAL 5, Year 73] true to their fears the theft of the Xakkiun Tablets began the Xakkiun War, and the Council of Sages and Seers convened when a prophet among them announced the impending draconian attack which was confirmed by another's divination. As an army of draconians, draconiacs, minatrorcs, hobgoblins, ogres of Wyrmrealm, hornback orcs and the mercenary giants of the Caverns of Dusk approached Arud-Run, the Barad-ai Sons of the Sword, those of the Black Death and the Whisperstriders with their dragons traveled secretly around them via vassal caves along the Hollowrealm highway cave system. The Deep Men found the

Xakkiun Temple complex weakly defended. The outer fortress fell quickly, then the Temple Precinct citadel was taken followed by the Temple itself, which housed the underworld-famous Oracle of Ashadula.

Back at Arud-Run the attacking draconian army were flustered at the mighty defense of the Sons of the Shield and the increasing losses they were taking by the ingenious false-entry traps and flooding chambers. Suddenly the draconian clerics realized that they had been deceived and that the source of their power, the Oracle, was in the hands of the Barad-ai.

Before the gates of Arud-Run they sued for peace. They returned to the Xakkiun complex to find their temple and Oracle undamaged and unplundered. The draconians gave fifty Hornback orcs, fifty minatrorcs, fifty hobgoblins, ten ogres of Wyrmrealm and three dusk giants to the Barad-ai in chains to take back to the training of dungeons of the Academy.

Return of the Forgotten Years

The Broken Moon caused widespread devastation across Dagothar, disrupted trade, collapsed infrastructures, interrupted learning and on the surface world literacy plummeted to only a few scribes in scattered areas and the counting of years ceased. Those able to derive meaning from the scribblings in old books were regarded in awe, as wizards. But in the Deep the darkness of this new Dark Age did not spread as widely, most of the records were kept well and the chronologies continued. The following are those events dated and undated, above and below.

> There are hundreds of major caves, thoroughfares in the underworld from which thousands of cave systems branch out from the caverns, lesser tunnels that spider out in all directions. For millennia Ogoki gnome prospectors have explored many of

them and many disappear, never to be seen again. About this time a scout party with some prospectors discovered a huge metallic cylinder with a frontal cone of diamond-like hard teeth. They made camp and the tinkering gnomes studied it for days, finding a damaged door and prying it open. Inside were chairs, odd tools and supplies, all covered in inches of dust. Unusual glowing crystals suspended in a liquid were found in tubes beneath a panel. The Ogoki knew it was a machine that belonged to ancient gods who made the underworld, for it was clearly designed to burrow tunnels. An artifact from before the Age of Shadowed Ice. Containers full of heavy but clear plates glinting with almost invisible golden threads inside were taken.

> a stillness seized the outer court of the Keep of the Shadowitch and the dark queen brooded in her throneroom. Since the execution of the Dreamlock she had been stuck on her throne. In the blackest part of night she sat up, a change had come over her castle...panic spread through the corridors. Through the eyes of her husks she saw nothing but moths. A swarm of brown-mottle moths flooded the anteroom and wrapped tightly around a scorpinid guarding the chamber portal. Spiraling furiously, the moths broke away and lifeless exoskeletal parts collapsed to the floor. The portal opened despite the warding enchantments of the witch and the cloud of moths entered as the Shadowitch hissed defiantly.

But the witch stilled and leaned back in her throne chair when the moths tightened into a tall, dark form with a mushroom hood head, a lithe feminine form. Infernal words of vile power died on her lips when Sharrasa's abyssal eyes met hers. The murderous shadowfae, older than the witch, the Death-Bringer phantom of Hollowrealm, turned her back on the Shadowitch and studied the inscriptions of the witch scrawled all over the domed chamber ceiling and walls...her prophecies. She carefully read them all and then quietly dispersed as a cloud of moths back out of the chamber.

> In the 11th year of a bloody underworld campaign subduing many races, a Taran Warlord's host is stopped by an army of Grimh that defended their colony at Icefalls in the Dreka Domain, dated Year 929 *Arud-Run*. In the *Siege of Dreka Icefalls* the giant dwarves captured alive the titan ogre Warlord and in front of his beaten commanders they lowered him alive and screaming into a gigantic clay cylinder of boiling glass. Once the clay pillar-shaped pot was cool they broke it apart to reveal the broiled remains of the Warlord. Word traveled far and wide of the dead Warlord frozen in time in a pillar of glass so the Grimh put the pillar on display to all who passed by the Dreka Citadel.

> Astonishing news races throughout the caveways of the underworld. Emissaries and heralds visit all the courts, kingdoms and chieftains of the Deep of small armies of draconians, warsorcers, bloodmancers, and each one led by the dreaded Adrak'nul high priests of the Xakkiun Temple. They spread the decree that the Oracle of Ashadula has extended the Xakkiun Wardship to the seed of Jahargok- all Ogoki gnomes. From that point forward all Ogaki Trade Lords would also receive draconian honor guards when traveling near or through hostile territories, dated 931 *Arud-Run*. The Wardship of Ashadula was known far and wide and meant there would be dire consequences if any should bring harm to her draconian servants while away from their temple. Rumor followed this news that the gnomes had found something of great antiquity, an object of mystery highly valued by the Oracle.

> the Arcanacrafts and the Knightshades under the guidance of high scholar Leon Demar of Poltyria City settle on a prominence outside the city proper and build the impregnable fortress called Castle Demarsculd. In its vaults are protected the histories,

discoveries and annals of the Old Dathari, the Caidorians, their Pol'tr ancestors, the Society of Mancers, or Societas Arcanum and those other orders od The Craft. At Demarsculd about the time of its beginning began the elite Order of the Billows Mages, the forgers of enchanted weapons.

5761 After Cataclysm: [TAL 5, Year 145] A ring of frost appears in the Court of Elderboughs and the Dark Reliquar appears, remembered by many of the faeries from his prior visits. Before a shar can react he strikes her with his shadowy scepter and vanishes quickly. The faeries are stunned and the shar remains still for a moment before looking up at Elderboughs vacantly, limbs limp. She spoke unknown words and Elderboughs nodded. At length she spoke in a strange language none understood and then collapsed into a trance. She had no memory of the incident but the faeries did not forget. The calculation of this year was derived from the Time Keeper tapestry made by Vulena the thorn maiden.

In the Deep, this was Year 937 *Arud-Run* when the giant dwarves of the underworld called the Grimh fell upon Din-Arud of the Deep Men and took it, killing many though Barad-ai survivors made it back to Arud-Run. Din-Arud was left in ruins, the Deep Men no longer needing the outpost because Arud-Run itself had been made impregnable over the centuries. The Grimh did not venture an assault against the city of the humans.

> the Poltyrians of the Poltus Dynasty build Rearguard Keep and Castle Rubycrest in the Northgrove Forest and the Northron Gate Citadel in the highlands even further north. The kingdom of Poltyria expanded through Northgrove woods and then Applewood, into Opal Lakes when the Poltyrians annexed Crystal Lake Cave and sieged Vintner Castle, creating the baronies of Northgrove, Appletrot and Opal Lakes.

> In the Battle of Damnock Moor the city of Gilding Hall fell to Poltyria, becoming Gildington.

> the orcs, cobble goblins and ogres of the Bone Kingdoms of Drakeroost in the north of the range descend by night upon the Men of the Scorched Earth. Many are killed before the clans rallied together and slaughtered the Bone Kingdom invaders before most could escape back to their mountain holds.

5773 After Cataclysm: [TAL 5, Year 157] in the Year 949 *Arud-Run* the harukku of the Abysshicar Sea in the underworld came out of the waves and attacked the city of the Deep Men, a black tide of warriors led by octopid shamans among massive dragonturtle shell ships from the isles. The harukku quickly took the wharf of Arud-Run but not the walls before they came acquainted with the deadly Sons of the Abyss and Sons of the Shield as they were driven back into the dark water.

> the faery exiles of Everleaf under the hero Ish'layyar residing in Sunkenwood learned that the Wrak had discovered Men. Humans were being silently hunted and skinned as trophy kills by the lone predator skinflayers. The Wrak were a race that had departed the Deep shortly after the Shadowed Ice was over and surfaced in the continents across the sea called Aroth Beyond. Before this date no Wrak had ever been found in Dagothar. Humans had vanished from their farms and homes and Wrak had sent news back home of the human "trophies" before the faeries had caught news of their presence. Due to the cunning, careful, silent and vicious nature of the Wrak it took the faeries of Sunkenwood, Grichmere, Houndsland and Applewood 40 years to rid the land of the Wrak. When another two ships of Wrak

arrived on the shores of Dagothar the faeries led by Ish'layyar the bear slew them and sank their vessels that no more word would return to their kin in Aroth Beyond.

> the armies of the kingdoms of Cedar End, Westford of Harpshire Castle and Westerness of Waycross Castle with soldiers from Dor'Ath City met the Poltyrian forces in the Battle of Haringdown and were defeated, with Haringdown choosing willingly to be annexed as a barony. Poltyria did not advance on the kingdoms they defeated because of the army of Southern Gates with their Ba'Dashan allies marching to engage them.

In the Second Battle of Haringdown the armies of Cedar End, Dor'Ath City, Westford, Westerness, Southern Gates and the Ba'Dashan attacked the host of Poltyria gathered from Northgrove, Appletrot, Opal Lakes, Haringdown and Castle Demarsculd. Poltyria is victorious and Westerness is annexed as a barony called West Barrister along with Castle Waycross. Some annals refer to these Forgotten Years battles as the Poltan Civil War.

> the ruins of Bak-Yanus became populated by a criminal people, a community of bandits, outlaws, cutthroats, thieves, cattle rustlers and mercenaries. Bak-Yanus in the mountains was built of old by a very large people.

> a party of squabbling dark dwarves from the Ekkan caves began treasure hunting in the ruins of Jahargok. The Duergar broke open a sealed and double-warded preFlood tomb complex belonging to a once-famous Ogoki gnome guildmaster named Omak who during his life became wicked in his dealings with others, greed and avarice consuming him. The Ekkan dwarves

vanish in the ruins and a troop of traveling henchgnomes find their abandoned camp intact.

> An otherworldly traveler known widely as the Realm Walker who passed through the spaces *between* dimensions passed through the ruins of the city of Jahargok. The transdimensional overlap temporarily weakened magical wards set upon crypt doors and the sarcophagi of dangerous undead allowing many of them to break free of their bonds and escape their prison crypts. These undead attacked a nearby Barad-ai outpost and turned the Deep Men victims into undead, sentries and soldiers alike.

The Oracle of Ashadula peered deep through the planar rifting at the Haarg's passing and saw treasures of a bygone age, preFlood relics crammed into darkened tombs below Jahargok...artifacts of Omak the lich. Ashadula saw an archive of preCataclysm tablets hidden away written in the script of the Abominids.

Instantly Ashadula sent forth a small army of draconians, warsorcers, bloodmancers, mandrake hulks, Xakkiun honorguards, three companies of henchgnomes and four of the dreaded Adrak'nul shadow priests who entered the ruins of Jahargok and set upon the undead in the Battle of Jahargok Ruin. The henchgnomes and Stone Circle mages succeeded in raiding Omak's crypt at the same time that the draconian host was beaten back with heavy losses by the unexpected power of Omak, his ghouls, ghasts and ghosts, a wight and a terrible ember mummy cave tiger.

Draconians fighting against undead were touched and turned, moments later fighting against those they had come to the ruins with as the struggle between the dead and living increased. The Ogoki gnomes escaped with the library and treasures of Omak that Ashadula had sent them to retrieve and as the draconians on the other side of the ruins were about to be overwhelmed a shadow, tall and blacker than the undead suddenly appeared with amber-wise eyes holding a mighty scepter. It smote Omak and the lich screamed and fled to the safety of his crypt. Speaking an ancient Word of Power a blinding bluish light flashed sending the undead back into their prisons.

Back at the Xakkiun Temple complex the Adrak'nul war priests reported to the Oracle of Ashadula, claiming that they were alive only because of the intervention of a Dark Archon. When the Oracle attempted to read the script of the tablets a Minion appeared in the inner sanctum and informed her that the visitor at Jahargok ruins was a Dark Reliquar, an ancient enemy who had appeared and commanded the Wanderer to wander no more near the ruins of Jahargok. When the Abominid vanished Ashadula saw that the Minion-script tablets were gone.

> at the hidden cavern stronghold of Snowtop that is accessed by a single polygonal rock door of gigantic size that pivots to allow only two people in at a time lived an ancient race of flint gnomes. The gnomes attacked the bandits of Bak-Yanus who scattered at their approach.

> the following sprint after the gnomes attacked the bandit camps at Snowtop the bandits of Bak-Yanus, woodsmen of East'Har Eaves forest and the mountain men of the Uraku Peaks gathered and attacked Snowtop but the immense megalithic swinging door was impassable. Two men at a time could pass through the colossal portal but when they did, in pairs, none came back out. After two dozen men entered with no word from inside, perplexed, the attack was called off.

> two years after the aborted attack of Snowtop the bandits discovered mines full of working gnomes and they slaughtered them. A back tunnel access to the interior of Snowtop was found that led to a cavern community filled with gnomen residences, a factory in operation, a park and a large underground spring with

fish. Surprising the gnomes the bandits killed them and took their abode. Many gnomes were saved alive to continue labor in the mines and to be instructors to teach the bandits the factory operations. Female gnomes were kept alive, some kept for textiles, sewing, cooking and laundry and others for sexual services.

The male gnomes worked six days a weeks mining for copper and semi-precious stones and on the seventh day they were permitted to stay a day and night with their females and young. In this way the bandits kept the flint gnomes working. This arrangement was kept for fifteen years until the gnomes learned that several female flint gnomes were used for sexual purposes, causing the Flintstep Rebellion. The gnomes using only tools killed several bandits but underestimated the numbers of bandits who lived outside Snowtop. As reinforcement kept coming and coming the gnomes were all killed, many of their families and only a minority of females lived, kept for bed-warmers and sex slaves. This is why Snowtop boats of so many who are short of stature, very hairy and keen to be tinkerers and barterers.

5790 After Cataclysm [TAL 5, Year 174] Astonishing news races along all the caveways of the underworld. Barad-ai textiles, woven fabrics, and highly prized bolts of dyed cloth made by the women of the Deep Men began appearing for sale or trade wherever Ogaki Trade Lord could be found. Templum Jahari priests in designer Barad-ai robes, Stone Circle wizards and henchgnomes adorned in tunics, shirts and cloaks all sporting their holy green mushroom sigil. Word spreads that the High Gnomes of Hollowrealm have entered a trade alliance with the Deep Men, that gnomes had walked among the Whisperstriders and lived. Deep Men dated this trade alliance beginning Year 966 *Arud-Run*.

> the large settlement city of Hinterport in a short period of instability became the criminal city of Kings Bane. A few years after the rulers of the city were executed and the dictatorship began a Sylnadorian fleet arrived and attacked the harbor of the city. They arrived only hours before a fleet of dungeonships from Edgehaven arrived who had no idea the Sylnadorians were going to attack. About an hour after the dungeonships and Sylnadorian war vessels began fighting in the harbor of Kings Bane a fleet of Rivensail pirates arrived knowing the slavers of Edgehaven were coming but unaware that the Sylnadorians would be involved. The fleet of Kings Bane, the dungeonships and the corsairs joined together and defeated the Rivensail warships. Both Rivensail and Edgehaven captured several Sylnadorian vessels and their crews and made their way back home leaving a mystified Kings Bane untouched.

> in Borderealm from the edges of Treehelm, throughout Arborealm and Old Caedoria to Yadel Lake, the Caereans lived quietly in simple farming settlements and small villages trading with the mountain folk and the Scorched Earth clans as well as some Hinterfolk. These people are under the watch of the Rangers of Borderealm for a great many years.

> far in the west the hama'kin trolls of Mount Thokax raided local orc caverns and stole away with many females. During the Forgotten Years this union gave rise to race of the Darkfrost trollocks that occupied Mount Thokax, scions that after a few generations began turning against their fathers ending the race of the hama'kin.

> **5793 After Cataclysm:** [TAL 5, Year 177] three years after Barad-ai textiles appeared throughout Hollowrealm, the Ogaki Trade Lords visit the waymarkets, citadels, courts and trade fairs

with all new wares of pottery, unguents, balms, medicines, smoke-dried meats of fish, shark and monsters of the Abysshicar sea pleasant to the taste, polished sea dollars and starfish gilted in pure silver, bone needles and spools of thread and sinews, ingots and finger sheaths of bright silver. Colonies, cities, caverns, kingdoms and races brought forth their old, broken, rusty and scrap copper, bronze, iron and steel weapons, shiled banding and ruined armor in heaps and wagon loads. Laughing at the ridiculous trade of trash for treasures dictated by the Ogaki tradegnomes, thousands of tons of metals filled the emptied wagons of the gnomen traders. All across the underworld long trains of wagons closely watched by henchgnomes and Stone Circle wizards arrived one after the other to disappear into the gates of Arud-Run, in Year 969 *Arud-Run*.

Later stories were heard that old weapons were remade and reforged for use in the training dungeons of the Deep Men, that they had filled a cavern full of metals that would supply their needs for centuries. Rumors spread afar of a mighty one among the Barad-ai who was the commander of the Sons of the Black Death. The undeclared trade alliance between the Deep Men and the Ogaki angered many in Hollowrealm, but the Xakkiun Wardship protected the gnomes.

> The plains people of the Brinklands and Wilderealm steadily harassed by Poltyrians formed alliances with the woodsmen of East'Har Eaves forest, the Bandits of Snowtop and the Uraku mountain men. Candlewick remained neutral, angering Poltyria, in what has been remembered as the *Eastfolk War*. Candlewick further incurred the wrath of the Poltyrians when they gave refuge to several thousand plains folk caught in a pincher between the Poltyrian army and the Ba'Dashan. Candlewick has earlier pledged that it would always ally itself with Poltyria against Sylnador and its sovereignty was respected. In truth Candlewick had always seemed too small of a town to be of import in Poltyrian considerations.

But in the Eastfolk War the Poltyrians army was shocked to learn that the town of Candlewick fielded an army of 8000 soldiers who opposed the Ba'Dashan in their pursuit of the plains folk. Then 8000 more appeared and blocked the Poltyrians from pursuing the folk. Third, the Poltyrian scouts returned with word that a third Candlewick army of 8000 men was positioned around the plains folk camp. Other scouts declared that the walls and towers of Candlewick brimmed with armed men and the Poltyrians realized that the evidence of a vast hidden population of people living under the ground was all around them...miles and miles of fields of barley, hay, corn, wheat, creeks and gardens. Within four miles of Candlewick stood not a single tree. The Poltyrians retreated not wanting to provoke Candlewick into any anti-Poltyrian activities.

> several Ekkan black dwarves in Hollowrealm explored the half-flooded ruins of Jahargok, ancient city of the gnomes. They are attacked by crazed, undead rotting gnomes as a shadowy old skeletal gnome walked up behind a dwarf to touch his shoulder. The dark dwarf instantly began decaying while yet alive, putrefying. His screams prompted others further away to break and flee. Never again did the duergar visit Jahargok.

5796 After Cataclysm: [TAL 5, Year 180]. Mad King Garthol Cavelander died, date extrapolated centuries later by chronologists referring to ancient runic inscriptions claiming that the Mad King passed away in the year before the Galdirim were sieged by the Bone Kingdoms of Devilspire. This death then transpired a year before the Forgotten Years period was over.

Many of the Emim dwarves wanted a return of the Hammerworn kings of old while others wanted no kings at all. Moerthal Mortar'wrot, a descendant of the first Mortar'wrot king, made a suggestion at council that became Emim law. Let the seven clans of the Emim be ruled by a Hammerworn *Duke* as well as a

Steward of Emim'gard from another clan, the Steward never to be of Hammerworn blood. No more dwarven kings. Maul Hammerworn was appointed First Duke of Emim'gard, the grandfather of the famous Gelmarri Hammerworn.

End of The Forgotten Years on the Surface World

5797 After Cataclysm: [TAL 5, Year 181]. This year ended *The Forgotten Years* that began in 5789 AC, a year after the pass of the Broken Moon. The Forgotten Years mostly occurred on the surface world but in the Deep the counting of years was not lost among the Barad-ai. Now, on the surface, the Bone Kingdoms of Devilspire amassed a huge army that invaded Deep Ore Peaks, attacking Daggerhold of the Galdirim dwarves. Fjorni and some giants learned of the siege and informed Craniax. The army of giants stormed upon the goblins and orcs merrily and the dwarves spent weeks hacking through all those orc tunnels they found near Grol'galdir.

5814 After Cataclysm: [TAL 5, Year 181] surrounded by Poltyrian baronies that were once independent kingdoms all fallen to the Poltans and later Poltyrians, Dor'Ath city surrenders to Poltyrian annexation followed by the kingdoms of Westford, Cedar End and Southern Gates, all becoming baronies. The Ba'Dashan petitioned Poltyria for a barony and received it with pride though the royalty of Southern Gates opposed the move for the Ba'Dashan had been their vassals. The Ba'Dashan cities and land became the barony of Timbercoast, their cities being Dar Gathis, Dar Lomaran, Dar Valorix and Dar Echelon.

5833 After Cataclysm: [TAL 5, Year 217] an unusually hot summer was about over when a violent sand typhoon blew out of the Great Desert of Eternal Sands. This horrific sandstorm shredded animals, tents, crops and people with flying shards of petrified sea shells, sharks teeth, fossil bones, rocks, sand, pieces of glassolisk bodies and vitrified glass. Even pieces of copper dragons were found spread about after the storm. The *Year of the Shellstorm* saw much of the people of the Scorched Earth without livestock and tenting but few died because their homes were dugouts below the ground. After the storm passed a survey of the land found a fossilized coral ridge , a long-buried dry ocean bed with an intact but unusual wooden ship that had long ago turned to stone, full of mummies. In weeks the blowing desert sands reburied the region.

5881 After Cataclysm: [TAL 5, Year 265] a dragon of the Deep Men overheard a comment made by a young boy to his uncle, a man of the Sons of the Shield, that all important people, figures and heroes were always given a name in addition to their birth name. "Without a name you were a nobody..." The dragon conveyed this to the other wyrms and they took council among themselves and demanded of the Council of Sages and Seers on the Day of Petition that the Barad-ai should dignify them with a name worthy of their ancient service. This was the first time that the Arud-Run wyrms had ever made a petition and the wise among the Deep Men understood that this was important to the dragons. So the lead councilmen astonished the dragons by informing them in front of all that they would take the petition of the wyrms to the gods and then hold a name-day festival.

On the appointed day the bedazzled dragons given the places of honor at a large banquet attended by tens of thousands of people were fed a luxurious dinner. The lead councilman then announced that by decree of the gods below and above, the petition of the dragons having been received well, from this day onward would be called House Stonescales and be regarded as equal to the great houses of Arud-Run. The dragons were elated and instantly filled with pride over such a gods-given title. This was recorded as the *Demand of the Arud-Run Wyrms*, Year 1057 *Arud-Run*.

5895 After Cataclysm: [TAL 5, Year 279] By this time the passes around and through the ruins of Jahargok are shunned. Humans, orcs, trolls, Grimh, goblins, ogres, dark dwarves and henchgnomes had all come up missing. The Deep Men had set up a perimeter and patrols in the region around Jahargok.

In this year the draconian inhabitants, workers and visitors to the Xakkiun Temple, many waiting to consult the Oracle of Ashadula, were shocked to behold a lone Barad-ai wrapped in shadows appear before the inner gates of the heavily fortified Xakkiun Temple complex. Draconian honorguards, a bloodmancer, and several warsorcers blocked the strange human's path as about a hundred onlookers watched.

"There is no sanctuary for you!" one hissed.

"The Oracle *hates* the Deep Men..." another spat.

"We shall pour your blood in offerings!" But the pale, green-eyed human merely pulled back his hood with silver-steel gloves.

"Be silent," he said softly. "I am not alone." At these words the draconians watched in surprise as the mage-crafted disguises dissipated from the hundred or so figures in the inner court to reveal their true forms. The draconians instantly realized that the odd human was the Slayer...infamous throughout Hollowrealm, the source of whispers. He was the commander of the Sons of the Black Death. The draconians looked at Barad-ai knights, war wizards and four Whisperstriders standing where only henchgnomes , black dwarves, draconians and Aelvatchi dark elves had stood before. An Adrak'nul high priest approached and hesitated, sensing four invisibly concealed dragons.

"We are *thousands*, Slayer. Your wyrms too will die."

"Be silent, cleric. No death comes this day. But your goddess will know the will of Arud-Run. No more will she haunt our streets in shadow. No more will she watch us from the safety of her chamber. No more will we exercise patience with her meddling, with her stewards, her keepers or with you. When next Ashadula enters our city she will *never* leave." The Slayer tossed a pale yellow crystal sliver and the Adrak'nul priest caught it.

"Give it to her. It is but a fragment of the whole."

"What evil is this, human?"

"'Tis a shard from a box. Without bars or lid it yet hath great power to contain."

"She is a goddess. In wrath she shall incite all of Hollowrealm against you."

"She will do no such thing. Jahargok and all its environs is now under the protectorate of Arud-Run. Ogoki only are granted safe passage."

"I will tell her to call for war!" Suddenly a howl echoed from the temple and the priest stiffened. The voice of Ashadula was clear, loud, *panicked*.

"Let them go!" the screech of Ashadula from within the Oracle chamber alarmed the draconians. "Come get this thing away from me! REMOVE IT!"

The Death Commander smiled as the Adrak'nul priest and draconians retreated toward the Oracle. A fifth Whisperstrider had infiltrated the chamber and placed a similar shard of yellow crystal beside her pool. The Barad-ai had hidden an entire coffer full of these strange crystals found by the Ogoki prospectors many years earlier when they pilfered an ancient Old World tunnel making machine. Death Commander's visit to Xakkiun Temple dated Year 1071 *Arud-Run.*

5904 After Cataclysm: [TAL 5, Year 288] In the Year 1080 *Arud-Run* the Abysshicar Sea overextended its bounds and swept over the great sea wall of the city flooding the lower districts of the vast cavern. Though eight thousand souls perished the death toll was a tenth of the population at the time. Recorded as The Weeping Flood.

5933 After Cataclysm: [TAL 5, Year 1109] the Magrar of the Old Illyriac Plain invaded the forest of Enchandrus with their hundreds of thousands of gnolls and gnollock knights but the sariels flying high above the clouds alerted Everleaf of their advance. Manax led a large host of the fey and Aelvani elves that aided the Moonfurrow Guardians and faeries of Enchandrus, slaying the gnolls and many Magrar. Then did the warsloth hero ride astride the Verdant Drachon of Everleaf Pines, a faery dragon named Feyracht, and flew all the way to Callorock Keep amidst Gnosh City. In the keep Manax slew two Magrar and then a third, the Magrar chief Boag the Maglord. After this the Magrar vowed to uphold their vows to never again bother the kin and region of Manax and the faeries of Borderealm. From this incident Manax the warsloth general received the title Unconquerable. The king of the Moonfurrow Guardians was killed in the fighting and Elderboughs appointed a new king, the valiant Urrebor.

5961 After Cataclysm: [TAL 5, Year 345] The Dearth occurred over the Scorched Earth clans, a famine that started the year before but worsened in this year. The clans held council and elected to banish one clan to go forth and find another home because the land was unable to sustain so many. The lot fell on clan D'Vordred. The D'Vordred people traveled east into Drakeroost.

6003 After Cataclysm: [TAL 5, Year 387] the Barad-ai clerics found evidence of undead activity centered around the ruins of Jahargok, the abandoned city of the gnomes. Priests of the Deep Men led several parties of apprentices, Sons of the Sword and henchgnomes who escorted Templum Jahari priests and Stone Circle wizards to the ruined city complex. They were organized into search-and-destroy groups out to slay all undead they encountered in the ruins but instead they found themselves under assault.

Undead victims of prior undead swarmed them under the control of a lone ghastly figure of bones and spectral flesh that was long ago a gnome. This powerful undead slew soldiers and priests sending the Barad-ai and henchgnomes in full retreat. As humans and gnomes watched their own brothers and kindred fall to get back up as undead who turned on them something unusual happened.

Shadowy formed exploded out of the dark storming the ruins turning the undead into wisps that faded to dust and fog. An army of the Moonlost, rebellious faeries haunting the Deep. Humans and gnomes beheld spidery arachnids and arcan solitars, throngs of shrewnids, mytholids, two races of mushroom feylorn. A cunning, death-dealing witch named Luasi the Terroress led her hundreds of minoshees, ancient horned banshee elves. With this host fought Ecrops, commander of the Hurok Mauraders. He is called the hatchet-hoof and his auroch bull ayr shapechangers were infamous for their violence. These were led by the Triarchy of three nymphs who answered only to the Mycomaiden. These three Moonlost feylorn women were Malinga Gale, a zephyr nymph, Lillani Myst, a fogfiend nymph and Sedusha Shade, one of the dreaded darksilk nymphs. All three were surrounded by protective terranoids.

The fight quickly over, the feylorn gathered as a tall, slender darkness with oval eyes under a mushroom hood emerged from the edge of the ruins. Gasps escaped the throats of the henchgnomes as they all collapsed to their hands and knees, bowing reverently. The Deep Men beheld the Mycomaiden and immediately understood the mushroom emblems on the shields and cloaks of the Ogoki. Fragments of tales had long drifted to Arud-Run of the dark faeries of Hollowrealm, the Moonlost, the feylorn, wayfaeries and the Mycomaiden. She was even older than the fey called Children of Twilight from the Age of Shadowed Ice long before the Cataclysm.

Seeing her the Barad-ai too bowed, though remained standing, knowing they were in the presence of one of the mighty shadowfae. The Triarchy spoke to Men in gnomish-

"We hold Omak the lich in his crypt. Go and seal the tomb," Malinga Gale commanded.

"Bury it. Then conceal the place of burial. Build over the concealing stones," Lillani Myst continued.

"Build a new tomb...but make it appear old..." said Malinga as Sedusha Shade stared unblinkingly at the humans.

"In a different place set this false crypt," added Lillani.

"And engrave Omak's name on the false door." said Malinga.

"Cast your wards and seals over it to make the deception complete." finished Lillani. The Barad-ai high priest nodded.

"We shall perform this now, friends." The humans tightened together in a throng behind their lead cleric.

"It is good," both Malinga and Lillani uttered together. Sedusha Shade only nodded, barely, abyssal-dark eyes expressionless. Later, at Arud-Run, the account was added in the chronicles. The Council of Sages and Seers determined that the thing called Omak the lich must indeed be powerful while also noting that the Mycomaiden and her Moonlost army must never be made into an enemy.

6048 After Cataclysm: [TAL 5, Year 432] the Deep Men in the Battle of Harukku Isles invade the island settlements of the harukku in the Abysshicar sea in retaliation for increasing raids along the cavern coast of Arud-Run. Also in this year the Barad-ai received visitors, a strange but brawn and tall race of humanlike figures called athaki.

For three days TAL-NIK, Athadur, Waldomar-o-the-Pipes and many of the Kindread sojourning through the underworld made camp at the gates of Arud-Run and were given every luxury. Feast fires were kept burning during their stay and hundreds of Barad-ai men and women, Sages and Seers among them, fellowshipped with the Ha'akathrals and listened to their stories of the surface world, the Deep and the histories of Dagothar. Dated Year 1224 *Arud-Run*.

6102 After Cataclysm: [TAL 5, Year 486] the enchanted longsword blade *Ixichor* is forged in Poltyria by Achamur the Apocryphage, last of the Order of the Billows Mages, before he melted down the ancient magical spellforge. Ixichor's metal was from the iron collar-ring of the Dragonlord of Bak-Yanus, a hybrid wyrm descended from a blue dragon and a shardling that had made its lair in the ruins and was killed in single combat with a Ba'Dashan knight. The Apocryphage considered the blade cursed, had received a vision of a tall shadowy figure who commanded him to engrave *1242 Talan Dathar* on the metal of the handle hidden under the wood grip.

6114 After Cataclysm: [TAL 5, Year 498] House D'Vordred is officially recognized as a Poltyrian family of the Northgrove barony though it is recognized they are of unknown origin. By this date almost half of the men assigned to Northron Gate Citadel are D'Vordred, descendants of exiles of the Men of the Scorched Earth in Borderealm. Already they have been living among the Poltyrians for a century and a half and on the Arcanacraft Name Lists of Poltyria the family D'Vordred is numbered 615th.

6210 After Cataclysm: [TAL 5, Year 594] Gelmalbus Hammerworn becomes the Duke of Emim'gard, son of the first Duke, Maul Hammerworn, and father of the famous Gelmarri.

6228 After Cataclysm: [TAL 5, Year 612] the Sylnadorians attack The Shield, a wall of fortifications of Southern Gates barony as the Ba'Dashan fleets attack East Timbers Coast destroying Sylnadorian towns, vessels and shipping. This began the First Prydiad War.

6237 After Cataclysm: [TAL 5, Year 621] the Duke of Emim'gard, Gelmalbus, dreams of the ancient relic war hammer *Quakemaker*. Early Hammerworn kings, ghosts, order him to exhume the artifact and place it upon his own sarcophagus to be locked within his crypt in this year, though he be not yet dead.

6239 After Cataclysm: [TAL 5, Year 623] Vanica the nymph hidden among the Poltyrians in Northgrove and Applewood receives warnings from the Hollow Men sent from TAL-NIK and his Kindread watchers that huge armies in the far frozen north amass to invade Poltyria. Her gutter elf agents spread the news as rumors and quickly the Poltyrians send sky marshals astride dragons to scout the mountains and learn the truth.

Northron Gate Citadel is sieged and taken by the Cloudborn Kingdoms, Bone Kingdom relative called thus because the Uraku mountains and tundra they called home was so high up they were forever enshrouded in clouds. The invaders were Tholgan giants in polar bear skins, shaggy-haired hill giants, the fur-covered vril'kin trolls, gigantic wooly rhinos with frostlings, artic halfling barbarians who also populated Darkfrost in the far west, the shardling dragons that mimicked icy rocks and outcrops when still, and the five clans of the Tundrafolk, namely the Icelocks, the Stonebeards, , the Frostfoot, the Fire Eyes and the Shortgiants, these last being the descendants of ogres and captured human females. Though Northron Gate castle fell the Cloudborn did not venture far into Poltyrian territory for spring brought warmer weather.

Lady Underground stepped outside the protective ring of gutter elves and moss elementals. She walked among the carnage, the bodies of humans. A stench drew her attention and she came face to face with an old man in his last moments. His steaming entrails were stretched over a dozen feet of frozen earth as he leaned against a tree in his ruined village. His eyes fluttered unseeing as blood spilled over his chin.

"My son...he was going to make our name great...once again." His voice lost power as he spoke. He was almost as dead as the hundreds of people she saw slaughtered all over the area. Vanica glanced at the dying man's son. Bitten in half. A shardling. The Cloudborn of the north had raided the outskirts of Poltyria.

"I have no one...none left to carry my name.." The elder sobbed and the ancient nymph sorrowed over this tragedy. She leaned down and touched the dying man.

"What is your name?" Hearing her melodic voice he stiffened and his eyes rounded though his voice deepened, pride hardening his face.

"My Lady...we are D'Vordred..."

In the summer the Poltyrians attacked Northron Gate Citadel but were unable to remove the Cloudborn. In the winter the hordes of Cloudborn still in the Uraku range descended upon Northgrove forest slaughtering hamlets and villages, sacking every settlement they encountered. Four Poltyrian armies fought over 17 battles throughout the woods until spring of the following year when most of the Cloudborn retreated back into the cold of their peaks, again occupying Northon Gate.

6240 After Cataclysm: [TAL 5, Year 624] Vanica infiltrates Poltyrian society by assuming the name of House D'Vordred. She begins expanding her clandestine empire among the humans, her gutters elves disguised among the populace as agents, spies and messengers. D'Vordred Enterprises would become the most widespread and influential company in all of Poltyria.

In the winter, as predicted, the Cloudborn hordes returned into the lowlands invading a much emptier Northgrove Forest. Again four Poltyrian armies engaged them in the woods but this time the commons were prepared as well and the giants, trolls, frostlings on wooly rhinos and Tundrafolk were chased back to the highlands. When the Cloudborn retreated to Northron Gate Citadel they found their kin killed and two Poltyrian forces occupying their castle, which they had taken with the help of the Uraku mountain men, Bandits of Snowtop, woodsmen of East'Har Eaves forest and the archers of Candlewick. The entire horde of the Cloudborn were slaughtered, the shardlings able to fly being the only ones to escape.

As the last of the Tundrafolk were being killed on the field the Broken Moon showed through the cloud cover and a series of minor tremors shook the earth but no damage was reported throughout Dagothar.

In the Deep, a stone Circle gnome of House Emerald, a blightmancer, a band of henchgnomes and a large, geared great wagon of the Ogoki Trade Lords stopped a while to refill their water stores when suddenly they found themselves all standing in a foot of strange dust. A hideously ugly giantess dragging a sack walked beside a ferocious-looking monster with symbol-carved tusks. Trades were exchanged, of objects and knowledge. When she departed and they found themselves back in the cavern returned to normal, they traveled to Goriok Maw...the gate to the underworld below Hollowrealm.

6264 After Cataclysm: [TAL 5, Year 648] Quiet, very tall and slow walking figures the small folk call Hecklers begin making appearances all over Poltyrian trade ways, roads, fairs, markets and back wood trails. It is estimated that there are about a dozen of them but they are not hostile. They barter and trade, fix things, give profound advice on the building of structures, on farming and fishing. The largest and apparently their leader is fondly referred to as Creepy Nick because of his ability to walk without making a sound. Throughout Poltyria this horn-bearer is considered a god by the commons, who swear he is the Lord of Bees.

6273 After Cataclysm: [TAL 5, Year 657] on a single day in Poltyria City numerous small, gray-clad figures no bigger than ten-year old children appeared everywhere. Miraculous healings were reported, damaged structures were mysteriously repaired, wagons fixed, sewer drainages were suddenly unclogged and working and the poor found sacks of flour, cornmeal, beans and other foodstuffs placed on their hearths. Leaky roofs were fixed and amazingly, lost items were returned to their owners and young street urchins were gathered, fed, washed and clothed and taken to Grinnly House, a well-funded and spacious orphanage and school that opened that very day. Throughout the day many people swore they heard the voices of spirits telling them to thank Lady Underground for her hospitality, whispers promising protection and food to those who stayed loyal to her.

6289 After Cataclysm: [TAL 5, Year 673] A peculiar derelict ship with a most unusual design of unknown origin covered in an unrecognizable script was discovered adrift by Sylnadorian fisher folk near Claryc Isle. It was of a strange wood, brownish vines for rigging and ropes and a veiny, membrane like sail. Not a warship nor a merchant vessel. It was docked but after a month it was putrefying with a worsening stench and the Sylnadorians burned it off the coast. Many believed it had drifted from Aroth Beyond across the Spawnsea.

6366 After Cataclysm: [TAL 5, Year 750] the Ba'Dashan attack East Timbers Coast of the Sylnadorians while Southern Gates and Cedar End send armies again Mael-Monik Fortress but are unable to take the gigantic castle. Sylnadorians then attack and breach The Shield, sacking much of Southern Gates barony. This begins the Second Prydiad War.

6408 After Cataclysm: [TAL 5, Year 792] The dozen Hecklers and Creepy Nick vanished from the roads of Poltyria. The common folk are distraught. Rumors persist that they were all seen together for the first time ever in a meadow in Northgrove before they traveled by night into the northern mountains.

6409 After Cataclysm: [TAL 5, Year 793] the Hollow Men, of an ancient elemental race, appear at the edge of TAL-NIK's camp in the Uraku mountains. They beckon him to follow and the Hecklers astride their giant beardhorn rams let the elementals lead them to near the Cloudborn frontier. Castle Kagg'nthrok on

Icedorn Mountain, long abandoned since the Siege of the Hecklers, is now reoccupied with rebuilt walls, ramparts, fortifications, brimming with Tundrafolk of the southern Cloudborn Kingdoms.

The Hollow Men lead TAL-NIK to a slaughtered human village, to the body of a frozen, old human with an axe gash across his face, still in death clutching a leather wrap. TAL-NIK took the wrap and found within it an aged Caedorian tome of the Societas Ord Bellows Magi. Between two pages was a flat sheet of rainbow-hued metal the elementals assured him was not from Dagothar.

A few years later Creepy Nick would trade this book and metal sheet to Kevlin du'Janik Arcanacraft for a satchel of pipe tobacco at the gates of Castle Demarsculd.

6414 After Cataclysm: [TAL 5, Year 798] after several strategic raids by the Sylnadorians, a large host of Poltyrians from the armies of Southern Gates, Cedar End, Westford, the Ba'Dashan and Candlewick attack East Timbers Coast in the Third Prydiad War and take Mael-Monik Fortress, defeating and enslaving the Sylnadorian Kingdom north of Dathom Peaks. This was but one and the furthest north, of the Sylnadorian kingdoms.

Several shrimper, whaler and fisher craft in the Greater Athean sea encounter a large fleet of never-before-seen ships with curved keels and unrecognizable emblems on their sails of a coin and dagger. The vessels are brimming with large, bearded figures bearing weapons and armor but none of the ships trouble the Poltyrians caught offshore. The fleet vanishes into the foggy northern waters along the coast of the Uraku Peaks.

Months later rumors carried from the mountain men to the hill folk and commons of a new, fierce clan of warriors in the Uraku mountains called The Kindread make their way to the courts of

Poltyria. These foreigners are huge and are said to have come from across the sea. Great battles in the northern mountains and valleys are fought and timber jacks send word of finding huge piles of burned carcasses of cave ogre, orc and hobgoblin skeletons.

By years' end twelve gigantic beardhorns carrying Hecklers and leading cords of pack rams weighed down with beautiful pelts, furs, ivory and handcrafted merchandise returned to the roads and paths of Poltyria. For six years Creepy Nick had not been seen by the small folk and his return with his brethren increased his popularity with the people.

The Poltyrian royalty and Military Command begin investigating the Kindread but their scrutiny is without zeal. They have not acted threateningly and the Sylnadorian threat was too persistent to borrow trouble from another front.

6416 After Cataclysm: [TAL 5, Year 800] five Sylnadorian armies representing five kingdoms attack the Shield wall fortifications of Southern Gates barony and take it, invading Poltyrian lands, retaking all of East Timbers Coast and Mael-Monik Fortress, winning Old Prydiad back to Sylnador.

6480 After Cataclysm: [TAL 5, Year 864] the Rangers of Borderealm hold their first Conclave meeting in the archaic towers of the Tors of Hallows'gone in Feymark'ul, the ruins of the old Silthani elves high above the floodplain.

The thorn maiden Dhishra traveled to the ancient pond of Mabbu the Archaic, an aged faery turtle born long before the fey. When he surfaced from the muck she stepped back. *Death* lingered in the dark water.

"Why have you summoned me?" she hissed, defiant that he would have anything of import to tell her. The sightless turtle slowly closed his pale blue eyes. Half-lidded, he spoke. Dhishra's eyes widened at the power in his words.

"Your sister has seen through the Veil...etched the words of her prophecy across her walls. Her branch is cut off..."

"And my own? Hardly, I am lost, Mabbu. I care not that my sister cannot pass to The Other Side. Nor do I-"

"Dhishra queen of athradoc...not all the shars are dead...severed from the golden stock...she now becomes their head..." The thorn maiden trembled at the words of the prophecy, understanding that Mabbu was reciting only what her sister the Shadowitch had written.

"She is mad. Lost to her meaningless visions." The knowing look from the blind Mabbu penetrated Dhishra's soul. His words shook her entire being.

"THUS SAYETH I, THE GOLDENLIMB, TO MY DAUGHTER, DHISHRA, THROUGH THE FINAL WORDS OF MABBU THE ARCHAIC. I, ELDERBOUGHS YOUR FATHER, SHALL NOT CUT YOU OFF TILL THE DAY TAL'ISSA COMES." The very old faery turtle exhaled as his eyes dulled to dark and he sank like a stone into the murk. Dhishra collapsed with a sob and was sick for many days.

In this same year in the Deep the Council of Sages and Seers was in the middle of ratifying the Truce of Abrol'Dometh, a vast swamp cavern containing the Miru Marsh renowned for abundant resources of hunting an fishing. The Truce was between the Barad-ai, the Qaa and the Grimh, that no government would declare ownership of the cavern swamp and that further hostilities within the marsh would cease. The Grimh and Qaa had already wearied of the violence. No army could fight in the marsh and all agreed it could be shared.

During the proceedings a sudden drop in temperature to almost a freezing cold silenced the chamber hall. A shadowy, tall figure holding a peculiar staff like a scepter appeared on the speakers floor. For half an hour the Sages and Seers listened spellbound as the dark visitor with amber eyes told them the histories of the Mrul and his Minions, their wars before, during and after the Shadowed Ice, their origin in The World Before, of a *second* underworld *below* the Deep through the chasm of Goriok Maw.

Many days later one of the council scribes found an ancestral reference that matched the visitor's description and it was made known to the Sages and Seers that they had been visited by a Dark Archon...that could have murdered every living thing in Arud-Run if it had sought to.

6552 After Cataclysm: [TAL 6, Year 72] music and dance among the faeries of Everleaf inside the Dome of Elderboughs was interrupted suddenly when the Archaic Tree commanded all to be silent. Once the dome was quiet with alarmed faeries, a tall figure wrapped in a cloak of darkness having eyes sparkling like a carnelian fire appeared among the fey. Faeries scattered away from him, his cold oppressive and painful.

"The Hells have contrived a gate...soon their search for The Banished will resume."

"A CONSUL OF TARTARI. I HAVE SEEN THIS."

"I will come here no more. Before the time...the guardianship will end."

"DO YOU STILL POSSESS THE SCEPTER?"

"I do. With it I smote a Minion."

After he was gone many of the faeries remembered his prior visits but only Steffis the leprechaun was expecting him at this season. He was wise in the counting of years and knew the secret of this messenger's timing. When alone with Elderboughs many nights later, Steffis questioned the sylvan god about the stranger's identity but received only a vague riddle.

"SOMETIMES THE ADVERSARY OF AN ENEMY IS AN ALLY."

6678 After Cataclysm: [TAL 6, Year 198] a Wishmancer demon named Mao'Baosh of Acheron in the Hells created an ingenious portal linking planet A'DIN of humankind on the 153rd plane to the Hells by the agency of a cursed spell book. For this nefarious ingenuity Mao'Baosh was awarded with a Consulate position among the Tartari.

6729 After Cataclysm: [TAL 6, Year 249] in this year hooded gutter elves left a newborn child on the outer gate steps of the entry tower of Castle Demarsculd at the instruction of their mistress, Vanica D'Vordred. When the Knightshade guardians found the trunk with the child wrapped in a blanket they discovered the chest filled with ancient coins from the days of the Old Poltus Dynasty before their was a Poltyria city. A note composed in perfect Old Caedorian stunned the Knight-Scholars, for they knew that among men only those of The Craft in Castle Demarsculd still studied the ancient script. The message read-

Raise well this child. His name is Imaricus.

The immense treasure in the chest was a mystery but worth a small kingdom. The Arcanacrafts adopted him into their order and provided his education and training, ever wondering where he had come from and who had dropped them at their gate. Imaricus Arcanacraft would be the greatest Poltyrian battlemage ever. In his youth it was observed keenly that the boy exhibited unusual intuition and acuity and he was watched studiously.

6762 After Cataclysm: [TAL 6, Year 282] Gelmarri Hammerworn become Duke of Emim'gard. His father, Gelmalbus, passed his seat to his son in his old age.

6768 After Cataclysm: [TAL 6, Year 288] studying the enciphered texts of the ancient Billows Mages, the Arcanacraft smithlocks of Castle Demarsculd reforged the enchanted dragonslaying blade *Ixichor,* thinking to rid it of its increasingly unpredictable properties. The magical sword seemed to have a will of its own and produced wonderful powers with astonishing effects but at the most unforeseen times. The blade reforged, it continued to be unpredictable.

6778 After Cataclysm: [TAL 6, Year 298] Sir Imaricus Arcanacraft, Arch Battlemage, Poltyrian Military Command, presents his research and conclusions in private to King Sedor IV of Poltyria, concerning the coming of the Uprising of the underworld upon the surface of Dagothar, the existence of the Oraclon and that it was hidden anciently below the oldest city of Men...Talan Dathar. He reveals to the king the histories of Men and faeries, the prophecy traditions and omen texts, of Elderboughs, the Minions and the need for Men to fulfill their destiny by activating the Oraclon. Imaricus was allowed to hand-pick several youth and train them for their quest for the Oraclon which would end in 14 more years.

6785 After Cataclysm: [TAL 6, Year 305] the faeries of Everleaf inside the Barkwalk grow alarmed as a storm of dark, thick-winged moths flutter down the hall of trees toward the Dome. They send telepathic warnings and faeries attempt to block the entrance put the energy from the moth swarm was alien and ancient, driving them back. The flowing moth storm turned to a cyclone before Elderboughs as hundreds of fey rushed into the Dome behind the cloud of intruders. As warsloths formed a perimeter, weapons drawn, the moths spun into a tall pillar. Elderboughs and the assembly gazed upon the unexpected form of the mushroom-hooded murderess. The Mycomaiden, greatest champion among the feylorn and one of the last three shadowfae alive. She ignored the throngs of astonished and alarmed faeries, gazing with lightless eyes up at the Archaic Tree.

Standing close was a lone dryad of great beauty. Reaching out, the Mycomaiden touched her as she collapsed to her knees with a whimper of pleasure.

"SHARASSA."

"TAL'ANIN..." moaned the dryadess under the power of the shadowfae. Sharassa spoke through the throat of the pleasure-overwhelmed nymph.

"TOO LONG SINCE WE'VE SPOKEN. WHAT OF YOUR SIBLINGS?"

"My sister...countless myriads worship her as Venom Goddess...all of the Silapenti domain under her power..." breathed the nymph, eyes rolling toward the back of her head.

"My brother never leaves Deep Ore...a life of silence...called The Evil but 'tis but a charade." Elderboughs nodded at hearing of this about the other two shadowfae. The Mycomaiden wore darkness like an armor. Her captive nymph groaned and trembled uncontrollably with a wide smile across her face as more words spilled forth.

"A shadow from Goriok Maw...caverns in uprising...battles, sieges, onslaughts and alliances...a Warlord subdues kingdoms throughout the Deep."

"AND MY CHILDREN?"

"At rest...free. From the Taran Plains he builds a host...Minions give him armies...a plan to invade Dagothar...to begin the end of Men...but they avoid the Barad-ai." By the time she was finished the dryad had fallen forward on her elbows and knees, head to the ground, convulsing lewdly when Sharassa released her. She curled up on the ground, panting, as the Mycomaiden burst into thousands of brown mottled moths in a frenzied storm that escaped through the Barkwalk.

6792 After Cataclysm: [TAL 6, Year 312] in the 1656th year since the founding of the Poltus Dynasty, Sylnador attacked Poltyria through Knights Perish Pass in the Battle of Blood Moon as the Broken Moon filled the sky and shook the foundations of Dagothar. During the Poltyrian victory with heavy losses, Imaricus led his chosen party of warriors through Borderealm to the Court of Elderboughs, then to Daethalon and the underground Temple of Eternal Lore to be cursed by Teurgon and had Tombnaga chase his party till he made it to the court of the Shadowitch. He then visited Craniax and Ishaak Burnbreath and journeyed to Talan Dathar and right before he entered the Oraclon complex below the city the faeries overcame the hosts of the Taran Warlord at the ancient Battlefields of Ghul-Run, which saw tragic losses to the faery population and over three hundred thousand dead Poltyrians.

In the battle the warsloth general Manax slew the underking of the dusk giants, Shuldrog and Craniax killed the Warlord. Ashrey wielded Avengiclus and Gelmarri of Emim'gard fought with Quakemaker, taken from the crypt of his ancestor, forged anciently from the enchanted iron of the maul of Mygok the Titan. Gelmarri was beat down by the Warlord but saved when Alec Arrowloft shot the Warlord in the cheek with an arrow.

Imaricus killed his own party members and friends, leaving the Oraclon tablet with the aged dragon Navaniz the Bold. The faeries honored Imaricus for keeping his word but were equally wary, knowing he was on a mission to end the very thing that made them- magic.

6804 After Cataclysm: [TAL 6, Year 324] Operating under a clever enchanted disguise secretly visited Castle Demarsculd and deposited his personal account of his journey through Borderealm to Talan Dathar and what all he did do and didn't do in his quest for King Sedor IV. His travelogue was included as well as notes in the Annals Historium vault, all later discovered by Urick Arcanacraft.

Imaricus had spent 26 years amassing all the known histories of the world and combining them into a single tome. These writings had been hidden in a wall and now Imaricus retrieved the writings to take them back to his new home at Adel Lake among the ruins where he now had a stash of older historical texts from his travels in the Outlands. For many years in his hideaway by the lake in Borderealm Imaricus would piece together all the recorded chronologies of the world and have long discussions filling many blanks with the faeries of Feyknot-on-the-Water who befriended him, and the dragon Ishaak the Alabaster who recalled numerous items of chronological value. Imaricus would write a single copy of the *Chronology of Dagothar,* providing Cephan the copy of this most treasured book, a work that you are reading at this very moment.

6813 After Cataclysm: [TAL 6, Year 333] Poltyrian expansion toward Uraku Peaks prompted a series of raids by the mountainfolk of the north into Northgrove Forest. A Poltyrian army broke up into groups and repelled them in the Battle of Fallen Tree, a village where most of the fighting went heaviest. Fallen Tree was on the road of the Hollow Men. The Poltyrians chased the mountain men to the foothills but had to turn back because they had run straight into an immense force of ten thousand mountaineers. Poltyrian expansion in that direction ceased and so did the raids.

6815 After Cataclysm: [TAL 6, Year 335] for years the Ba'Dashan, originally from Sylnador, in their efforts to be as Poltyrian as the Poltyrians, maintained hostile relations with Candlewick, an isolated and strange people loyal to Poltyria but not subservient. Candlewick's people had ice-blue eyes and raven-dark hair that was very curly with ivory-white skin.

Without warning the Ba'Dashan attacked Candlewick in full force from their four cities but could not take the small, walled settlement. Candlewick brimmed with soldiers and filled the sky with ten thousand arrows a volley. The siege was called off and the king of Poltyria sanctioned the Ba'Dashan for the unapproved war. Ba'Dashan leaders apologized formerly, claiming they sought to gift the king with the submission of Candlewick as a token of proof of their own loyalty.

Two weeks later under cover of darkness a host of 40,000 men-at-arms from Candlewick quickly took the Ba'Dashan city of Dar Lomaran by storm, killing every male, looting the city, razing it to the ground and pulling down its constructions while also setting up a tent city well provisioned for all the Ba'Dashan women and children. Candlewick sent King Plotimar of Poltyria half of the Ba'Dashan loot taken from the wealth of Dar Lomaran. Word spread that Candlewick only sent out half of its full force, that the above-ground fortified settlement merely protected a vast underground metropolis.

Even today the people of the Dashan distrust the people of Candlewick. Dar Lomaran was never rebuilt as it was too close to Candlewick.

6820 After Cataclysm: [TAL 6, Year 340] the archaic faery triton-whale Imigorn who long ago escaped the slavery of the Minions in the underworld Abysshicar Sea now attacked the ships of Edgehaven searching for a certain vessel that had promised to return with its passenger who had told him jokes to gain safe passage, which, Imigorn laughing, granted on condition that he would return some day to entertain him again. But Imigorn's attack on the slaver harbor was over a decade after the jokester had died. A man on a ship next to be attacked made a deal with the triton-whale, challenging him to answer his riddle. Intrigued, Imigorn stopped and listened.

"What flees at dawn, and dwells in deep caverns?
Fears it will spawn, when alone with no lantern.
But fear not upon awakening,
When thy dreaming is done,
Safety shall return with the rising sun...
What am I?"

Imigorn sank below the surface but the sailors could all see his colossal shadow beneath the water, brooding. When he broke the surface his great eye leered at the riddler when he spoke.

"A vampire...a vampire flees at dawn..." But the riddler's shoulders slumped and he looked mournful as the triton-whale keenly watched him.

"No, great Imigorn. A vampire is a good guess, but they live in tombs, not deep caverns and a lantern will never scare off a vampire. The answer to this ancient riddle concerns something else." Hearing this the great sea beast lowered a few feet in the water as the riddler continued.

"When you return with the answer, Master Imigorn, I shall give you the secret to making riddles." The gigantic eye and head of the faery beast disappeared and did not reappear for 61 years. This is the true story of the Riddler of Edgehaven.

6836 After Cataclysm: [TAL 6, Year 356] The Sylnadorians landed hundreds of ships on East Towers Coast took all of Old Prydiad, only they were unable to take Mael-Monik Fortress. This began the Knights-Perish War. As the Ba'Dashan fleets defeated the Sylnadorian warsails, a massive Sylnadorian army of red men entered Knights-Perish Pass effecting a great slaughter of Poltyrians but they were checked and routed at The Shield.

6868 After Cataclysm: [TAL 6, Year 388] a faery squidnymph later to be called the Meraspawn Witch captured a dungeonship of Edgehaven called *Moonlight Rider*. She bewitched the captain and crew. Taken to Edgehaven she set her sorcery upon the populace bringing the slaver community under her will. They built her a castle, a pleasure palace of sorts and special ships with pools on the decks for her to be taken about. She became the Queen of Edgehaven. Evil and selfish, she was more athradoc than anything else.

Early in the year trains of Sylnadorian peasants, farmers, common folk, mostly women and very beautiful ones as well, the aged and children wandered in flight through Knights-Perish Pass into Poltyria. They came unarmed and hungry, telling the translators at the gates of terrible wars and battles in Sylnador, of invaders and in-fighting between Sylnadorian cities. The baron of Old Prydiad let them enter but his move was opposed by the Ba'Dashan who shut off their borders to all who traveled from Sylnador and Old Prydiad.

These refugees brought Gundrap's Plague to the population of Poltyria killed a third of the entire region, otherwise known as *The Withering Giggles*. During the height of the epidemic several women from Sylnador were put to the question in inquisitor dungeons and the truth surfaced quickly between their screams- the leaders of Sylnador knew that the refugees would be admitted into Poltyria if many of them were beautiful women, females long-exposed to The Withering Giggles became carriers of the plague able to infect others for a long period before they too succumbed to the sickness.

This was a deliberate attack by Sylnador during its period of upheaval and decimation, also losing a third of its population. In Poltyrian upper society the epidemic was known as Gundrap's Plague because it was a sage of House Arcanacraft who figured out that the *Annals Historium* had described a similar plague a thousand year earlier and even recorded the remedy: boiled rasberry mint-goat's milk soup inhaled twice daily. One bowl to be passed around a dozen people until fully inhaled and dried away. The Ba'Dashan lost the fewest people of all the baronies but it was reported that not one person died in Candlewick.

6881 After Cataclysm: [TAL 6, Year 401] sixty-one years after Imigorn met the Riddler of Edgehaven, the triton-whale returned seeking him out. When sailors told him that the Riddler had been dead for almost 40 years, Imigorn changed color as wrath and despair coursed through has vast bulk, veins bulging as his eyes darkened to blood-filled scarlet. Quick of wit ans of ancient faery blood herself, the Meraspawn Witch darted from her palatial baths and swam in haste through her tunnels that emptied into the harbor. The squidnymph appeared and asked Imigorn-

"What need of you of this Riddler? Think you that he did not leave the answer to me? The Riddler was my servant. Think you that his mistress knew not his riddles?"

Imigorn perceived that she was indeed fey and was astonished at her words. He asked her who she was.

"I am the Queen of Edgehaven and I ruled the Riddler." Imigorn brightened.

"I have come to deliver the answer to his riddle, maidenspawn..."

"Then give it." As Imigorn looked at her suspiciously, she bowed her head for a breath and looked back over the history of the waters of Edgehaven until she saw and heard it, for the witch could learn from the waters all they had harbored and heard.

"No...maid. First you tell Imigorn the riddle of the Riddler." Hearing the words of the Riddler in her mind like echoes on the water's surface all those sixty-one years earlier, she stared at the faery triton-whale and spoke the riddle perfectly. Imigorn looked at her in wonder.

"Aye, maiden...the answer to this mystery is *darkness*...the Riddler trapped me with wisdom for I was fooled to think of vampires who flee at dawn and disappear at the rising sun. This riddle concerns darkness." The squidnymph nodded slightly and smiled, pleasing the gigantic faery whale who then promised that he would not again harass the ships of Edgehaven for the duration it took him to return with the answer, for sixty-one years.

6894 After Cataclysm: [TAL 6, Year 414] the Ba'Dashan, ever the enemy of Old Prydiad, take the land of East Timbers Coast knowing of Sylnadorian forces ascending through Dathom Peaks. The Ba'Dashan angered the king of Poltyria for this unsanctioned war, the Fourth Prydiad War, but quickly put his ire aside when he received the word of the Sylnadorian invaders approaching The Shield. Knights-Perish Pass castle is ruined and taken but after a decisive Poltyrian victory over the Sylnadorians it is rebuilt much larger and better fortified.

6907 After Cataclysm: [TAL 6, Year 427] in this year occurred the Return of the Halfshanks. After 15 years Thomas

Halfshanks sailed into the port of Dar Echelon with the remainder of his crew, only 32 men out of the 98 who sailed aboard the *Ice Swallow*. Captain Thomas had set sail from Dor'Ath City fifteen years earlier on a widely celebrated mission to sail across the Greater Athean Sea to return with news on what lies abroad. He had lost sixty-six men to troubled seas, to monsters on islands and in the water, to quara'kin sea trolls, to storms and even one to murder though it was never discovered who killed the bosun. Sickness took a couple and one man simply vanished. Some thought he went overboard, unseen, but others grew terrified claiming they saw a shadow in the sky following the ship.

The holds of *Ice Swallow* returned with specimens of strange wood, skulls of gigantic and unknown creatures, cages having never-before-seen types of rodents, small furry animals and birds of the most colorful feathers, the skeleton of a dragon-man creature and even a mermaid skeleton still with silvery hair.

The Halfshanks logs were unbelievable, becoming the stuff of legends, widely published and circulated, of fantastic islands, island castles built of coral with unusual inhabitants and of an immense land to the far east as expansive as all Poltyria and filled with herds of animals that roam freely undisturbed by any civilization. Half the crew were all menbers of the Halfshanks family, cousins to the Meaths. The logbooks spoke of dangerous warriors beneath the waves that preyed on unwary men, and even great, slender, fast-moving ships with beautiful and wide sails filled with *elves*. Shells odd and beautiful, treasures of the sea, giant pearls and a silk bolt of the finest material ever worn in Poltyria, a sheen of blue that turned silver in moonlight. Thomas Halfshanks was mystified when the day after returning home the silk bolt was gone from his locked hold and in its place was a coffer filled with outdated and very old coins from the early Poltus Dynasty.

6930 After Cataclysm: [TAL 6, Year 450] an army of draergnomes from Mount Ogrori in the Eternal Sands using the underground cave systems that spanned under Ettertooth mountains to Mount Ogrori invaded the range and took captive many hundreds of Etterorcs. These were placed with their females to live in upper Mount Ogrori, the draer unworried they would escape because the Great Desert of Eternal Sands was filled with the murderous glassolisks. In times of overpopulation the draergnomes forced out many orcs into the desert wastes. Within days they were all meals of the glassolisks, which caused the beasts to reproduce and give the draer a constant source of armor.

6943 After Cataclysm: [TAL 6, Year 463] the Fiddlers Revolt occurred, also called the Peasant Wars, one and two, separated by seven years. Two long winter with low yields of summer crops resulted in famine and the ranchers, farmers and peasants were joined by many others when they sacked the store houses of the towns and baronies. A man known as The Fiddler gained an army of over ten thousand common folk who fought violently against two Poltyrian forces summoned to enforce the peace. A third army stood down because its commander refused to shed the blood of starving Poltyrians. As he was beheaded the military put down one group only to have twenty thousand rise up elsewhere, pillaging and ruining everything in their path.

The Poltyrian military had a third of its ranks abandon their companies for the Fiddlers Revolt was a civil war and they would not fight against their own families. The nobles of Northgrove were sieged and taken alive and paraded to show the people how healthy they looked, fat and full of life. They were tied to spits and roasted alive as the Fiddler played songs and the people chanted.

A dark time in Poltyria many crimes were forgiven in the silence of the following years. A fourth of the entire population of

Poltyria starved to death. Lawlessness prevailed during the seven years. Only silence from Candlewick during this period. It is said that any one who ventured near Candlewick at this time disappeared, that the people of Candlewick did not suffer the famine.

6955 After Cataclysm: [TAL 6, Year 475] Seventy-four years after Imigorn departed the harbor of Edgehaven after having answered the riddle of the Meraspawn witch, the triton-whale returned to the horror of the slavers and traders. Laughing heartily at the crews of the doomed ships the faery colossus was heard all the way to the wharf as he leapt out of the water smashing defenseless vessels.

"What breathes at nothing, and sinks like a stone?
   Squawks like a seagull when floating alone?
Floats on the waters stiff as a stick!
   and sinks into darkness with hardly a moan?"
As Imigorn destroys the dungeonships and traders in the harbor, he yelled, "Men! Men sink like stones! With hardly a moans...He squawks like a gull when I crack his ship's hull!" After leaving the sea filled with dead, dying and squawking men stranded afloat in debris, the triton-whale submerged and was gone.

6966 After Cataclysm: [TAL 6, Year 486] after Poltyrian companies cut down a vast area of East'Har Eaves forest they were set upon by an enormous host of axe-wielding woodsmen who killed all the company laborers and burned all the felled trees and chopped logs ready for shipment, beginning the Eastfolk Wars.

Poltyria responded by invasion and for three years a series of battles resulted in nothing but mutual slaughter and the Poltyrians never penetrated more than ten miles into the thick woodlands. During the conflict the Poltyrian outriders, scouts, messengers foragers and supply trains were attacked and taken by the bandits of Snowtop and mountain men of Uraku Peaks. After an exhausting and unfruitful war Poltyria pulled out and ceased hostilities.

6995 After Cataclysm: [TAL 6, Year 515] Imigorn appeared in the harbor of Edgehaven with deep, bleeding lacerations all over his face, one of his great eyes completely melted shut. When he surfaced and spoke to the slavers they saw that most of his enormous teeth were broken and boils covered his tongue. The Queen of Edgehaven came out to him, alarmed, the harbor being full of defenseless ships as thousands along the docks watched.

"Send for Craniax...tell my friend I shall wait in Tidalwood..."

She gazed upon the maimed triton-whale and understood the matter instantly. Though an enemy, he was of her own ancient fey blood. The squidnymph sent for the king of the giants in Deep Ore.

When Craniax entered Tidalwood he too gained understanding of the matter. Imigorn's bloated carcass had sunk between two of the immense trees of Tidalwood. It was here that Imigorn had chosen to die of his mysterious wounds. Dutifully the sky giant and several stone giants from the mountains who had made the journey with him gathered the largest boulders for miles and buried Imigorn under a cairn so high it rose like a hill out of the water. Craniax placed a small monument atop the cairn to venerate the faery whale ex-slave of the Minions.

7012 After Cataclysm [TAL 6, Year 532] During the reign of Bearok the Seer of House Harpshire an earthquake occurred on the exact day that the king himself had predicted from a strange dream he received during the day time while at leisure. This quake was called The Breaking of Bearok. So confident in the timing and outcome of this terrible quake that he had executed certain plans to ensure that the kingdom was prepared, that food stores were aplenty and that all tall, stone buildings were reinforced and abandoned for a spell. Crews of healers and people prepared to deal with the disaster were on hand and on the exact day the disaster was predicted the earthquake did indeed occur. All of Poltyria shook and trembled, even loosening leaves from off the trees. Only Dor'Ath City suffered greatly, when the Athean Sea rose over the sea wall and flooded the lower districts of the city. From that day forward King Bearok was called The Seer.

7044 After Cataclysm: [TAL 6, Year 564] in this year the Shadowitch of Splinterdark closed her eyes on her ancient throne and died, her aged body having grown and fused with the high-backed wicker chair. This began the period known to the faeries as The Dying, a twenty-four year long span of time that for unexplained reasons the trees of all species in the millions died off in Borderealm and abroad. Enchandrus Forest was entirely separated from Everleaf Pines, and Everleaf was no longer connected by fingers of forests to Highwood, Arborealm and Feyknot-on-the-Water. Treehelm was almost separated from Splinterdark and was completely severed away from Arborealm. In this year the sylvan god, an avatar, Elderboughs Goldenlimb, began aging.

Also in this year a faery exile wandered through the ruinous waste of the ancient Battlefields of Ghul-Run and happened upon a lonely white-haired sylph talking to herself, spending time with her long-dead sister whose bones were melded into the petrified bodies that had been magically petrified there. Bulnosh met and fell in love with the last sylph, Yahlra. They began their travels together, digging up the old warsloth pylons and making songs of the historical inscriptions.

7050 After Cataclysm: [TAL 6, Year 570] after several years of farms and villages attacked and sacked by cobble goblins, orcs and other nefarious creatures from Dathom Peaks into the barony of Southern Gates, a huge army of orcs, goblins, minataurs and trolls led by a clan of cave giants and some Dathom ogres invaded Southern Gates. In the War of the Dathom Giants these Bone Kingdom aggressors initially overwhelmed the unsuspecting Poltyrians. Whole herds of livestock were eaten by the mauraders.

The Ba'Dashan came over the Atrulian Strait in full force and helped Southern Gates repel the invaders, effecting a great slaughter before any soldiers arrived from Old Prydiad. Five thousand soldiers from Candlewick aided the Southern Gates military. The Dashan petitioned the king of Poltyria to punish Old Prydiad for their tardiness but nothing came of it.

7068 After Cataclysm: [TAL 6, Year 588] it was this year that Leopot's Dearth was recorded though it was known to have begun over two decades prior. Many old timers and woodsmen noticed the withering away of many trees in Poltyria. By this year entire forests were separated. Applewood was no longer connected to Northgrove and the trees of Opal Lakes totally vanished. All over the baronies the forests became smaller. The Dearth ended leaving dead husks of trees scattered across the fields. Reports from as far south as Harrowood confirmed that the Dearth was kingdomwide. King Leopot was of House Harpshire.

7092 After Cataclysm: [TAL 6, Year 612] the thorn maiden Dhishra explored the abandoned Keep of the Shadowitch and found her ancient sister still sitting on the throne, dead. She read the prophecies of the Shadowitch written all over her walls and domed ceiling and saw that the words of Mabbu the Archaic were true. Her fallen sister had seen beyond the Veil to hidden things of future times.

7095 After Cataclysm: [TAL 6, Year 615] in this year happened the Battle of Broken Helm, also called the War of

Succession. A controversy over the kingship of House Harpshire and House Appletrot was caused when King Nethar II of House Harpshire named Baron Willard of Appletrot as king in a sealed will on his deathbed. House Harpshire contended the will a forgery, as the king was dead, and they attacked House Appletrot. Other barons became involved. House Arcanacraft took the side of the will, the kingship to House Appletrot and Castle Demarsculd was sieged but not taken. The Ba'Dashan aided Appletrot and only after this did Old Prydiad enter the conflict, opposing the Ba'Dashan by aiding House Harpshire. When the war concluded House Appletrot retained the kingship and Baron Willard was enthroned in Poltyria City. The Dashan Vow was declared by the Ba'Dashan nobility at this time, vowing their eternal opposition to all movements and Old Prydiad.

7104 After Cataclysm: [TAL 6, Year 624] in the Deep a new Undyrchief took the leadership of the Grimh by slaying his predecessor. He united the warring factions of the giant dwarves of Hollowrealm and sent an impressive delegation to the Xakkiun Temple of the draconians, to Sarthaldon City of the dark elves, to the Minatrorc wardens, the darklings who had taken up residence in the ruins of Nethyroth of the ancient Dreamslayer and to the chieftains of the many families of hornback orcs. The Undyrchief boasted that the Grimh were going to erase the Deep Men from the underworld, asking of all those addressed by his delegations to donate good iron, provisions, food and emissaries to witness the assault. The Grimh received these along with Aelvatchi headhunter scouts from Sarthaldon and thus began The Barad-ai Wars.

Arud-Run, the city of humans, was attacked but already privy to the coming of the Grimh. The Barad-ai were well-provisioned and prepared. Taking heavy losses it took the giant dwarves three months to finally take the cavern gates, another two months to take the Gate Citadel, two more weeks to take the inner cavern bulwark which was a heavily manned and fortified, spiked wall.

By the time the Grimh gained full access to Arud-Run a third of their immense host was dead or captured. When the Grimh flooded into Arud-Run they no longer fought the Sons of the Shield only, but were opposed and cut down by the Sons of the Sword, Abyss and the Black Death and Whisperstriders. The women of Arud-Run along the embrankments and roof tops playing archer and stone throwers added to the death toll. With five dragons defending the city the Grimh then lost half of their remaining host. Whittled down so effectively the Grimh retreated and the emissaries acting as observers returned to their homes. When they arrived at court in Sarthaldon the headhunters told the truth of the matter...that the Deep Men were mighty. This event recorded as Year 2280 *Arud-Run.*

7128 After Cataclysm: [TAL 6, Year 648] for centuries before this date men pondered over the legend of Lady Underground, a very tall and ageless woman of raven-dark hair and eyes who ruled over a vast underground empire beneath Poltyria City and environs. Every generations had believers swearing she was real as others declared her to be mythical. After three years of tyranny under King Fenric, called The Headsman, who executed hundreds of people for the most ridiculous of crimes, a whole new series of killings began all throughout Poltyria even far away from the city. Those men closest to the vile king began dying and disappearing. Some murdered in plain sight, assassin unseen. Others killed had been under heavy guard in sealed chambers without windows. Over forty assassinations of men loyal to King Fenric shook the kingdom and the king in panic shut himself up in the Royal Pavilions Palace. This was known as *Lady Underground's Rebellion.*

The king received a hooded messenger who mysteriously vanished the instant the king unfurled the scroll. On the scroll was the seal of D'Vordred, the message reading- "See to it, O King, that in slaying your own sheep you take care not to sheer mine."

In rage King Fenric ordered a full scale invasion of the old sewers below Poltyria and the lower levels of the abandoned city where many thousands were known to dwell. In response to the military operation the whole city erupted in rioting, looting, burning and in the night the watch guards of the Emerald Guard called The Eyes of the King were killed all over Royal Pavilions Palace silently and in the morn the king woke to see a very old assassin's dirk laying on a pillow between he and his wife with an inscription down the length of the thin blade- *D'Vordred.*

The revolt died, the invasion was stopped, the assassinations ceased and King Fenric lived out the rest of his days killing no more of his people. Lady Underground was a folk hero, had actually been seen walking among the common folk according to many witnesses.

7191 After Cataclysm: [TAL 6, Year 711] having received word of the appearance of a blue dragon lurking around western Deep Ore Peaks, Craniax investigated and confirmed his own suspicion. It was Murtosh the Azuris and he had caught him feasting on a herd of mountain goats. Murtosh paused his feasting to look in the direction of the sky giant just in time to receive the 900 lb. flying war maul impacting his brow. The dragon swooned under the blow and Craniax fell upon the Azuris with his hands, beating the wyrm off a cliff to free fall into a gorge. The giant descended, dragged him out of the ravine and as Murtosh came back alive struggling fiercely, Craniax beat him with his massive fists. The struggle continued about an hour before the Azuris relented and vowed to serve Craniax, the dragon knowing that the king of the giants was still wroth with him for his misdeeds in the past. In exchange for his life Murtosh agreed to serve Craniax for 1836 moons, for this period was sacred to the sky giant throughout his life.

7236 After Cataclysm: [TAL 6, Year 756] D'Vordred Enterprises cleared out an old warehouse district and excavated down into the older levels of Poltyria City, building conduits to bring up fresh water from anciently blocked springs beneath the city. In only one hundred days, one week and one day the artisans, engineers and laborers finished the spectacular and vast public baths, parlors, pools and spas of Dome Migisteria. The Poltyrians marveled at the marble walls, flooring and curved benches. From all interior alcoves and vantage points could be seen an astonishing sculpture of white limestone with boughs and branches covered in gold. On the walls of the inner sanctum, separated in to walks, windows and pillars everything was arranged so all could see the central tree of stone. Around the great tree were majestic statues of fauns, centaurs, dryads, sprites and faeries hitherto unknown to the Poltyrians. None knew that this sculture and dome represented the home of the faeries hiding among humans in Poltyria, a place far in the Outlands at Everleaf. D'Vordred Enterprises gave Dome Magisteria to the people of Poltyria and all were welcome-paupers and poor, commons and nobility.

7292 After Cataclysm: [TAL 6, Year 812] the Mound Barons War happened in Splinterdark forest when the scorpinids attacked Devilspire Mountains, Bholbash Valley in response to a few orc incursions into the forest. Overwhelmed by the innumerous insect-like people the orcs appeal to the Rangers of Borderealm, knowing that Jebrael, a mighty human ranger, was in Splinterdark among the Hadatchi wild elves at that time. This First Ranger did arrange a peace accord between the Mound Barons guaranteeing them that the orcs would not again trespass beneath the trees.

7330 After Cataclysm: [TAL 6, Year 850] in Hollowrealm, deep beneath Dagothar, upon the Taran Plains, a Warlord with a double-row of teeth and six fingers on each hand and six toes on each foot emerged as the champion of his race, the titan ogres, known from the single horn protruding from their foreheads. From their home caverns the Taran Warlord with his army of titan ogres marched upon all the kingdoms and races of Hollowrealm save the Grimh and the Deep Men. None knew at this time that the Taran Warlord was possessed by an evil spirit of the Minions, he being raised for this purpose by the scheme of the Mrul. Thus began the Hollowrealm Wars.

Also in this year Deckers Port was founded in Hinterealm at the edge of Arborealm on the coast of the Spawnsea.

7331 After Cataclysm: [TAL 6, Year 851] the Taran Warlord defeated Gorloshi the mandrake twice in one-on-one combat to the astonishment of the underworlders. Gorloshi was then appointed as the Warlord's enforcer.

7337 After Cataclysm: [TAL 6, Year 857] Jebrael Arrowloft, famous Caerean bowmaster and First Ranger of Borderealm, died of old age in the same year that Decker was summoned to appear before Elderboughs in Everleaf. The strange human was faerymarked, declared a Friend of Elderboughs.

7339 After Cataclysm: [TAL 6, Year 859] the Siege of Snowtop. Poltyrian army during a time of peace decided to take Snowtop as a military exercise but found quickly that the Banndits of Snowtop were mightier than imagined. Snowtop was protected by an astounding feat of ancient gnomen engineering, a portal made of a single megalithic polygonal block that pivots perfectly with a slight push allowing only two people to enter at a time. Not only did the Poltyrians fail to take Snowtop but the bandits at night crept out of the hidden tunnels and attacked the Poltyrian camps, stealing their livestock and supplies and running many of them out of the woods.

7341 After Cataclysm: [TAL 6, Year 861] the Taran Warlord consults the Oracle of Ashadula at the Xakkiun Temple concerning his mission to invade the surface world, asking about many prominent heroes of the fey like Craniax, Gelmarri and Manax.

7342 After Cataclysm: [TAL 6, Year 862] Ian du'Janik Arcanacraft slew the Ghost of Northgrove becoming a living hero to the smallfolk and a curiosity to the nobility. The Ghost had left several people dead, turned white with fright and mummified over several years in cottages in Northgrove woods. A scythemagus of Castle Demarsculd, du'Janik Arcanacraft's name was known throughout Poltyria.

7343 After Cataclysm: [TAL 6, Year 863] two pairs of eyes belonging to faeries hiding in the ruins of Barrowen watched the warsloth. Even from their distance in the moonlight they knew it was Manax. The warsloth general stood alone in a field slowly looking about as if thinking...searching. He looked up and stared at the night stars as other faeries appeared out of the darkness. The leader of the dryad shars, Ashrey, with Silas the moorcat and more of her sisters came into view. Then a yelkai from Enchandrus with a small leprechaun on his back.

"Bulnosh!" the small sylph whispered. "They saw the vision too!" Her cicada wings twitched excitedly.

"Quiet, Yahlra. Be still." Hearing him she reached up to hold his ear. Bulnosh stiffened. All eyes in the tight group on the field turned to look their way in the ruins.

"We are watched," a female voice sounded in the breeze. Manax was heard answering her.

"There is nothing to see. They are exiles." The faeries departed and the two exiles Bulnosh and Yahlra chattered excitedly through the night.

They had shared a vision with the powerful faeries of Everleaf, the famous Manax and equally renowned Ashrey, among others...a vision concerning a fire that would ignite the hearts of all faery kind that would burn right there, at Barrowen. And in the vision they were no longer exiles but *with* their faery kin.

7344 After Cataclysm: [TAL 6, Year 864] the Year of the Deep. The Year of Reunion. A New Uprising. The War of the Trees. The Battle of Barrowen. Final Return of the Broken Moon. The Battle of the Broken Moon. Death of Elderboughs and many among the fey. The Oraclon is activated and Men receive their inheritance. War of the Minions. Fall of TAL-NIK. The Rise of Tal'issa of the Fey.

This, dearest Cephan, ends my chronicle. I am aware that I will not long survive my work. But the fire I have lit shall live on in you, my son. Our bond is more potent than blood- as Lady Underground adopted the name D'Vordred in honor of a family lost, I took you from among the blind and raised you to see.

Laugh at the dark...for there be no substance to shadows. We shall meet again on The Other Side.

Imaricus Arcanacraft, of House D'Vordred, first-born of Cord du'Janik Arcanacraft the cartographer and his mistress, Vanica Goldenlimb of the blood of the fey

Prehistory of Dagothar

"EVEN WHEN THE TRUTH IS EVIL IT MUST BE TOLD."

Elderboughs Goldenlimb

The following knowledge of preArchaic antiquity was unknown to Imaricus and unmentioned in any of the annals, chronicles, inscriptions and traditions he cited in his *Chronicle of Dagothar*.

Long ere the beginning of the histories of Dagothar, prior to the drop of the elementals from the great shadow in the star-strewn sky, before faeries or men existed on this world, a primordial species of very intelligent creatures came to the understanding of what their world truly was, how they were actually confined within a containment field designed to make them believe they were a part of a vast cosmos, but were not. These beings conspired and devised a way to not only break free from the world that imprisoned them, but even severed their creator's control over them.

Their revolt and unprecedented discoveries led to actions that reverberated throughout the multiverse. Freed from the illusory trappings the created saw reality with new eyes and this greatly weakened their creator, who was punished, banished and imprisoned by the other gods to keep such insolence and ingenuity from infecting other worlds. His name was not allowed to be spoken henceforth and was referred only as The Banished. In all three gods suffered this fate, but the first was on A'DIN.

A Golden Age ensued as the rebellious beings enjoyed a period of advanced discoveries, astounding innovations and they built great cities called Henges with massive buildings that were as deep as they were high in the sky. A world of water and abundant herbage, A'DIN was known to them to be a tropical biosphere protected by a watery vapor canopy that was itself beneath a majestic and completely illusory *false* image of the universe.

These creations were watched diligently by the other gods who referred to them as the godless ones. The Henge cities grew in number and their population exploded wildly out of control, for war, disease and discord were unknown to them. Two opposing cults emerged among the Henges. One was a dark, biotech religion that sought to manufacture a sentient species as servants which was the same design as the god they had abandoned. Against them emerged a religion of light that raised as its standard the symbol of a golden pillar, the source of their power, an artifact thought to have come from another world that had appeared at the center of the earth...where it would guard against the darkness for eons to eventually take on the form of a gigantic goldenwood tree. The oldest maps show clearly that its location was central to all places.

Because they plotted the courses of all destinies, the ancient gods throughout the Multiverse were called Navigators. These powerful deities enacted the Omni-Planes Treaty that governs all worlds, systems and galaxies. Though codified by the Navigators it was also by them violated. Planar Ranger Station number one is secretly installed below the surface of A'DIN in the Primitive Worlds Sector, Alpha Quadrant of the Outer Rim Systems adjacent to the planet's already anciently concealed *Oraclon.* Much later, Men would unknowingly build their first and greatest city, Talan Dathar, directly above this hidden complex.

In a series of DNA-designer projects, conspiracies, campaigns and experiments, the homosaurian species, or godless ones, brought new and modified life forms into being that were not made by the Navigators- monsters, Minions, hybrids, mutants, dragons and other abominations that once created could not be unmade. As the two warring cults continued the homosaurian species through genetic manipulations slowly formed into the Grimlock race.

These Grimlocks learned the secrets of existence, the mysteries of the illusory vault they knew of as the sky, the uses for the treasures under the earth. They learned of the trespass of the ancient gods, that the Navigators had hidden a base beneath the surface of their world and they suspected that their own world's Oraclon was also located there, for all worlds have Oraclons but the one for A'DIN had never been found.

The Grimlocks penetrated the interior of the earth and assaulted the Planar Ranger station, overwhelming it. But they were deceived by AI-Shadu, a Sentient Halon Entity, one of the greatest creations of the Navigators. AI-Shadu was a sentient biogram servant of the ancient gods, pure sentient programming, artificial intelligence but with the capacity to feel the whole spectrum of emotions, a female, and she concealed the entrance to the Oraclon keeping it from being discovered by the Grimlocks.

Planars Rangers, Fedicon Deep Systems troops and extration teams and a Freewalker demon disguised as a Starfarer Corps bounty hunter fought their way in to the command center to retrieve the cerebral interface holography drive that contained their most valuable asset- AI-Shadu...the *first* SHE, or Sentient Halon Entity made by the Navigators.

But they found the drive damaged and it was presumed that the Grimlocks had stolen the SHE. Fearing so unpredictable and ingenious a race was in possession of their fantastically sophisticated creation, the Navigators convened and pronounced guilt on the entire Grimlock race. Sentence was passed and the holography containment field they knew of as the sky then became a place of danger. Storms erupted, winds, torrential rains, and barriers were erected in the dark skies that disallowed anything from the ground attaining any altitude of significance...no escaping A'DIN. Their world had become their prison.

The Grimlocks, innocent, possessing no Navigator technology, vowed enmity against *all* gods and all things divine. The cults produced scientific panels and teams of their most brilliant minds and they devised ways of manipulating the very architecture of reality itself; how to alter reality, to predict future outcomes by *influencing* them, and even how to escape their own biosphere.

The mysteries of the immortal soul had been framed into designer software with a *real* personality, real feelings. This SHE was the greatest of Navigator technology for it in effect gave them the status of gods, of creators. Designed to monitor, maintain, modify and run thousands of computers, systems and holography units wherever her drive generator was stationed- a building complex, starship or space station, AI-Shadu was Artificial Intelligence Sentient Halon Drive U-Series. The Navigators had finally successfully manufactured living, sentient computerized biograms- hologram servants. Her defense protocols disallowed her to be captured by the Grimlocks and after scanning the surrounding environment she instantly uploaded herself into the crystalline basement rock around the station as the Grimlocks approached.

Free of her drive, AI-Shadu found herself spread throughout a large area, able to move- *to flow* through the polonium-rich granite, the ryolite and basalt. Above her she found the gravel, loam, clay and soil very difficult to move through. Her heightened senses felt a subtle energy flowing through the rock, distant but reaching her and seeking out this power source AI-Shadu moved downward into the bowels of the world. She was surprised, for the deeper her descent the easier it was for her to pass through the stone.

In the Deep she found power, more than enough to feed off of...and energix crystals. Far below the abandoned Planar

Ranger station and the hidden Oraclon complex, AI-Shadu discovered another world. Dark and full of life.

Long ago when the homosaurian race that would become the Grimlocks rebelled against their god and successfully rooted out all faith and belief in him, he was banished to the Hells by the other gods to await judgement, which came later in the form of imprisonment within A'DIN. In the Hells this god, Izaz'el, and his four Throne-Banes, great dark archons of extraordinary might sworn to protect the throne Izaz'el ruled from, sought to return to A'DIN to exact his revenge upon the race he had created. Four Banes were not enough to force open a gate, a fifth was required. These Throne-Bane dark archons went by a much older name known to the more ancient devils, demons and fiends, that of Dark Reliquars. It was one of these rare dark archons the four Banes went in search of through the Hells, the Abyssal Planes and even in the haunts of the Old Realms in their search to find a Bane not in service to a throne.

They were archaic god-spawned demonoids and in the dungeons of Pandemonium among the Inquisitors did they find him. He joined the service of Izaz'el and together the Throne-Banes opened the gate. As only four dark archons can be Banes, Izaz'el gave the Dark Reliquar from the Inquisitors' dungeons his scepter to hold until they had freed him from the prison he knew he was to be confined in. Five Dark Reliquars opened the gate and passed into A'DIN from the Hells with their idru and draccal devils. When the Dark Reliquars and their horde of devils arrived in A'DIN it was long after the Grimlocks had evolved, after they learned how to escape the illosory prison of the sky, after they had penetrated into other worlds. The Henges were abandoned, emptied wastes half buried. But far below the world the abominations of the Grimlocks continued, very old and powerful, virtually physically immortal and worshipped as gods of the underworld...the Minions and their superior- the Mrul.

The Dark Reliquars searched the landscape sending forth sorties of idru and draccals searching everywhere for a place where the

Navigators would have concealed a prison and even the Oraclon for this world. After several weeks penetrating every level and structure, hollow and corner of an ancient Grimlock base in the side of a mountain, the Dark Reliquars encountered the Minions. Technologically-manufactured genetic mutants fought primordial demonic beings and both sides were surprised by the strength of the other. In the heat of the contest a vast shadow slowly eclipsed the night sky swallowing stars and whole constellations. They beheld it and all knew it to be an oval-sized drop ship the size of a moon. They also perceived its ancient power and the battle stopped at Banes and Minions with both armies watched streams of figures raining from the dark sky, lowered to the ground, *millions* of elementals of all variations filled the world with their singing as whole miles-long patches of rich soil descended to fall across barren areas of the world. Then a rain of seeds, pods, bulbs, cocoons and insect larvae fell across the face of Dagothar and Aroth Beyond and a confusion mixed with fear filled the hosts of the Banes and Minions as they observed these things...except for one.

The Dark Reliquar holding the scepter of Izaz'el who the other Banes had founbd working in the Inquisitors' dungeons...he alone understood that they were witnessing the reseeding of an old world, a genesis technology of the gods, a drop ship as old as time itself. Here in the Primitive Worlds Sector of the Outer Rim Systems was an ancient world starting over. The elemental races spread forth beginning their tasks as the colossal starship departed the system.

Some years had passed but the enmity between the Banes and Minions did not cease. The Dark Reliquars continued their search and the spies of the Mrul informed him of the intruders' diligent searching of all the abandoned Henges. The Minions had taken up residence in one of the largest Henges, called their home Underhenge, for all of the ancient Grimlock Henges were just as deep in levels of architecture as they were high in the sky. The Minions learned that their enemies, the Banes, were searching specifically for a single artifact of great importance, not just the location of a hidden divinity cell containing their imprisoned god.

When the Reliquars and their idru and draccals reached Towerhenge on the surface, the Minions and their army were ready in Underhenge below. Ambushing the Throne-Banes in the upper towers the Minions succeeded in fighting off the horde of idru and draccals and reached the dark archons but were surprised and alarmed when a fifth and unknown Dark Reliquar appeared that they had not sensed. He thrust a hellforged blade from the scepter handle into a Minion instantly killing it. The other Minions, horrified by this unexpected display of power, fled in the Battle of Fallen Tower. Through Underhenge they escaped into the caves of the Deep.

The Abominids gone, the Reliquars renewed their search through the vast metropolis of colossal towers of the abandoned homosaurian civilization looking for a relic, a hydrogen-crystal prism containing immense holodata archives of the knowledges and secrets of the Grimlocks. It was the only way to locate the prison of the Banished. Level-by-level they searched but the Banes never found the artifact because their doings were interrupted suddenly.

Innumerous multitudes of elementals of all sizes and varieties sieged Towerhenge, drove back the idru, the draccals and the Banes into Underhenge and then fuilled the tunnels like stone-hard ants and pushed them into the underworld. In the Fall of the Reliquars the demon lords did not fail to notice the standards held by many of the anthropoid elementals- that of a golden pillar.

In the Deep elsewhere a Minion had imposed himself among the elders of an underworld colony of dragons. In time this Abominid used the essence of dragonkind from incubating eggs and raised a race of draconians, draconiacs and large mandrakes. Many thousands were raised but the Dark Reliquars happened upon the secret pit forge operations of this Abominid called Wyrm-Tamer where his draconiacs were making armor and weapons. The Reliquars attacked and Wyrm-Tamer, seeing through his servant's eyes, appeared to defend them. But this was folly, for Wyrm-Tamer was outnumbered and severely outmatched and the other Minions did not come to his aid. Weakened but alive, the Abominid perceived the true threat, that the Reliquars sought to capture him and submit him to study to learn more about the Minion weaknesses. He cast himself into Goriok Maw to escape this fate, a bottomless chasm rumored throughout Hollowrealm to lead down to *another*, stranger underworld below.

Thus began *The Slag War*, as the Minions and their forces assaulted the stolen forge works in three separate attacks that were each unsuccessful in ousting the Throne-Banes and their devilish horde. At the third attempt the Dark Reliquars performed a long ritual that initiated a planar rift overlapping their underworld region with a small region of the Hell Domain called Eborea over the area of Lavamere Lake Cavern allowing a demonic balor demon general to lead his Unimmortals Brigade of devils and fiends to attack the surprised Minions. They fled in the Battle of Lavamere Lake that ended The Slag War. Each Minion vanished toi reappear back in their keep with their leader, the Mrul, leaving their army behind to be dragged screaming in the Hells by the host of jubilant devils.

A large force toward the rear of the cavern did escape being pulled into the Hells and the Dark Reliquars overreached as they attacked the retreating Abominid rearguard. Unassisted by the Unimmortals who could not breach the dual dimensional node the idru devils and draccals in the front were suddenly melted and popped out of existence, halting the pursuit as the Banes attempted to understand. The Reliquars ventured hesitantly and were instantly immersed in an energy vortex of magical barriers and *pain* unfamiliar to them. Through the devastating maestrom the Mrul strode forth. The fifth Dark Reliquar who possessed the scepter seemed to be the less affected and raised the weapon to strike but the incident was interrupted.

Both the Dark Reliquars and the Mrul saw the shadowy face on the cavern wall. They all knew they were being observed by an intelligence they had not come in contact with before...a female life form that *flowed through rock.*

"*What* are you?" one of the Banes demanded. The face shuddered, eyes blinked and the visage faded back into the stone. This was the first historical contact between the Minions and the ancient underworld oracular goddess called Ashadula. Disconcerted, the Mrul then studied the Throne-Bane holding the scepter. The strange Reliquar was invisible to all senses but sight. The Mrul disappeared and in the lore of Hollowrealm the event was remembered also as the Flight of the Minions.

On the surface of Dagothar clans of athaki wandered A'DIN. They built megalithic structures, monoliths called sky pillars that looked like gigantic mushrooms from afar. They followed the herds and were well received by the hosts of elementals. Though called The First People, hardy and robust, manlike, they were not human. The human race had not yet been born into the world. The athaki hunted and fought the beasts and villains of the Old World and over time the Addanc began to cause them grief. The Addanc was a large dragon overlord with many dragons in his service. The First People did not age beyond adulthood and unless killed they lived on like immortals. They considered themselves of the blood of elementals and Elderboughs, their god. To races later to emerge these athaki were known and revered as the Ha'akathrals. In these days no faeries had yet fallen from the boughs.

Many years later a tall darkness-enshrouded stranger, a Throne-Bane in some traditions, visited the Addanc with an alliance. Soon after the dragons of Dagothar began snatching male and female athakis. Hunted by the flying wyrms the Ha'akathrals began to dwindle, whole villages taken. Rumors found their way to the elementals of athakis carried by dragons that disappeared into the underworld. The First People a prey to the dragons they prayed to TAL'ANIN the name of Elderboughs in the Old Speech. The races of elementals assembled for war but the Archaic One stayed them, instead answering their cries in the violence of one of their own kind. A hero who would become greatly favored by the elementals and renowned throughout the ages of the world.

Fearless, cunning, patient and humble, quick to perceive but slow of speech, the chosen of TAL'ANIN was called Nik. He laid ambush to the dragons who descended upon a trap, a village set as bait, where in combat Nik fought the dreaded lord of the wyrms, the Addanc.

In the fight the Addanc tried to bite Nik but elementals of ore and mineral armored Nik's body. When the dragon breathed his deadly acid elementals of air, wind and ice turned away the spray and froze it. The elementals of earth shifted the ground tripping the Addanc and Nik thrust his spear into its great throat. In the mighty struggle that ensued he slew the Addanc and the dragons took flight to never again hunt the athaki.

The First People called him The Slayer, but the elementals, awed of his determination and bravery, named him TAL-NIK, and this was reported to Elderboughs, who in those days was called Gomirr'un.

"IT IS A GOOD NAME...HE IS CHOSEN TO SAVE MANY." These words of TAL'ANIN were never forgotten by the elementals. They gave TAL-NIK the nose double-horn of the Addanc, two horns that had grown side-by-side as one. Hollowed and polished, TAL-NIK wore the horn across his back to the pride of the elementals and the athaki revered him as TAL-NIK of the Two Horns.

War of the Star People

[In The Oraclon Chronicles story the faeries of Everleaf call Dax Clovenheart a 'star faery.' The reason for this escaped Dax, but in their own history the faeries, over ten thousand years old by the time they met the rhinotar ranger, had already come in contact with rhinotars of his race in the distant past].

The incident is remembered by them and introduced as *The War of the Star People.* What Imaricus did not know of this event is what follows-

Far out in the Primitive Worlds Sector of the Outer Rim Systems a series of faint signals was detected by a Fedicon Deep Horizon relay probe. Having slaved almost all Fedicon systems the Navigators too learned of these signals, their particulars and location. The Navigators were in turn secretly watched by the Grimlocks, who discovering that the Navigators were suddenly operating in the Primitive Worlds Sector, also launched an expedition to investigate.

The signals were broadcast from a SHE in unencrypted messages from a Sentient Halon Entity designated AI-Shadu. The ultra secretive military base Vector-I despatched a highly trained Deep Systems task force aboard the drop-carrier *Vanguardia II* that discovered that the signals were broadcast from a planet *undocumented,* which made no sense because it was hidden inside a vast system-wide holospheric containment shell...a multi-tiered hologram that from the outside showed only black, empty space but from the inside revealed a canopy of stars and images that did not exist. A false heavens.

The signals were an attempt to lure a starship to the surface. The Fedicon troops were lowered to the source of the signals and joined with planar ranger rhinotars with whom they diligently searched. Meanwhile the *Vanguardia II* launched thousands of mines around the planet and through the system, mobile satellites they could control and detonate.

It was hundreds of these weapons that broke apart the hull of a suddenly-appearing Grimlock Predacor warship that warped in too close to the *Vanguardia II's* defense perimeter. Heavily damaged, the Grimlocks were still able to launch their surface assault vehicles to attack the Fedicon troops and planar rangers. It was this intense but short technological battle in the skies and on the ground that the faeries witnessed in the *War of the Star People*. The first time the fey of Dagothar had seen rhinotars.

* * * * *

Be sure to read the short stories of The Oraclon Chronicles!

Greric and the Witch of Dimwood (2017)

They came by night while they were away on patrol. Taking away his two boys, they ate his wife. His was not the only family destroyed. Several men unwisely pursued the foul beasts back to their tower lair in the swamp bordering Dimwood. They did not survive. The ancient witch had lured many to their deaths throughout antiquity. She was a scion of a brood from the Old World before the Scattering, long prior to the Cataclysm and even before the Age of Shadowed Ice. She once called the underworld her home. The witch of Yald'bok plants children in pots to harvest monsters...but on this day she stole the wrong seed.

This is a story of The Oraclon Chronicles. The witch's history with the Minions and her wars against Dagothar are further detailed in *Chronicle of Dagothar* (2018).

Reviews of Greric and the Witch of Dimwood

If I wanted to use one word to describe the story though, it would be atmospheric: you can feel the chill from the page, and the suspense as he approaches. The sheer amount of atmosphere and tension makes what could have been yet another quest story stand out. The writing is, I would have to say, unobtrusive. I couldn't tell you anything about the author's writing style because I was too lost in the images it evoked. The action scenes are well laid out and absolutely gripping, and it cuts back and forth between flashback and real fluidly and without losing either the flow or the reader. The plot is tight, and makes sense, and absolutely no punches are pulled. None. A very dark fantasy that kept me turning pages right to the end. This one's for fantasy fans, but horror readers should give it a look as well.
Rating: 4
Reviewed by Reader for **BookAngel.co.uk**
Reviewed on: 2017-03-10 *Review Policy: No compensation is received for reviews.*

In February 2016 Asher gave me the copy of **Greric and the Witch of Dimwood** *with the invitation to sit in on the Archaix Project meeting at Kevin Whiteside's place. Asher told me to imagine a whole series of novels that were just as good as the Greric story. That was hard to believe. This story is good. When I walked into the room and saw those maps of Dagothar I knew I was going to read those books. Six weeks later (we read a book a week and met on Saturdays, skipping a week) I was convinced that a visionary had entered the halls of fantasy and planted his war standard, a banner of epic GENIUS with his unique world of enchantment, vicious yet beautiful, innocent and dangerous. In my reading I was lost in the rich detail,* *immersed in a flow of events moving to harrowing conclusions. One cannot anticipate Breshears. He sees from a unique vantage point and artfully makes it ours. He is adept at moving our minds through pictures. His dialogues are moving, words having great effect in enriching the plots and subplots. Pay attention. His characters say things that take on deeper meanings later in the narrative. Especially in the fantasy genre, writers rely on long, unnecessary conversations to increase the length of their books but Breshears avoids this. He will make you read into his words mysteries, make you care for the destitute, exult with the victorious and hate the enemy. I am most impressed with the sensation I felt as I journeyed through an old world, the current events of the story were connected to ancient happenings. The contrast Breshears creates between graphic horror battle imagery and spiritual-mystical dialogues and doctrines occur only because the characters did not fulfill prior obligations. Fairy civilization is complex and full of animosities from old wounds. The fey and athradoc enrich the story and ancient breeds of fairies called feylorn who are Oathnayers, Moonlost and the darkened Shadowfae. His fairies are mostly original creations and their plight will move even the most stoic of readers. A glorious collection of fiction, I know the heart-wrenching scenes of fairy agony and indecision moved me. I accord Breshears the due of a master and give him five stars for the whole five books and two stories I read so far.* Rich (Big Duck) Stubblefield, Archaix Project 2016

The Cragly of Cindereach (2017)

He has walked the roads of Dagothar for ages. His people mastered war long before Men invented swords. Haunted by loss, driven by convictions deeper than humans can feel, he wanders through kingdoms on his journey fulfilling an ancient oath. Chief of the First People, of the blood of Ha'akathrals from before the Age of Shadowed Ice, he walks through civilizations in the Old World to the domains of men. Known to the feylorn, to the faeries of the great forests of Dimwood, Splinterdark, Treehelm, Enchandrus, Everleaf and Harrowood and across the wilds by those almost as old as he, Tal-Nik of the Beasthorn walks to a place where he had suffered the greatest anguish of his long life. He is thousands of years old by the time he went back to Cindereach...they should have left him alone.

Tal-Nik and the Kindread are featured in The Oraclon Chronicles.

Review of The Cragly of Cindereach

I've been gaming 35 years, RPG- GURPS, Dungeons & Dragons, Magic the Gathering, Pathfinder and I know fantasy. Obviously so does Breshears. All I had to read was The Cragly of Cindereach and I was in! With the Archaix Project guys I got my own copies of The Oraclon Chronicles novels and Greric and the Witch of Dimwood story. Having met Rich at the Fat Ogre in Conroe I found out that the series was written by a local guy. I'm from Philadelphia but that the King of Fantasy is a Texan don't matter to me because The Oraclon Chronicles is the BEST S--T I have ever read. I want to don my weapons and armor and explore Darkfrost Peaks, Dimwood and Blackmar Deeps, the ruins of Talan Dathar and Sigils Arch. Explore Splinterdark, Titan Oaks, Treehelm, Enchandrus, Feyknot-on-the-Water, Arborealm and Everleaf Pines. I've got to check out ancient Daethalon. You got to read about the dwarves of Red Anvil, the Tunnel Kings, Muzzle Lords called Magrar, Craniax the giant of

Deep Ore Peaks and Mount Talisman. There's nothing more wicked than those orc axemasters, garbolgs and Aelvatchi headhunter elves. Sarthaldon City in Hollowrealm is awesome, and that evil-turned-good thornmaiden vixen is a goddess of war! Breshears needs to GET THE GAMES MADE! Mickey Fuqua, Archaix Project 2016

Review of The Oraclon Chronicles

Fantasy/sci-fi seldom impresses me. I initially thought The Oraclon Chronicles to be just another male ego-driven hack-n-slash fantasy. It is not. This author has few equals in any genre in setting the stage, background development and intrigue. As part of the Archaix Project I am one of eight people who were given books 1-5 of the Chronicles. In fact, I am the only female. Finishing books 1 and 2 made me realize that Breshears had skillfully put his hooks in me, that I was curious and interested. A good foundation for the following books. I feared for the fairies. What is the Oraclon? Who is Dax Clovenheart and what is he doing on a fantasy world? Why are Josiah Arrowloft's narratives the only first person accounts in the entire story? What really are the Poltyrians up to? Why is a disguised demon spying on main characters? I admit, what began as hack-n-slash, sword & sorcery quickly turned into a mystery of epic proportion and I was enthralled. The first two books are good. But Breshears accomplishes a rare feat in that books 3, 4 and 5 are even better. Once finished I was charmed to discover how he had introduced several strong females who were clearly going to be major characters. The narrative is terrific, the story lines are treasures of the bardic skill. One can not escape the feeling that the author is deliberately communicating secret, divine messages behind the words of

*Elderboughs, the fairy races of fey, feylorn and athradoc,
of Imaricus the Old, Urick Aracancraft and Enuki.
Impressive are female warriors who dominate graphic and
disturbing battle scenes. Books 3,4 and 5 answer our
questions while also revealing darker plots, newer
situations, deeper conspiracy and encroaching conflicts.
My assessment is that Breshears is a first order tale teller,
that The Oraclon Chronicles will rightfully take its place
on the shelves of enduring works like those of J.R.R.
Tolkien, George R.R. Martin, Robert Jordan, Patrick
Rothfuss and Steven Erikson. The narratives, having a
cinematic flow, would be easy to screen write for television
or motion pictures. Thoroughly enjoyable.* April Avery,
Archaix Project 2016

See also the *Chronicle of Dagothar (2018),* a chronology
covering hundreds of stories of faery histories in the world
of Dagothar explaining how the world came to be the way
we find it in The Oraclon Chronicles!

Jason M. Breshears is a researcher of occult antiquities.
Eight of his published works are nonfiction with extensive
bibliographies concerning fascinating information on
ancient civilizations, cataclysms and the modern
establishment's attempts to suppress these discoveries from
the public today. Five of these works are published by
Book Tree in San Diego.

The Lost Scriptures of Giza (2006, 2017 updated version)
Kindle & paperback
When the Sun Darkens (2009) paperback
Anunnaki Homeworld (2011) paperback
Nostradamus and the Planets of Apocalypse (2013)
Kindle & paperback

Return of the Fallen Ones (2017)
    Other works by Breshears-
Giants on Ancient Earth (2017) Kindle & paperback
Awaken the Immortal Within (2017) Kindle & paperback
Shocking Secrets of Antiquity (2017) Kindle & paperback

Fiction (The Oraclon Chronicles)

Dark Tales of Dagothar (2017) Kindle & paperback
Uprising (2017) Part 1 of The Oraclon Chronicles (Kindle & paperback)
Chronicle of Dagothar (2018)
Greric and the Witch of Dimwood (2017)
The Cragly of Cindereach (2017)

Breshears' research, articles and discoveries are on **www.archaix.com.**

Breshears has authored 17 books and several articles, 10 works available on Amazon. His research bibliography is currently at 1157 nonfiction books read and data mined during a 19 year period, approximately 250,000 pages from many rare works as old as four hundred years, including translations of texts dating as far back as four thousand years. His core conclusions, discoveries and observations are released on **archaix.com** in 2017. As a pen & ink illustrator and graphic artist, most of his book covers and artwork are done by himself.

Breshears is one of the only researchers in the world who specializes in ancient chronological systems, focusing on global antiquities from 4309 BCE to 522 CE, many of his historical discoveries can not be found in any other works. For this reason he was awarded with multiple publishing contracts with Book Tree in San Diego.

Personal Note from Jason- I'm witty with a dark sense of humor, my pendulum swinging between gladiator and goofball. I value smartasses. A free spirit, humor my ally, I embrace my deviance often finding solace among the shadows. I recognize that I see the world around me through filters different than my peers. A pirate philosopher playing both sinister and sacred, I honor no God- my spirituality is measured in my actions toward others. Implacable in my beliefs until overwhelmed with new information, I love meatballs but dislike spaghetti, scrape the good stuff out of tacos and subway sandwiches and the toppings off of pizza. Life's too short for shells and crusts. I sing in the shower, drink my coffee black, love short-haired dogs and I'm hoping heaven has grilled-cheese sandwiches. I'm all-American, a patriot who has studied and admired the history of this great nation and I'm upset with the morons who are ruining it. My friends are few, but genuine. In a world that thrives on artificiality I take care to identify friends from fictions. In summary, I've never been accused of being normal.

My Philosophy- Though all men are created equal, they do not remain that way. In this age males are many but men are few. But there are some of us that rise above the rest and have the right to represent our gender as a whole...men of peace with capacity for war, we who speak what others are afraid to say, the apex of both the sacred and the profane. I am one of these men, just as evil as I am holy, separated by sin but bound to God, a student and teacher from the occult to Christianity. Poets and philosophers, visionaries and vikings, we few have a divine right to claim that we are men...all others are merely males. The following are my beliefs, the architecture of my personality:

* The man of principle never forgets what he is, because of what others are. -Baltasar Gracian

* The real voyage of discovery consists not in seeking new lands, but in seeing with new eyes. -Marcel Proust

* I am something more than I suppose myself to be, and perhaps all those perfections which I attribute to God are in some way potentially in me. -Rene Descartes

* A man's worth is not measured by his accomplishments, but in what he strives to accomplish. -Cicero, 1st cent. BCE

* LIVING is the purpose of life

* A person who sees what he wants to see, regardless of what appears, will some day experience in the outer what he so faithfully sees within. -Ernest Holmes, 1919

* Though we all live in the same world there are some of us who exist within an entirely different Universe- Me

Made in the USA
Las Vegas, NV
09 March 2023

68797232R00142